SINMISOLA OGÚNYINKA

ROGUE

A NOVEL

DEDICATION

For Sandra Ubong Nta (RIP January 2022)
Thanks for being my friend!
For Ebaye Akonjom (RIP January 2022)
The failure in our health system needs to stop!
For Olufadeke Iluyomade (RIP November 2024)
My dearest big sis, I miss you!

WARNING: 16 SNL

THIS NOVEL CONTAINS SEX, NUDITY AND STRONG LAN‑
GUAGE. READER DISCRETION IS ADVISED.

You don't make good choices, babe! You fell for that bastard. Damn.

You fell for me.

***

You see, God does not do threesomes. When you are with him, he wants

all your attention to be on him.

***

DURU

Chapter 1

"The type of banga they cook in this Lagos tires me. Let my grandmother cook banga for you, ehn..."

"Duru! Duru."

"Yeah."

"I have bad news."

I have bad news. I have bad news...

"Duru!"

I turned to Ahmed, my eyes hurt at the back. "I'm listening, Ahmed," I said.

"They asked for a dress. For Belema." Ahmed motioned to the nurse at the nurse's station. "To dress her."

"Of course. A dress for Belema." I nodded. "A dress."

My mother ran into the lobby, her stilt heels clattering on the tiled floor of the private hospital.

"Ewoo! What am I hearing? What happened, Stanley?" She gripped my shirt front. "What happeeened? Where is she?"

For a moment, I thought something may be wrong. The last one hour seemed to be a hallucination. I stared at my mother who freed me and went to Ahmed.

"I am finished." she fell on her knees and then her back.

Ahmed tried to hold her, but she rolled around. "Nurse, please help here," he said.

The nurse remained right where she had been all along. "Please, sir. We need to get the dress," the nurse said in a clipped tone.

Boma ran in too. "Stan!" She hugged my neck. "I came as soon as I heard."

That is quite soon, because everyone came as soon as the news broke.

"Boma," I stammered. "Boma..." the words got stuck in my throat. My head pounded even more if that was possible.

I glanced at Ahmed who now had my mother under some control. She sat on the hospital floor, her scarf and wig thrown to one side. Her high-heeled shoes at least ten feet apart in different directions.

"What are they saying? Where is she?" Boma's calm voice came as though from a far place. She cupped my face with stone cold hands. They chilled my hot skin. "Stan."

"We need a dress for her," the nurse said.

"Okay. Umm, yeah, we'll get a dress right now," Boma said. "Huh, Stan, do you want to come with me to get a dress?"

I shook my head.

"I think you should come with me," Boma looked at our mother. "What about Belema's family? Her. Her parents?"

I shrugged. Who would know? They live in Rivers State.

"Come with me, Stan." Boma pulled my hand.

Tears slid from my eyes. My sister was the family rock. Always sure of what to do. I didn't understand how she managed but right now, I just had to trust her. As I always did.

We walked out into the open. To the car park. To Boma's car. She opened the doors with her car remote and then opened the front passenger's seat for me. I got inside and sat.

Boma got into the driver's seat but did not drive. She turned and cupped my face again.

"John is coming on the next available flight from Abuja," she said. "Tonye is offshore, but I sent a message. He may not get it until evening. Dad. We can't tell him for a bit, you know."

I nodded. Huge tears dropped on to my cheeks of their own accord. Boma let them. I thought she had tears in her eyes too. At least, her voice sounded as though she did.

"I don't know what they need a dress for. But we should get one." She sniffed. "We can't drive to your house or mine."

Then she sat back and said nothing. I said nothing too. Growing up, Boma always took charge of everything. Perhaps it was one of the reasons she and our mum hardly saw eye to eye now. They differed in every way. The mum and the oldest daughter. Always striving for the more powerful – queen versus princess. I never chose a side until I was married, then mummy never could say the right thing. Boma was boss. She always came up with a solution.

When John, our first born, denied paternity of his child with Eugenia. When Daddy had his first stroke. When I brought Belema home.

"There are shops around here. Do you want me to get a nice gown for her?"

I shrugged.

"Go back inside," she said. "I don't want to leave you out here in the car. Alone."

I nodded.

I got out of her car and sure, she stood there until I went into the hospital.

My mother sat on a bench against the wall, wailing, and Ahmed walked over to me.

"Boma has gone to get it?"

I nodded.

"Just sit here. We have to wait until she returns. With the dress. I paid the bill. Your mum wants to see her. Belema. The nurse said no."

Ahmed's voice blended with the first words that started all of this. *I have bad news.*

Boma returned four hours later with John and a short stunning maternity wedding dress.

"Well, the nurse who made the mistake has been fired," Ahmed said.

I sat in the lying-in-state room, with Boma, and her husband, Tonye, and John, and Ahmed. It once was our master bedroom. I disvirgined Belema in this room. As though that made a difference now. But I liked to think this room was important. I'd never heard of anyone lie-in-state in the bedroom. Everything was taken out. To the parlour. Belema was here. Just this morning. In the beautiful dress Boma bought for her.

"Guys, please. This is not the time or the place to talk about this," Boma said.

She normally had the final say. Not today.

"Let's talk about it." I cleared my throat. "Let's talk about it." I seemed to have to repeat myself every time these days.

With all the furniture moved out, we all sat on the floor. The room wasn't all that big and now it showed.

Boma sighed. "I think we should talk about your next plans, Stan. Belema's clothes..."

"I'm taking them all to her mother." I nodded towards the wardrobe. "We were decluttering just last week."

Boma does always have her way. The talk about the erring nurse is shoved to the back but I can't get it out of my mind. This time last week, Belema was arranging her wardrobe to give out all the clothes she wore before her stomach and every other part of her body expanded.

"I look like a sack of beans..." Her laughter rang out.

Just last week, she packed her bag, and I dropped her at the expensive and elite hospital we both chose because of how expensive it was. I always thought the more expensive a hospital the better the services would be. Huh. Belema's doctor did not like the way her feet swell up so easily and wanted to monitor her because she was due.

"They like money too much," my mother had said. "Which feet swelling? Every day you stay in that hospital, how much will they take?"

"About twenty-five kay. I think. Bed alone," I said. "But what does it matter? Better safe than sorry."

Better safe than sorry. Better safe than sorry.

"I hate taking things out of my wardrobe. I know I am a hoarder," Boma said. Her words hung in the air like an uncompleted music note.

"What happened to the patient whose medication Belema got?" I said.

"We are not talking about that now!" Boma snapped. "Stan, stop!"

I turned dead eyes on her. "But I want to."

"It's important to talk about it," Boma's laid-back husband, Tonye, said. The guy seemed to have something ...an invisible remote that controlled his wife. "If that's what Stan wants."

Boma shrugged. "I'll see to the cleaners." She rose, patted my cheek, and left.

She did that too. Walk away when things were not to her command.

"Go ahead, Ahmed," I said.

The hospital, without consultation, chose to speak to Ahmed since the disaster, well, since Belema had his and my names as the contact people. But I was husband, and Ahmed was friend. My friend. My best friend from primary school. My best man.

Ahmed sighed. "The patient must have gotten another dose."

"I heard the patient was charged for both doses," John said. "Protested because it wasn't his fault, he didn't get the first shot."

"You shouldn't say things like that, John. To Stan," Boma was back. Something else she liked to do. Return if she didn't have her way and command the conversation.

"Shut the *f**k* up!" I snapped.

Silence everywhere. Boma opened her mouth to speak, trust her to always think she knew but Tonye's hand went up to give her the stop sign. Her mouth remained hanging open.

"Go on, Ahmed," John said.

Boma did her next best thing. She stomped out. No one followed her and she didn't return. It was past everyone's bedtime anyway. Close to three in the morning. Close to twenty-four hours since we put Belema in the ground. At eight in the morning. We all needed to sleep but a short twenty-four hours ago, Belema lay inside her coffin, in her beautiful maternity wedding gown. In this room.

"The nurse was fired," Ahmed said.

"I personally think the hospital should be shut down," John said. "When will medical personnel pay dearly for a simple mistake?"

"Not that it will bring Belema back, right?" Ahmed stole a glance at me. "Ehn, Duru? Did you say something?"

I locked my gaze with Ahmed's. "No."

"She didn't suffer. That's consolation. Her heart just…" Ahmed broke down.

I realized Ahmed really hadn't cried since last week when in the middle of a silly discussion about banga soup, he took a call from the hospital. He delivered the bad news. Sitting in our bank's cafeteria where we both worked as bankers, eating starch and banga. I forgot my phone in my cubicle. In my mad rush to get banga before it finished.

"That's consolation," I said. I bent my head between my knees and wept with Ahmed.

The guys let me.

Chapter 2

"What is suing the hospital going to do? It's not going to bring my daughter or her baby back." Belema's mother stood. "Goodbye when you and your family decide to leave our house."

"Mama Belema," Belema's father said. "Wait."

But the woman went inside, sobbing aloud.

I trained my gaze between my feet. Tears clouded my eyes and soon dropped on the sides of my leather-slippered feet.

"We know it won't bring her back, but it will send a strong message to that hospital," John said. "They cannot just make a mistake like that."

No one said anything.

After almost an hour of sitting down and nothing else, John stood, and Tonye with him.

"We will be going, sir. Stan?" John said.

I stood too. Belema's father remained in the old cane chair, one of five in their village home sitting room. The four suitcases with Belema and the baby's things sat at the corner of the floor. By the door. I felt a strange attachment to them. I remembered two of the suitcases were part of Belema's marriage gift. She loved those suitcases as if they were made with gold.

Tonye passed first, then John. Out into the October sun of the tropical rain forest, which could so easily turn to days of heavy rainfall.

I paused beside the suitcases. My shoulders shook with my silent sobbing. This was like lowering Belema into the ground at Atan cemetery all over again. Leaving her there inside the ground with my unborn daughter. The hospital had offered to take the 8-plus-month foetus out, at no additional cost, they said, as though I was going to pay after they mistakenly killed my wife and baby! I was leaving every single thing that remained of Belema's here, in Kalabari land. I may never be back here.

"Perebo!" Belema's mother shouted from whichever part of the house she was. "See when that man leave, go and carry your sister cloth to the market. We go get better money."

Nothing harder could have pushed my feet out of the house.

There's definitely madness in grief, I thought.

"Well, Belema left a will."

"I didn't know she had a will," I said. "She told me everything." I gazed into the soulful eyes of the female lawyer who called earlier to see me in my house.

"When you didn't contact me, I thought you probably didn't know about it," she said.

I couldn't remember her name. Peju? Dupe? Apeke? A "pe" somewhere.

"Sorry, what's your name again?"

"Bimpe Olajuwonlo. I work with Olajuwonlo and Olajuwonlo," she said.

Good, I could never remember such a confused name.

"Okay. So, do you want to read the will?"

"It has to be in the presence of two witnesses," Bimpe said. "Belema left it to your discretion to find those two witnesses."

"You could have said all of this on the phone, so I'd be ready," I said.

She rubbed me wrong.

"I know. I will come back for that at your..."

I stood. "My mother is here. I'll get my neighbour." I strode out before she could stop me.

We returned and sat. The neighbour had her hands in dish washing soap and tried to dry them off her "Ankara" wrapper. My mother had been "praying" when I barged in on her in my guest room.

"I told you to go back to your house, and leave me alone, but you do not want to listen. So, take anything you get…" I tried to ensure I said that at least once a day, since I buried Belema two weeks earlier and my mother insisted on staying with me, when she had a very sick husband at home.

"There are people to take care of him," she had said.

Bimpe took out an official envelope and pressed the record button on her phone. After pleasantries, she introduced the meeting and the people in attendance and tore the envelope. She took out only a sheet of paper.

"The final testament of I, Tamunobelema Agnes Duru, dated this day, the 3rd of August, 2010…"

I blanked out for a minute. Two and a half months ago. Belema must have feared she would die! I breathed through my mouth and all I heard were my mother's soft sobs and the neighbour's incessant hissing.

"She has nothing. Why would she write a will?" I spoke.

Bimpe folded the paper. "She felt it was important for her family to understand her thoughts." She put the will back in the envelope and gave me.

I hadn't heard anything from the will, so I took it out of the envelope. I could cry over it later. There may be need to ask a question or two.

Bimpe stood.

"Hold on," I said.

Belema's will said only one thing. *Leave everything I own to my daughter, Agbani Promise Duru.*

"Why did she do this?" I looked up at the lawyer.

Bimpe heaved a sigh. "She had her reasons for..."

I rumpled the paper and threw it across the room. Bent my head between my feet and allowed my tears to flow without reservation. I didn't even want to be silent about it, so I raised my head and wailed. So loud, I didn't hear anything for a long time except my own hoarse cries.

The lawyer left. Followed by the neighbour. Then my mother.

My mother left my house. Which was really good. Because there was nothing she was doing for me or vice versa. Since Belema died, I had done exactly what I wanted. I was rude, disrespectful, disengaged. I cursed. I never cursed before. Even after I returned to work just a day before. I didn't have a care in the world. My soul had been snatched from me. Belema had been my everything.

Everything.

She left her worldly goods to her daughter. She had feared she would die, and she never told me. To the last minute I left her at the hospital, she was laughing and teasing.

I kicked my expensive leather couch, and the stool, and the wall. I sat on the floor and cried even more.

Chapter 3

"Their lawyer wants to settle out of court. Ruled as accidental."

Ahmed sighed. "How much?"

I gasped. "Is that the point, Ahmed? How much?"

I still couldn't believe I called that lawyer Bimpe with the complicated Yoruba name and even more annoying chambers name. But when I started to really think about the injustice... The pain of losing Belema and our baby who was due to be born at any time, the thought that my life was suddenly in shambles, I thought of Bimpe. I knew many lawyers, but this was the one Belema found and trusted so why couldn't I. And I called her, and she filed a suit, and I liked the way she worked. Very professional.

And it was a good fact that she was a partner at her father's law firm, and the father was a big man and a SAN. Respect there, for her to have her own cases and stand her ground.

Ahmed threw his hands up in the air. "I just want to know, Duru, don't bite me."

"One million," Bimpe said softly. "Of course, I rejected it."

"One million." I gasped as tears gathered in my eyes. "For?"

"That was exactly what I asked. It doesn't even cover my fees," Bimpe said.

"That's ridiculous," Ahmed said. "Are they stupid? A life... no, two lives were lost by their stupid nurse's carelessness."

"Speaking of, your fees," I cut in. "I want your invoice. The next one."

Bimpe nodded. "I'll send it." She sighed. "So, as we stand, I'm pressing forward with the suit."

"There is no amount of money they can offer," Ahmed said. "They are stupid."

"From dust to dust."

I took a handful of the sand, from the bucket full I got off the mound Belema was covered with and rubbed it over my face. Then, I returned the bucket into my wardrobe.

It was the first anniversary of Belema and Agbani's deaths, and I wanted to be on my own, so, early in the morning, I went to the graveside, sat on it for several minutes, and then drove to the beach. I turned my phone off.

Family was everything but ever since Belema died, many things had changed.

Boma was still cold after I swore at her a year ago.

Tonye stood by his wife, though he called once in a while and they both spoke to me with their kind-of-kind-tone.

John had forgotten and his life had returned to normal.

Ahmed whined just like before, but all the reasons I liked him were now the same for which I hated him.

My job was the only thing which sort of made some sense, and I hated smiling at customers when my insides were a mess.

I hadn't tasted banga soup in one year, since the day I got the news of my wife's death while I was eating it and hated it more than living.

Bimpe just seemed so slow. I had never had a lawsuit before, had no clue what the process was, but this lady seemed so slow. So slow. But she was the only one who meant anything to me in recent times. Because she was fighting a cause for me.

When I got back to my flat, Boma and my mother were in her car, waiting for me.

"Good evening," I said and strolled by to open the front door.

Each time I came here, which technically was at least twice a day, going out and coming back in, except for Sundays, which I dedicated to "family time" with my late wife and baby, I saw the sign. The flat next door was vacant. When it first became available, I'd thought of moving in. The old neighbour, the one who witnessed Belema's will reading, had moved with her family to another part of town. Their space was smaller, a one-bedroom unlike mine that was two-bed, and I had toyed with the idea of taking it. Pay less and leave the memories behind. But I couldn't. My life remained in this flat. If I left, it would be like burying the last memories. Putting my wife and child in the ground again and leaving them there. All alone.

"You should move next door," Boma said beside me.

She still threw her opinions in occasionally. Not as frequently as before the ef-word saga. I hadn't imagined it would hurt her so badly. *Sorry, sis.*

"Yes?" I mumbled, and let them in.

I left scented candles burning and stepping in after at least sixteen hours of being away from the house, the scent had settled in nicely. I flipped on the switch and light flooded my nice sitting room. Belema's amateur interior decorations but the best I'd seen of any home I visited.

"Change. It's time for change. Hmm. I like this cinnamon scent every time." Boma dropped her bag on the couch and sat beside it.

Our mother sat next to her.

I walked into the empty bedroom I once shared with Belema and did not turn on the light. The only thing that remained was the carpet. I slept on it like that. I took off my clothes and lay on my back, naked. My sister and mother chatted mutedly but that mattered none. When they were done, they would leave.

I turned on my phone in the dark. Bimpe had promised to have news today. She basically usually kept her word and with my pressure, she had impressed my case on her chambers so her father could pull some strings and get the case going. I believed it was a very strong case. Absolute neglect. The defence had no wriggle room in this one, especially after they offered to settle.

"Bimpe."

"Hello, Stan. Huh."

"You said you will definitely have some news today."

"I do. I called earlier." She paused. She did that when she wanted me to be accountable. Tell her why she couldn't reach me when she called.

I wasn't going to be. Not to her. Or anyone. "And?"

"Defence umm presented new evidence. Which I had an inkling about." She sucked in her breath.

"If they get away, I'm going to appeal," I said.

"It's on a technicality. Belema's maiden name was wrongly spelt in your marriage certificate," she said. Paused and sighed. "A missing alphabet. One b instead of two. So, she wasn't properly identified for the court to have a verdict for her."

"That's *bullsh*t!*"

There was movement at my bedroom door. To hell with whoever was rude enough to enter without knocking. I could feel my muscles sag. I had a workout routine from last year. My muscles seemed tired out from lack of exercise. But then, I didn't need to keep fit anymore.

"The judge has thrown the case out," Bimpe said. "I want to pursue a civil suit. Those things will not matter…"

"Wait a minute. A civil *f**king* suit means no one will go to jail. And some cash will be paid to me. Right?" I knew how to maintain a deep, soft voice even when I was mad as hell. I needed to learn how to yell, for goodness' sake. "If you win it. Right?"

"Precisely."

"I don't want the blood money…"

"It will pay off my fees at least and…"

"I can pay your *sh*tty, f**king* fees, Bimpe. Why did you not see this misspelling and they did?"

She drew in a long deep breath. "Like I told you, I saw it. But this was a mistake already made. We could withdraw that document and get an affidavit to correct it, but the law doesn't always work like that. It would seem we were trying to, like, you know, change the figures or something."

"No. No." I sniffed. "The truth is that you submitted that document without cross-checking. This was your mistake. Belema's birth certificate and degree certificate have her maiden name correctly spelled." I paused for effect. "You did not double-check the documents and only noticed after it was too late and prayed the other lawyer will be stupid enough not to notice."

"Pretty much."

"I pay you a *f**king* seven-figures. I sell my *d*mn* television to pay you, and you did not notice there was a missing b, *b*tch*..."

"If you swear at me one more time, Stan, I'm going to hang up," she said softly.

Chapter 4

"**I**'m sorry to hear that, Stan."

I sobbed like a child after Bimpe actually hung up because I couldn't stop swearing at her. Boma sat on the carpet beside me in the dark. She placed her palm on my shoulder, and what a cold hand. Why were her hands so cold especially when my body burned? Did she know I was naked? Did it matter?

"Mummy has gone to bed," Boma said. "I can't drive home tonight. It's too late. We were here since like seven. Your phone was switched off."

She rambled in her complaints of my behaviour when all I just wanted was silence. Belema's killers were going to walk free. They would live their normal lives, and probably kill more people. The hospital was still rated one of the best in Lagos. Most expensive too. To think I sold my car, saved up and didn't buy another car just to pay that hospital's bills, and they would go scot free?

"I really don't know much about these cases, but can't we get a lawyer. Another lawyer to try again?" Boma did this when she didn't want to talk about an issue. She'd bring up the silliest ideas.

"I just want Belema and my Agbani." I wept. "Oh God, I just want them back. I want them back."

Boma hugged me and may have realized I didn't have clothes. She was four years older but what did I care?

"You will be alright, Stan. Everything will be fine." She let go and traced her way in the darkness to my wardrobe. "Wear something. I want us to talk."

Boma threw a shirt at me. I did not want to talk to her or anyone, but I wore the shirt anyway. But I did not sit up. I remained flat on my back. Boma turned on the light and got me my pyjama bottoms. I just wore it to get her out of my room. To say what she had to and leave. Today was for my family not her.

"We finished up our house in Port Harcourt. Tonye wants me to move there with the kids." She moaned. "I've been here in Lagos just because of you all, anyway. There's no use paying rent in Lagos when I have a house of my own in Port."

Her voice just droned on and on. I heard her but couldn't be bothered. She was telling her life's story, and obviously, I didn't seem to be a part of it. A house, really, when Agbani could have been celebrating her first birthday today or tomorrow or this week. A house was more important to my sister.

Did Boma expect me to jump and shout "hallelujah" to the king of kings and lord of lords? The extent of their insensitivity to me was alarming.

"So, we are moving at the end of the term. The children have schools already·so they will join in January. I could even move now. What am I doing here?"

What indeed?

"But you know children..."

As though I have any.

"They want to be with their friends a little longer." She sighed. "I am so tired of Lagos. And there is really nothing I am doing here. Just doing school runs, entering unnecessary traffic."

As though Port is not almost as bad.

"Anyway, are you hearing me? Stan?"

I nodded.

"Tonye wants you to move in with us."

That jolted me but only inside my chest. I remained mute and frozen. Not even a twitch gave away my thoughts.

"As a banker, you will easily get a job if your bank refuses to transfer you. And everybody will feel so much better if they know you're with me. Our BQ is even bigger than this your place, and Tonye is not taking any rent from you. We initially wanted to rent it out but until you don't need it anymore, it's all yours."

Rent it out, I don't need your charity.

"I will feel much better, and comfortable with you there. You'll be close to family. Frank and Pauline love you, you know that. You are their favourite uncle, and there is a way children make bad memories go away. So, what do you say?"

"I'll think about it," I said, knowing I would not.

This was Boma in her element. She figured out everything for everyone.

She let out a long breath as though she had been holding it. "Good, I know you will be reasonable."

"Thank you."

"Mummy has her hands full with daddy. And John too, whether we like to admit it or not. Did you know Eugenia has permanently moved back to Abuja again with Ada? So, your brother is back paying two rents from one job. I am tired. He is the big brother but not setting any examples for us. Big for nothing. Why won't he marry Eugenia and have a family. He's flying up and down every week. How can he concentrate? Anyway, Stan, when do you plan to move? The house is ready as we speak. Electricity, water, everything. We have security there. Generator. Tonye even got Wi-Fi." She giggled. "I was like, haba, let's come in first but honestly, it is ready. You can move tomorrow if you want."

"I'll think about it," I said.

Chapter 5

"Bimpe means well and stopping her at this point is going to harm you more. You won't have the closure you desire, and this anger I see building in you, Duru, hmm."

I snapped. "She hung up on me, Ahmed."

"She said you were shouting at her and..."

"I never shout. I wish I can."

"But you were calling her names and swearing at her," Ahmed said.

"I've also paid her eight hundred thousand naira, and I owe another five thereabout. I have bought the right to yell and curse if she messes up."

"It doesn't work like that, Duru." Ahmed shook his head. Eight more minutes until lunch is over. He cleaned the last spoon of rice on his plate.

I had not eaten in this cafeteria for more than a year, precisely one year and one day. "I plan to get another lawyer. See where that goes."

"You have to pay her. You need to pay up all of her money."

"I will." I heaved. "I already sold my furniture."

"Duru. I. I don't know what to say. You will self-destruct the way you're going."

"I know."

Ahmed sighed. "Take the offer from Boma. Go to Port Harcourt. Start over."

"I will. When Belema rests. I will." I stood. "I need to get back."

Ahmed stood too. "Me too. We work in the same office."

The old Duru would laugh and tease. I nodded curtly. "I know."

Grief breeds madness. So so true.

"There is some good news. My father helped to discover indeed that there was a correct marriage certificate, and it was carefully forged and replaced."

Bimpe sat with her hands clasped in her lap on one of four plastic chairs that replaced the old leather furniture I sold for a million naira, originally worth two and a half, and one of the crazy deals I got to please Belema.

"Agbani will be two next week, so I guess this good news is to celebrate that," I said.

Bimpe and Ahmed exchanged a glance. She was a pretty woman, in other thoughts. Dark-skinned, slim, just the way I used to like my women before I married "yellow" Belema. My eyes went to her hands. Not married, I thought. Upward mobile. She had demanded for an apology for calling her a b*tch, and I had given one without second thoughts, howbeit, without remorse.

Bimpe shrugged. "Great news to celebrate but there is no guarantee anything can happen yet. Just that we were duped and we…"

"You did your best and you were not wrong or careless, after all. I get it." I stood. "If anything comes up, let me know."

Bimpe stood too. "Of course. I understand you haven't been able to get a lawyer to replace me. I still consider myself working for you, anyway."

"Except that I'm free of fees in almost a year," I said.

"Take care of yourself, Stan." Bimpe headed for the door. "I should have some more news next week."

"The anniversary. Birthday. Deathday."

Bimpe waved at Ahmed. "I'll see you around."

Ahmed winked at her, and she left.

I glanced to see Bimpe's reaction to the wink. Maybe she would blow a kiss?

"Are you dating? Of course, it is none of my business." I sighed. "I don't know why she came here. She doesn't have news." I paced. "She asked you to bring her, right? Because she knows what she did? Now she wants to cover up with a fake story."

Ahmed arched an eyebrow. "Cool down, Duru."

"I'm as cool as a cucumber."

"You need to let Bimpe continue this case, and she told me she's not charging anymore. Until the case is won one way or the other," Ahmed said.

I nodded.

"I miss you, Duru! Where's my bud for heaven's sake. You've not mistakenly smiled in two years."

"What is funny?"

"Look, you remember this babe, this girl who was at your wedding. Umm, we used to call her udari." Ahmed chuckled.

Old Duru would be singing a song about the girl. I nodded.

"She asked after you. Take her out, Duru."

"To where?"

"It's two years, Duru. You have to move on."

I stood. "I'll see you in the office tomorrow."

I strode into my room and closed the door. On second thoughts, I locked the door and burst into tears. Ahmed knocked several times, called me, pleaded with me, told me sorry, and left.

Chapter 6

"Congratulations, Stan Duru! You have done your bank, and your family proud!"

I stood stoically as the MD, and directors of my bank shook my hand, followed by my branch manager.

"Let's go out tonight, Duru. This calls for a big celebration," Ahmed came to stand beside me.

I nodded. "That's a great idea!"

"Awesome!" Ayobami, one of my colleagues said.

Ahmed slapped hands with Ayobami. "We go after work."

Banking Staff of the year award goes to Stan Duru for an outstanding performance of his duties. My bank didn't even get the bank of the year. I met my targets four times over in the past year for the first time in my life. I didn't even know it was happening. I got to work on time, worked every single possible overtime. Pursued every business lead as though my life depended on it. And it did anyway. Work was the only life I had.

"I think you need to get drunk and sleep with Udari," Ahmed slapped my shoulder, and strolled off to his cubicle.

"You need to marry Bimpe!" I called after him.

He laughed. "She won't marry me."

My head pounded. Nothing was funny, nothing was great. Nothing mattered.

I returned to my cubicle. The five-hundred-thousand-naira gift for the award was in my account seated. I logged in just to look at it again. Spent before arrival because no one knew this, but I did not only get a new lawyer, I also got a top private investigator. It was all what my income went to. The two were very expensive and I really didn't mind at this point. My monthly income could cater to them. As it were, I only had my stocks left in asset. And I was ready to liquidate it at a moment's notice.

When the guys signed off for the day, and prepared to go drinking to celebrate me, I stepped out of the bank building and followed Ahmed to the parking lot, to his car, to go out and eat suya, drink brandy and sleep with Udari. Only that I did not enter his car. I continued walking even after he shouted my name.

I got into another car, which was just a few feet away from Ahmed's. My private investigator, Walid, sat behind the wheel, waiting. He'd been waiting for at least ten minutes, running his engine because he couldn't find parking.

"Hey," I said.

Walid was a businessman to the core and didn't have time for frivolities. We were a perfect match.

"Good evening. I was with Barrister Ojong this afternoon, and he wants us to have a meeting. I didn't want to start saying all that when I called earlier." Walid drove off but slowed and looked at his rear-view mirror. "It's like someone is trying to..."

"Ignore." From the side-view mirror, I could see Ahmed run towards Walid's car, waving.

"Okay." He drove on and joined the evening traffic of mainland Ikeja. "There is a lot going on and I'm sure Barrister Ojong will give better perspective."

"Is it positive or negative?"

"Negative, mostly," Walid said. "The owner of the hospital is a younger brother to a senator. The nurse who made that mistake even, is a big man's daughter."

"Hmm."

"That marriage certificate thing was just a big fraud. From my findings, your former lawyer's father may have been told to calm down."

"Hmm."

"So, to fight this battle, you need a lot of money. I got a judge who is willing to reopen the case, but he's talking plenty things."

Walid was a great driver. He should be, I guessed. He moved around a lot and knew back roads to avoid horrible rush-hour traffic.

"I don't know if Barrister Ojong will be able to agree on some things."

Old Duru would want to know what things, but I just rested my head back and closed my eyes. I didn't sleep well most nights, and I wanted to be rested a bit after a long day of so many excitements at work.

We walked into Barrister Ojong's office in the heart of mainland, Lagos, a crowded office with an empty reception. It was almost ten o'clock and I wasn't surprised his clerk or secretary, whatever had gone.

Ojong was a slight man with big eyes, a flare of a nose, and thick lips. Amazing how all those big things fitted into his small, dark face.

Walid and I sat on two of four visitors' chairs crammed inside.

"First of all, the judiciary is a big mess. Second, there are powerful people involved and third, time has passed." Ojong yawned. He should be worn out but the last thing I wanted was a tired lawyer. "A corrupt judiciary can be of advantage and disadvantage. In this case, you need so much money to..."

"I will liquidate my stocks. At least I have more than three million there," I said.

Walid chuckled. "Three million is what one judge will take."

Ojong scowled. "Try not to interrupt me, okay, Duru? As I was saying, the senator's brother is not going to go down because of you."

"Is there a way around this *f**king sh*t*? Or I should do things my way?"

"Be patient, Duru." Walid snapped. "Let Barrister finish."

"If I cannot get them through the law, I will do it otherwise." I snapped back.

"Your wife is dead. As well as your daughter. Do you want justice for them or not?" Barrister Ojong glared at me. "Huh?"

I could not help it, and I started to sob. This crying surprised me. I may have cried every day since Belema died. To imagine I never thought of myself as so weak.

"I thought you did." Ojong sniffed. "Walid told me he found a judge willing to hear this case in his court. There is a procedure to reopen such a case, and we must go through it. And it is not a small task."

It was annoying and disruptive, sobbing aloud, and it was exactly what I did.

"You pull yourself together, please, I still have to drive far," Walid said.

No one understood. How could they? Their lives were normal. Happy. I sniffed and coughed and lowered my wailing.

"Walid may not have told you, but we have enough evidence to show the foul play the defence attorneys did to get the case thrown out. Once we prove that, the case will be re-opened and we will proceed," Ojong said.

"You are going to be spending money like water," Walid said. "If your late wife has gold, go and sell it."

As callous as that sounded, it seemed as though these men were trying to harden me. Mentioning Belema so flippantly aggravated me.

"I sent all her things to her mother," I said.

"I am not taking anything apart from the running costs," Ojong said. "When the case is over, you can settle me."

I found this generosity worrisome. Ojong was already charging me for different stuffs, which I believe would yield result, and I had no problem with them at all. For a second, my heart skipped. Three million in stocks, five hundred thousand award gift, two-fifty thousand monthly take-home after tax, and nothing but my clothes and shoes.

I heaved a heavy sigh. "I will pay anything."

Chapter 7

"Let this thing go, Duru, please now!"

I sat on the floor in my parlour and stared into space.

Ahmed paced. "Isn't it obvious you are fighting a lost battle? They are asking you to bring this and bring that. Look at where you live? You have punned everything like a man on hard drugs."

It did feel like an addiction, fighting for Belema and Agbani. The three million was gone plus the little change from my award, plus the bulk of my salary, and the case had still not gone far.

"You should be offering your help now, as a good friend."

It was the most unfair thing to say, and Ahmed let out a strangled cry. I did not spend a kobo for Belema's funeral. Ahmed and Boma took all the cost. And after then, some of Bimpe's fees were paid by these two.

"If you think I will sell my car, and stuff to help you, then you don't know me, Duru!" He stomped his feet. "You may be foolish, I am not. You are nothing to these people. They will crush you."

"It just remains a little. Just a little for us to be back on track. Ojong is fantastic. Can't you see?"

"Ojong is a lawyer. He is not sentimentally attached, and he will pull back if it by any chance will hurt him."

"And he hasn't pulled back."

"Yet! But he soon will."

I leaped to my feet. "Look, your negativity is getting at me. If you want to be my friend, you need to support this." I turned towards my bedroom. "Turn off the lights when you leave."

Ahmed stomped to my door. "Turn them off yourself."

I couldn't be moved by his emotional tirade. I had too much going. Ojong and Walid had me in their palms and asking for just a little more. Though Ojong said he wasn't charging me any fees, he was on a monthly running cost fee of fifty thousand naira. Which in itself was not beyond me, but my patience was running thin. It was getting close to the third year, and from my research, the longer it took, the worse for my case.

Ahmed got to the door and turned. "Two Christmases, New Years, birthdays, birthdays of friends and family, ileyas, Easters, and you have been a ghost of yourself. Have not celebrated with anyone. Two anniversaries of Belema's death, and you disappear the whole day. Duru, please." His throat worked up and down as though he tried to control tears. "Please. You don't have anything again. You need to stop here. At this point. Belema would have wanted you to move on…"

"Ahmed, please go!" I left him there and slammed my bedroom door after me.

My mistake was to carry him along as I took my decisions. Maybe if I shut him out too, he would back off. I couldn't understand why he did not see things my way. I pulled off my clothes and sat in the dark.

Belema would have wanted you to move on…

How would Ahmed know that? If Belema wanted me to move on, she would not have written a will and left my name out of it totally, like I never existed. Three years fast approached and much as I did not care about living a normal life ever again, I wanted to see justice, and the evil hospital shut down.

I called Ojong.

"Barrister, good evening."

"Good evening, Mr. Duru. I was just about to call you. I have some not too good news. The case cannot be reopened. Whatever your former lawyer agreed to, is sealed. But I have appealed the decision to throw out the case. It is unlikely to scale through the way we expect but it is a good way to keep your names in the radar…"

What nonsense was he saying? He hated being interrupted but how would I not at this point?

"What are you saying? What are you saying again?"

"You want to fight this matter, don't you? We are fighting it. Just calm down and let us do our job as best as we can. I have at least one judge in the appeal court, and he is happy to help."

I snapped. "For how much?"

"He will do the job first. Calm down." I heard him yawn. "He may not even take anything. I know him very well. He is a great man and a Christian. I will get feedback from him in the next few days. One thing I am doing is putting a lot of pressure so we will have a date. Getting a date is very difficult, but I have my people."

"Okay."

"I will want you to have some money on standby, though, because our friend is going to talk to some other judges and there may be cost implications."

I knew it would come to that. Cost implications, when I started this rough journey thirty-one months earlier, were Bimpe's fees alone. Now all manner of things went into that broad heading. But I wasn't deterred.

"No problem."

"Okay, I need to get to some other things. I'll give you update by weekend, latest."

"Thank you, Barrister," I said.

Or was it not polite to thank someone you could quickly begin to realize would rip you off? Weekend was three days away. I folded into a ball, like a child and allowed my tears to flow. There just had to be a way out of here. I didn't want to pray. God had not done me well, after all. What was my offence? I and Belema loved the Lord with all our hearts. We served him with everything we had. Why would this terrible thing happen to us? Why would these wicked people get away?

Chapter 8

"Sir, please let this not become a police case. Please sir, let this just be internal."

My branch manager shook his head. "I still can't believe that this time last week, we were celebrating this fool."

I stood with my head high, staring straight at nothing, unflinching, uncaring that tears rolled down my cheeks and soaked my chest. My smart supervisor, Wole, just caught me steal from the money meant to go to the ATM, and lucky him, reported it before I left the building. Otherwise, he'd probably be indicted too.

Wole sighed. "He's a good worker. This will never happen again, sir."

"Of course, he is going on an indefinite suspension." Eli, the branch manager, glared at me. "You better go and fix your life. I should sack and flag you immediately but because of your record, I will let it lie."

I swallowed. "Thank you, sir."

"Get out of my office. Clear out your desk. Wole, get security to escort him out!"

Wole nodded. "Yes, sir. Thank you, sir."

At least, it was proven. I was not a smart criminal. I stepped out of Eli's office behind Wole and walked to my cubicle. I could feel eyes on me. I passed Ahmed and he frowned but couldn't talk because he had a customer with him.

A security man stood at my desk with an empty carton. I took it and dropped all my personal stuff mainly Belema's pictures, into it. I walked by the others and out the door. Somehow, I knew I wasn't coming back even if they called me. This was the worst, definitely. No money, no job, no savings, no investments, no assets. All I waited and wanted was justice. All I could hope for. I did not want money. Just the hospital shut down and the nurse sent to jail. Then I'd be able to sleep.

"I'm in shock, Duru. I don't even know where to start. What to say. Please now, please for God's sake. For your mother's sake. Please."

I lay on my back in my dark room, and Ahmed sat beside me. There was no electricity and on and off, Ahmed tapped his phone to provide a little illumination.

"Stealing, ah! This is unbelievable. Look, you need to move to Port Harcourt. There is no other option." Ahmed moaned. "Ah, God, what is this? How can this be happening?"

Ahmed went on and on. I just lay there, naked as the day I was born. Since he arrived and I let him in, I had not said more than a greeting.

Ahmed tapped my shoulder. "Talk to me. What's your plan now?"

I sighed. "I will just wait until we get a verdict."

"What verdict? The case is not in court, now!" He smacked the carpeted floor. "You have finished everything you have trying to fight a lost battle. All these people are just using you to collect money. Even if this case enters another court now, how will you pay your lawyers?"

"Barrister Ojong is understanding."

"Oh, stop that! What nonsense understanding? But he collected all that money for what?"

"Listen, Ahmed. I don't care. In case you haven't noticed. I don't care."

"What did you need this money for this time? Because if I remember, it was to bribe judges." Ahmed snapped his fingers. "Chai. Chai. Those bastards just chop you, and now you have to steal. Twenty million! For what?"

"I just took out a zero. It wasn't twenty million."

Right there in the dark, my tear glands started acting up. Tears just started flowing down my eyes. I didn't bother to clean it.

"You took a zero. What does that mean?"

"Two million was what I took from the twenty." I sniffed. "For the last judge I was supposed to see before they can admit the case again."

"Anyway, you are just lucky the bank is not handing you over to the police. Right now, your best bet is to leave this house and this city. Go and start fresh with Boma."

"They gave out their BQ. Where will I live?"

"Inside their house of course. Do you think you can live on your own?" Ahmed snickered. "As it is, you need to move out of this house because how will you pay your rent?"

He had valid points. At some point, I realized I had gone over my head, yet a strong force seemed to pull me. I couldn't let this issue go. Why would justice not be served? Close to three years and I never imagined I would be here, still fighting for the case to even be heard. But I couldn't live in Boma's house. Living on my own, she bossed around. I was a year short of thirty. In my scheme of things, with Belema, I was supposed to be buying a piece of land on the outskirts of Lagos, a goal set to be completed by next year when our marriage would be hitting five. By the time we are ten years in, we would be moving to our own house. What happened to all those great plans?

"I'll sort myself out, Ahmed. Thanks for coming."

He growled. "Duru, please now! Oh my God. What is all this?"

I wiped tears from my eyes. His agony was touching but there was no way I could assure him.

"I said I will move to Port Harcourt."

"Hmm. When?"

"Tomorrow. I have some…" Then I remembered my account was immediately frozen when my theft was discovered. "I'll call Boma."

Ahmed tapped on his phone for the light, took out his wallet and counted twenty one-thousand-naira notes. "Take the first bus tomorrow, please."

"Thank you." I took the money. "I owe you."

"You don't." He stood. "I'll talk tomorrow evening after work. You should be in Port by then."

"Yeah, sure."

Chapter 9

"You should just thank God the medical director is not pressing any charges."

My mother and John stood at the counter while the officer in charge at the zonal police headquarters took out my cuffs and gave me back my clothing.

"Thank you, Officer," Mummy said. "Thank you."

The policemen had beaten me so badly my face was disfigured, and I had pains all over my body but at least, I could breathe. No broken bones, hopefully.

I slowly wore my belt and shirt and walked out of the police station barefooted because they didn't return my shoes. We went to John's 2000 Oldsmobile in silence. And onward to my parents' house. I could not protest at this point. When they were done with me, surely, I'd find my way to my house.

Boma was waiting at home, which made me realize this was much bigger than my small mind comprehended it. To make matters worse, she said nothing to me. She must have flown in from Port Harcourt.

"We put your things in you and John's old room," Mummy said. "Bath and sleep and we can talk later."

"Better talk now than later," Boma muttered.

My things? I walked into the room and saw two suitcases that contained all my clothes. All. My life's belongings. Now I knew why Boma did not come with them to the police station. She was packing me up. Probably had bought my ticket to Port Harcourt too. I felt so stupid and sad. What manner of end was this for me? Still no justice. No solution. Would I just give up on this fight like this? Disgraced. Packed up like a baby and sent to live with my big sister and her family?

I sat on the double bed I slept in until five years ago when I started living on my own just before I got married. I stank though, so I got in the bathroom and had a long bath. To avoid being hunted down, I wore a pair of jeans and t-shirt and went into the parlour.

My sick father had just been fed and put down for the night, and Mummy was still finishing this task up, but Boma was seated on the edge of the couch, as though impatient, which I deduced she was. I sat on a single chair and somehow, I knew Boma's silence was worse than her ranting. John walked in and sat with Boma on the couch, with a plate of rice and stew.

Oh, a family meeting. Just what I needed!

"Go and eat, Stan," John said around a mouthful of food. As though I was six years again.

"Thanks, I'm fine," I mumbled.

Mummy came to join us shortly and sat on a single chair.

"Start talking what happened, Stan," Boma said. "Because I am tired of this, and you may notice, all your things are in you people's room. I have cleared your things out of that house and handed your place back to the landlord. I have tidied everything. Your remaining rent will be used to fix the door I broke and any other thing. I am done with this news of Stan this Stan that. Ahmed told me you tried to steal money from your bank, and now this! I can't be living in Port and babysitting you in Lagos."

I sighed. "My lawyer called that the case was rejected, and the appeal of the other one was also thrown out."

John grunted. "Which other one?"

"Please, John, don't interrupt." Boma snapped. "Let him talk."

I frowned. "Anyway, I had three different cases I am pursuing and all just failed. They told me on Thursday night. So, I went to the hospital. I told them I wanted to see their MD. He wasn't in the hospital, according to them."

"And then?" Boma shouted. "Look, I want to go and sleep o, I don't have all night to be sitting here listening to nonsense."

"I beat the nurse up. I scattered the nursing station. I went into the hospital wards throwing anything I could before their security came." I gripped my head and looked down at my feet and fought tears. I did not want to cry now.

Boma snapped. "And then?"

"The security started beating me, and took me to the station with the ambulance," I said. "The police beat me some more. The prisoners in the cell beat me too."

"Which you deserve thoroughly," Boma said. "Ehn! You see your life? To what end, Stan? This is what you want. Your life in a mess. Are you the first person that will lose his wife?"

Mummy grunted. "Ah, Bomaemi, don't speak like that."

"Mummy, no. Is this what we will be dealing with for-ever?" Boma stood. "I am going to sleep. Tomorrow, you follow me to Port. Our flight is twelve noon."

Mummy started to sob. "Boma, please calm down."

"I was too calm. That's why he is where he is." She stomped into her room.

Mummy heaved. "Ah, Stanley, please now. Ehn, where is all this going?"

I stood. "I want to go and sleep," I walked out without waiting for their permission.

In the room, I emptied the two suitcases Boma packed. She had all my things, pretty much. I took two good changes of clothing and stuffed them in my laptop bag, and all of the twenty-thousand-naira Ahmed gave me the previous day before he left my house, and I got the call from Ojong, and I went to the hospital. When the house was quiet, close to midnight, I walked out into the night. I couldn't call a taxi because I wanted to be shrewd with money. I trekked into the night until I got to the main junction of the street. There, I got a commercial motorcycle willing to take me to my destination for one thousand naira.

Chapter 10

"Duru! This is ridiculous. This is absolutely unacceptable."

I sighed. "At least, I'm speaking to you now."

"Three days," Ahmed shouted on the phone. "Three days nobody had a clue where you were. Do you want to kill your mother?"

She can't die because of me. John's wahala did not kill her, or daddy's cheating and sickness. It is me. Hmm. But I said nothing because it did not matter.

Ahmed exhaled noisily. "Anyway, you are at the camp, right? Which one? Because there are like six of those places along the same area."

"I'm at Redemption camp."

"You need the total redemption of your soul," Ahmed said. "When are you coming back?"

"Today."

Ahmed scoffed. "It's evening already. Are you going to sneak in the same way you sneaked out?"

"Look, I'll come home."

"Do you know how worried Boma has been. She didn't go back to Port because she couldn't leave your mum and John to cope with all this. Why are you being so impossible? Huh?" His voice thickened. "You need to let go of this grief! Anyway, where in the camp are you?"

"I said I'm coming home tonight."

"No, no, no. I can't take your word again. Just let me know your exact location," Ahmed said.

"The first hall when you enter. It used to be the children's hall or something. You can't miss it."

"I am not coming. In fact, I'm going to bed now because I have work tomorrow but when you get home tonight, call or leave a message if I don't pick up."

"Okay," I said. "Thanks for everything."

I hung up before he could say more. It didn't feel good to be the centre of all this negative attention, but I just couldn't shake off my sadness, disappointment, and hunger for justice for Belema and Agbani. I wanted to shout and let the whole world know it hurt. Instead, I walked out of the hall and went in search of something to eat. At least, it would not be good to get home to more scolding on an empty stomach.

A special programme was scheduled for the weekend and the traders were already mostly around. I had not eaten anything since the night I was suspended at work, and I went on a rampage. Only been drinking water. My body however, seemed to have healed from all the battering. I was hungry.

I walked along a line of kiosks and finally found one that sold besides Christian books and resources, dry snacks, chinchin, biscuit and plantain chips, and soft drinks. I bought a lot and went to the back where a bench was kept, and a few people chatted. I sat down and woodenly chewed on biscuits, with sprite. I felt too tired to walk back to the hall and thought of just going to the road instead since I had my laptop bag and all my stuff with me. People came and went. To get a taxi back home would be easy.

"Good evening, ma. We are looking for a young man..."

I thought I was hearing double. That voice belonged to Ahmed, my friend of more than twenty years. From where I sat behind the kiosk, I peeped and saw Boma and Mummy with him as he gave a detailed description of me to the person, and I melted into the night. He lied to me. Ahmed never lied, and he did tonight. I was serious about going home. Why would he lie?

The salesperson said there were many young men around because people had started arriving for the programme starting the following day. Ahmed, Boma and Mummy moved to the next stall. I watched them go on and on, and then headed back to the hall. I knew this was definitely the end for me. There was no use stalling anymore. I took the opposite direction from them and vanished into the night.

DEMI

Chapter 11

"Hi. The lady from the bank?"

I looked up and smiled. Hmm, the cute dude I saw earlier in the banking hall stood beside me in the aisle of our small-town supermarket, smiling. He did look good. A very nice smile on a guy and such clear and expressive eyes. He had nicely shaped lips, though the upper lip was lost under his moustache.

"Hi," I said coolly.

"Her office voice is different." He chuckled. "My name is Idem Isong."

I hated to admit that I could remember clearly because his name, though foreign was a variation of my short form. I remember thinking my "I" is last while his is first.

"Ademilade Okuniyi. But you can call me Demi."

His hand stretched towards mine and I took a dry, strong hand.

"Huh," he grunted. "So soft."

I honestly didn't want to laugh but I did and tried to take my hand from his grip.

"Not so fast," he said. "Don't think I'm going to let go so fast, Demi."

The way he said my name sent the chills down my spine. Wow! This guy rubbed me right and I was seeing him only for the second time in my life.

"Guy, um, Idem, I need to go home. It's been a long day for me." But the soft way this came out of my belly and the silly smile on my face spoke a totally different thing. More like, *"Guy, you look so good. I'm all yours forever."*

"I can just imagine, in that bank of yours where the whole town banks." He smiled. "How about you tell me where the best joint in this town is, and I'll take you there..."

I was shaking my head before he could finish.

"Calm down. Let me finish. I would not have to ask but I'm new in town. In fact, I just moved in yesterday," he said.

"Yesterday? Wow."

"Yeah, I'm a contractor. Working on the renovations at the electoral commission complex," he said.

"Oh, you are the contractor?" I gasped. "But they started work on it a while back. So, you just came?"

"To tell you the truth, I have been dreading living in this little town of yours. I was operating from Akure," Idem said. "But we are at a crucial state and driving the stretch makes no sense."

"Oh wow." I frowned. "What was wrong with our town that you didn't want to live here?"

"The small hotel." He laughed. "Naa!"

His laughter was contagious, and I joined in. "It's not funny." I tried to look serious.

"I'm glad you are a bit relaxed. So, is it peppersoup your town is known for or ...?"

"Booli." I chuckled. "And roasted corn."

He laughed hard. "No kidding."

"And palmwine. And I don't drink."

"You see how we will have a problem. How am I going to spoil you? We need to travel to Akure or even Ilesa? Where is good enough?"

My eyes widened. "You know towns around here!"

"Well, a lonely young man, so far from home needs to find things to do, or what do you say?"

I tugged at my hand, and he let it go finally. I felt lonely without that connection and wondered what was wrong with me. Idem was quite overpowering, though.

"What I say is I'm pleased to meet you and do have a great evening." I smiled, picked the beverages I needed off the shelf, and walked to the next aisle.

He followed me as I hoped.

"Huh, not so fast, beautiful woman."

When a man called a woman "beautiful" not "pretty" it shows the man is serious and wants a commitment. I don't know where I got that from but that was what came to my mind.

"I need to get home, sir."

"Sir, not me. Call me Idem unless you have a more dramatic and romantic variation."

I could not help it, again, I laughed. After a long, stressful day in the bank, this sure was the kind of evening I wished for. He took a few cans of liquid milk and a loaf of bread.

We continued to banter about name-calling and how I found it unnecessary to use endearments and before I knew it, I was really running late. At the counter, he insisted he was paying, and then wanted to drive me home.

"I walk from here. My house is close," I said.

"When am I seeing you tomorrow, Demi?"

I shrugged. "I work late every day and now even on Saturdays."

"Let's make time. For us," Idem said.

I nodded. "Okay."

"Give me your number."

I did. For the life of me, I gave him my number. Someone I was just meeting. In 2013 not 1813 or some extinct world where anyone was safe and everything was fine with everyone!

I walked home that night with my head in the clouds. I hadn't had a man sweep me off my feet so swiftly. When I got home, my parents were surprised at how long it took me.

"I'm sorry, I just couldn't decide."

Mummy gasped. "Decide what?"

Daddy, my ever-present support, snickered. "Leave her. After working all day, you want to start nagging her?"

I smiled. As their last child and the only one at home, they loved my company and wouldn't trade it for anything. Owena was such a small town and divided by a river that also made us one town in two states. With the spate of democracies lasting this long, the town had been torn in two literally. Owena Osun, where we lived, voted so differently from Owena Ondo where our family roots were, and this consistently caused a lot of friction between friends and family. My father's brother and only living paternal uncle had not visited since the last elections and we were in another election year now. Daddy at some point had been the council chairman of the ruling party, and still had a lot of political influence.

"They didn't have our brand of bread, and I couldn't decide on those other ones," I said. True but not totally.

"Hmm, anyway, welcome. Your food is cold." Mummy squeezed her nose at me. "Go and eat."

"Yes ma. I'll just change first." I curtseyed and went into my room as my phone started to ring.

Chapter 12

"**A**re you in your room now?"

I chuckled. "Yes. How did you know?"

"Well, I reckoned you'd get home, put things away, and start your dinner. Then, go into your room, and change."

"I live with my parents. So, you are a little wrong but anyway, I just entered my room."

"Ah, you didn't tell me you have a curfew. Why do you still live with your parents?"

"Why? Because they have a house, and I have a nice big room in it." I dropped my handbag on my king-size bed. "And I love living with my parents."

"Do you have siblings living there too?"

"No, I am the last of three. The only girl too."

"No wonder, hmm. Nice."

I chuckled again. "What are you thinking?"

"Just calculating how I will beat this curfew of yours, darling."

I rolled my eyes and took off my shoes. "I'm a grown woman."

I needed to peel off my dirty skirt suit and shirt, so I put the phone on speaker.

"You are indeed." Idem chuckled. "And am I glad you are."

The jacket went first and the skirt, then the shirt in quick succession.

"Are you undressing?" He moaned. "Demi."

My hands on the clasp of my bra froze. Was it a video call? Goodness. My gaze shot to my phone screen, and I confirmed it wasn't.

"Demi? Are you there?"

I moaned. "Yes."

"Say my name. Say yes, Idem."

"Yes, Idem," I whispered.

Maybe I wasn't too experienced in these things. I was twenty-six, but Idem's voice however was so thick with emotion like nothing I had heard in my life. My knees weakened and I lowered myself on to my bed.

"God, Demi, I don't know what's happening to me." His voice deepened. "I want you so much. I can't believe we just met."

I didn't know what to say. This guy, this Idem Isong, was a man I saw for the first time in my life today in my bank. He came to open an account and deposit some money, and I attended to him. In essence, I was his account officer. Meeting him in the supermarket later in the evening couldn't count for these emotions whirling around my waist and lower stomach. My privates. Like him, I couldn't believe we just met either. I wanted so badly to lie with him. *What?*

"Demi?"

"Yes, Idem?"

I swallowed.

"Touch yourself for me, please." He paused. "Please."

I did. For the life of me, and for the first time in my life, I found myself following a man's voice and doing things I couldn't believe I was capable of. I had intercourse on the phone for the first time. It was crazy. I couldn't believe myself.

As we both panted in the aftermath, my mother knocked on my door and opened it. I was naked and too weak to do anything. Before Mummy entered, I turned on my side and pushed my phone under the pillow.

"Ademilade. Ah." Mummy walked in fully. "Poor girl. This bank work is too hard."

She took my wrapper and covered me and turned off the light after her. When she was gone, I took the phone close to my ear.

"I love you, Demi. I can't believe myself, but I do."

"I love you, too, Idem."

He blew a noisy kiss over the phone. "I'll see you after work tomorrow, darling. I'll send a message to know where."

"Okay, love."

"Sleep tight. My sweet."

Long after he hung up, I just lay in the dark. What just happened? My heart thudded. This wasn't real. I didn't just come from zero to "in love" with a man I just met. But deep inside I liked the way I felt. I hadn't been in a relationship for over a year and the dryness in my life was filled with work and family. Did I miss the emotions, maybe a little because my former boyfriend had not been a lot and after four months, I was tired. He had been a colleague at work and my work friends had thought it was ridiculous. My best friend, Lore, who worked and lived in Akure had joked that I was behaving like a desperate old maid. It made me wonder what they'd all think about Idem. This made me look more desperate. But when I closed my eyes to sleep, I had a sweet satisfactory smile on my face and joy in my heart.

"Good morning, Demi."

I blinked and there he was, Idem Isong, his face hovering over mine. What was Idem doing here in my room? I pushed my eyes open and saw Mummy opening the curtains.

"Demi, good morning. You really need to take a break from this job of yours," she said. "You are oversleeping now. Do you know the time?"

I jumped up. "Ye! Oh my God."

"You didn't even eat your supper. I came in last night and you couldn't even wear your nightdress."

As Mummy went on about my job, I ran into the bathroom and had a quick shower. I didn't check the time until I stepped into the sitting room. It was already a half past seven. The exact time I was supposed to sign in at work.

"I packed your dinner. It's yam porridge. Very sweet." Mummy handed me a food warmer inside a nylon bag.

"Thank you, Mummy. Bye!"

I ran to the road and waved down the first taxi I saw. Thankfully, there was nothing like rush hour in Owena, except that taxis would be full and drop people along the way. Finally, I got to work at a quarter to eight. The morning meeting we had every day where the manager briefed us and we signed for our cash was over, which I particularly hated because then I'd have to go and do the rounds alone or with any other latecomer. Our branch manager took lateness seriously too, and I knew this would count against me someday soon.

Bukky, my best office friend was already in her "cage" ready to start receiving customers at eight, and I waved hurriedly at her.

"What happened to you, Demi?"

"Sleep o!" I said and rushed off.

She called out. "Sorry o!"

I was still at the customer service desk for another month. The branch manager liked to rotate us in operations around all the time, which helped to develop everyone in all the units. I was just sitting down when the first customer stood in front of me.

Idem.

My heart dropped into my stomach and shame flushed me like a blast of hot sun. I remembered his voice. How I woke up dreaming about him and how my mother's voice seemed like his own.

"Good morning, Demi."

Goodness, that voice had me sweating between my thighs. What on earth was this?

I smiled. "Who could have imagined that I will sleep late, and my first customer would be you." I opened my drawer and kept some of the forms and cards for the day's job. "Please, have a seat," I said.

He sat across from me. "I overslept too. Hmm, Demi." He looked away, and then down at his feet, probably, because my table was between us, and I couldn't see what he would have been looking at.

His gesture and tone confused me. I was at work. Whatever magic powers he had...I couldn't afford to have their effects on me. Not after what happened the previous night.

"How may I help you today?" I said in my best professional voice, though it still came out thin, and shaky.

He looked up and my heart shifted. His eyes were red and the veins at his temples seemed to stand on their ends. He locked his gaze with mine.

"What did you do to me, Demi?"

I swallowed. If his eyes didn't suck me in, I'd have thought he was teasing or pretending, but the fear I saw in his eyes mirrored the one in mine. In my heart.

"We can't talk about us here," I mumbled.

Behind him, the line of customers quickly grew. Before I could stop myself, I muttered, "My lunch time is at four. I could..."

"I'll pick you at four." He stood. "Thank you."

My gaze followed him as he left. He did turn to look at me just before he was out of view, and there was no smile or gloating on his face. I dragged in a deep breath and tried to compose myself. I further confirmed this Idem was as flustered about what was going on between us as I was because once, Bukky came to my desk to get a form, with a frown.

"The first guy who came to your desk. What did you tell him?"

"Huh?"

"As if you told him off?" Bukky held the form she need-ed. "The very first..."

"I know. I'll gist you later."

Chapter 13

"**Y**ou look so beautiful."

Idem's eyes lit up on my face and a lazy smile played around his lips, yet there was an intensity about the moment. A connection I could not explain. I got into his Nissan Sunny, and he got back inside and drove out of the bank's parking lot.

A lot was on my mind, but words failed me. I didn't even know where we were going and somehow, I could not ask. Was I under a spell or what? I stared out and saw we were leaving town. I had only a thirty-minute break. Just as I turned to ask what was going on, Idem pulled over by the side of the road, just on the outskirt of town.

He pulled me into his embrace and before I could agree or disagree, kissed me on my mouth.

"Hmm, Demi." He moaned. "I can't help myself. My love."

I couldn't help myself too and when he went in for another kiss, I yielded totally. When the kiss ended, he turned away, and then started laughing. I felt so embarrassed and laughed with him to cover it too. *What was funny?* I did not know.

"Last night," he said. "After we got off the phone, I stood in front of my mirror and just laughed."

"Huh, why?"

"I had never felt so good in my life, Demi. You are like a superior drug. I'm high on you." He lowered his voice and stared into my eyes. "I am high on you, Demi."

"I'm high on you too."

His face crumpled as though he would cry, but then he smiled, and I could feel exactly the same. The fear. The joy. The confusion. The hope. All mixed into a laughter-tearful emotion too complex to aggregate. I had never been here before.

"That makes me so happy." He cupped my face. "I know this must be so confusing for you, and it is for me too, but I'm just happy you feel this way."

I nodded, too unsure of the right thing to say.

"When I was done laughing last night, I started crying and went to sleep crying," he said.

"Why?"

"You know, this fear just gripped my heart, and I asked the question, what if Demi thinks I'm a pervert and doesn't feel what I feel?" He chuckled. "And I started to cry. And when I woke up this morning, I knew I had to see you."

I smiled. "I was so scared when I saw you in front of me."

He laughed. "Everyone else disappeared. I just wanted to grab you and kiss you."

"You would have got me fired."

He took my hands and kissed each one. "You can't imagine how glad I was when you told me to come back. At least, I knew you felt something too."

We were seated in his car, having this lame conversation by the side of the expressway as cars sped by, and I didn't think I was supposed to be anywhere else in the world. After about twenty minutes, which Idem brought to my attention, he asked to take me back so I could still get something to eat before my lunch break was over. *How thoughtful of him!*

"Can I pick you up from work when you close? And we can go and find roasted corn to eat together," he said as he pulled back on to the road.

I laughed. "Wow, so romantic. Dinner by the...what will we call it now? By the charcoal fire."

He laughed hard. "That is very romantic indeed. Hmm."

"I'll post it on social media and tag you."

"I am not on social media, my dear. Too toxic."

"I know, right?" I sighed. "Even me, I'm hardly there."

"Doesn't make any sense. I started one, and just decided it wasn't worth all the drama my ex-girlfriend took there."

"When was that?"

"About four years ago. I had just been redundant there, but that awful experience chased me out."

"I won't be there if not for my friends. But my job doesn't even give me time," I said.

We got back to my office in less than five minutes, and how incredulous because I had thought Idem drove far out of town.

When he stopped the car, he kissed his index finger and placed it on my cheek. "Call me when you're about to close."

"I'll be done at eight, but my colleagues and I normally car-pool."

"Not today, please. Please," he said softly. "I need to eat that roasted corn with you tonight."

We both laughed.

"Okay," I said. "See you at eight."

Bukky bumped into me purposely at the side entrance of the bank where we all used. "What is going on, Demilade?"

I covered my face with both hands and laughed. "Your friend is in trouble."

"Ehn? Trouble? What happened?"

"That guy." I lowered my hands and sighed. "He just came in yesterday and I think I'm in love with him."

"Yee!" Bukky raised her hands above her head. "How? Where did you meet him? Just that yesterday morning he came in looking around like a peacock?"

I laughed hard. "Bukky, please don't kill me. See, we need to get back to work."

"Did he take you to eat, or where did you go? I saw him when he picked you. And dropped you."

"Are you a stalker now?" I started walking to my desk and she followed.

"Yes o, how can someone just come and sweep my friend like that? Is he a Christian?"

Oh, Bukky, the over-spiritual one. Why was I not surprised that would be her first question?

"Huh! You didn't even ask for his name!"

Our branch manager walked into the banking hall.

"We'll gist after work," Bukky said and briskly walked to her cage.

I couldn't tell her Idem had me after work, and once he arrived, I didn't plan to introduce him to anyone. One-day lover? No way. So, as soon as work closed, I carried my bag and hurried out of the building before Bukky or any of the others could get to me.

Idem was waiting outside by his car.

I got into the passenger's side in front, and he seemed to get the message. He hopped in and zoomed off as my colleagues trooped out of the bank, both of us laughing like delinquent kids.

Chapter 14

"**W**hen are you going to tell us about him?"

"Aha, Mummy! She is a grown up." Daddy gasped. "Is it because she is still living in your house?'

"Don't mind your father o, he wants to know as much as I do. So, tell us."

This was just Saturday morning at breakfast. I only met Idem the Tuesday before, but we had been out together every evening and today, I was going to his house for the first time to help him arrange and decorate.

I laughed. "Well, his name is Idem Isong."

Daddy's eyes widened. "Ah, Calabar?"

Mummy laughed. "I thought you said I should leave her alone."

"He doesn't even look like a Calabar man," Daddy said.

"Have you seen him before?"

"Of course, I see him when he drops her off."

"He's actually from Akwa Ibom," I said.

Daddy frowned. "Are they not the same?"

I chuckled. "No, Daddy."

Daddy grunted. "But they are from the same side. He is not Yoruba."

"He's Ibibio," I said.

"All of them are the same." Daddy growled. "Huh. So, how will someone find out about his family?"

Mummy laughed. "So says the man who said I should leave the grown up alone. Did she tell you they are getting married? Someone she just met."

"But he has been bringing her home every day for the past one week," Daddy said. "Is that not enough?"

"Actually, the past three days," I said.

"And so? Is three days not a lot?" Daddy shook his head. "You are not getting any younger. You don't need unnecessary relationships."

"Yes, sir," I murmured.

"Hmm, it seems your father is the one who really wants to find out about this Inden," Mummy said.

"Idem," I said.

"What does he do?"

"He's a federal government contractor," I said calmly. "They are renovating the old electoral commission building."

It seemed as though I had repeated this same answer a million times in the last three days. Bukky had wanted full details, and Lore, when I spoke with her on the phone, and my immediate older brother in Ibadan, Kayode, who I had no idea how he got to know I was seeing someone.

"I see the work going on at the building. But it's been on for several weeks," Daddy said.

"Yes, sir. He said he didn't want to live here so he commuted from Akure."

"Why? Why didn't he want to live here?" Daddy snapped. "Is Calabar better?"

"Uyo, actually. Daddy, you're making me laugh," I said.

Mummy laughed too. "Your father was forming strong man since, asking me all the questions. Now, see him." Mummy shrugged. "As if you want to marry tomorrow."

"They are working longer hours and it's telling on him to return to Akure every day. And also, he was banking in Akure, and his bank doesn't have a branch here," I said.

Mummy nodded. "Ahh, so that is how he met you?"

"Yes, ma."

"Hmm, I haven't met him of course, but he seems like a very nice person." Mummy shrugged. "Dropping you off every day."

"Thank you, ma." They didn't know he picked me in the morning too, but that information was for later.

I stood and cleared the empty plates in front of everyone. "I'll do the dishes and go to his house today."

Daddy's face jerked to mine. "His house?"

"He moved in on Tuesday and hadn't had time to really unpack and decorate the place," I said.

"Hmm. Okay."

"Thank you, sir."

Mummy laughed. "It is not easy on your father. His only daughter will soon marry."

Daddy snapped at Mummy. "You know that is not the issue. She's old enough to marry."

"Sorry, sir." She stood and we both went into the kitchen.

Mummy burst into laughter. "I have never seen your father so sad. As if you should never marry." She shook her head. "Meanwhile, he was telling me not to bother you about it."

It kind of bothered me that Daddy was like that. The last time I dated a guy, I was much younger, and Daddy was okay with both of us until the relationship ended.

"Maybe it's because Idem is not Yoruba," I said. "He'll get used to it."

"He has no choice." Mummy giggled. "So, when are you going to...?"

"Going to what? Mummy, we just met this week! Heh?"

"I have never seen you this happy. See how you are glowing!"

"Thank you, ma." I started washing the plates.

"I hope he is in love with you too."

"Mummy!"

"My dear, it is important. You need to marry a man who loves you more than you love him. Look at your brother, Kayode, the way he is following that small girl he married all over. Leaving his good job in Lagos to go and live with her in Ibadan because her family is there."

"Mummy! Ah. But won't you want me to live close to you too?"

"Yes, but she was in Lagos, and he went there only for her to move to Ibadan! Anyway, you get my point. This one that is from faraway Calabar..."

"Uyo."

"Wherever. Let him know quickly you are not moving from Yorubaland. At most, Lagos," Mummy said.

"Okay, ma." I scoffed. "If it gets to that."

"And of course, you know men like that, they want everything quick quick so don't be slack. Don't allow him to start having second thoughts."

"Aha, Mummy. But you said I should be sure he loves me more than I love him."

"Yes, I said so." Mummy nodded. "But once you establish that, you two can marry. You are not a child anymore."

"Yes, ma." I laughed. "I have heard you." I rinsed the last plate and put it on the rack. "Let me go and get ready. He will soon come."

Mummy smiled. "Okay, dear. Greet him for us."

I nodded and hurried to prepare. I knew my parents would really like Idem's personality. He was outgoing and respectful, and hopefully, Daddy's issues about him not being Yoruba would fade fast once they met him.

Idem arrived on time to pick me, and I went out to the roadside to him, with a big smile on my face. As soon as I entered the car, he said,

"Is Daddy at home? And Mummy?"

I nodded. I looked back at our closed-in compound with the big gate.

"Will it be okay to just come in and say hello?"

My mouth dropped open for a second. "Of course," I said.

Chapter 15

"**I**dem, Idem!"

I looked at my father for like the hundredth time and wondered what magic Idem had performed on him. From the moment they were introduced, they talked non-stop for almost an hour, and Mummy and I had to even leave them to do other things. To say my mother was so excited would be an understatement. She swooned and hugged me.

Finally, my father let Idem go, and we went back into his car.

"You want to go out with my father or me?" I said.

"Jealousy!" He chuckled. "Wow, he is a fascinating man. Can you believe he worked with my father on a committee that campaigned for the first democratic president?" He pulled on to the road smoothly.

My eyes widened. "Really? Daddy is a wonder, honestly."

"He worked with many people I knew. You know I told you I'm active in politics back in Akwa Ibom."

"You did. Hmm. I'm just wondering, you know, politics in this country is tough," I said.

"I know. And so dirty too."

"I lived all my life being a politician's daughter. Huh, it's not a life I want for my children," I said.

"So, I should leave politics?"

The implication took a second to dawn. I laughed. "No. I'm just saying."

"I will leave politics in a fast jiffy if you don't want any part of it."

I threw back my head and laughed. "Well, I thought you were just doing politics because your father did."

"I introduced my father to politics, but he can enjoy it to the fullest, I don't care." He stole a glance at me. "I only want what my woman wants."

"Yes, sir," I said.

"I mean it," he said as he pulled up in front of a one-storey house in a high-income part of town where many of the old Owena money sank in huge family buildings.

For the sake of politics, my father had not owned a property here in order to display his moderation as a "man of the people." Our house was more in the centre of town, but Daddy had built a mansion in Owena Ondo where his widowed sister lived with her children.

"I didn't know you would get accommodation around here."

Idem parked at the side of the house. "Apparently, the owner up until now didn't want to rent it out. I think it belonged to the father, and he died."

"Yes, the Ominirans. Chief Ominiran died two years ago, and the kids came and took their mother to Lagos to live with them. And the house has been empty," I said, and got out of the car.

"Apparently. But it's newly renovated and costs an arm and a leg," Idem said.

"I can imagine. My father was the old man's acquaintance but so much younger, so I don't know any of the children."

We went into the house. The white-painted wall smelt fresh, and Idem had some simple furniture already set up, two couches and four single chairs, a centre table, and a seven-piece dining set in the adjoining dining area.

I exclaimed. "The sitting room is huge!"

"And there's another one upstairs. Costs as much as what I was paying in Akure for a three-bedroom." Idem snickered. "I thought I'd pay half or less."

"But this is so much bigger."

"Yes, sure. So, I slashed some of the money I pay my staff and gave them accommodation here. Very cost effective, right?"

"Yeah." I dropped my bag on one couch. "How many rooms are here?"

"Three down, three up. There's a kitchen down here, and each room is en-suite, so the guys I put upstairs cook on the balcony, or sometimes they come and use my kitchen. And there's a BQ, with two rooms and a toilet."

I smiled. "Wow! Very big and nice."

"Let me take you round, and then we can eat, unpack and do small fun stuff together." He planted a quick, surprising kiss on my lips.

"Okay." I giggled.

He took my hand, and we walked into the rooms he had told me about. We entered his bedroom last. It was the only one with a double bed, and not much else. Several boxes and suitcases were on the floor.

Idem pulled me into his arms and kissed me hungrily. For several minutes, we just kissed and touched each other.

"I want you," he moaned. "So much. So much." He raised his head and stared into my eyes. "Do you want me?"

I nodded, too overwhelmed to speak. He covered my mouth again with a kiss, and his hands covered my breasts. I groaned but he continued to knead me, making me want him so much. Unable to breathe, I tore my mouth off, and he bent his head to kiss my neck, and his mouth just kept going down until it caught my hardened nipple through my blouse.

I cried. "Oh, Idem."

He picked me and lay me on the bed. I felt so helpless to stop him from unbuttoning my blouse and freeing my breasts from the cups of my bra.

"I love you so much, Demi. My own. My love," he said.

As he sucked on each breast, he unbuttoned his shirt too and pulled it off. I spread my palms over his back and moaned with every dart of his tongue.

"Tell me you want me, Demi. Please."

I sobbed. "I want you. I want you."

He came up and took my mouth in his as I felt his hands pull down my skirt with my underwear. There was no way I could stop him now. Totally naked, I lay beneath him and allowed him to take me. Own me.

Completely.

Chapter 16

"**Y**ou didn't tell me you're a virgin."

"You didn't ask," I mumbled.

He wrapped me in his arms. "I am so blessed to have you, my love. I still can't believe it."

I couldn't believe myself. Less than one week of knowing a man and I had given my body to him. The fascinating part was that I didn't feel bad about it. It felt like the right thing to do. I knew this would never come out in the open because I was a serious Christian and none of my friends or church people or my pastor would understand the love and urges I had for this man. Or the way he reacted to me too. I was madly in love with Idem and he with me. Did I love him more than he loved me like my mother advised, at this point, it was hard to say.

"I feel so hungry now, I don't know if I can stand up to unpack," he said softly.

He nestled his head in my neck and took lazy love bites off my skin, and I threw my leg over his thigh. It was the comfiest position on earth. Sweat from our lovemaking started to dry off my body and I shivered a little from the cool air from the air conditioning.

"Are you cold?" He pulled me even more into his warmth. "I don't ever want to stand up from here."

I dozed off but I could hear him on and off. I didn't want to stand up from here either. Ever. Idem was the best thing that happened to me. I could feel the thudding in my chest, the longing, wanting. Perhaps if this happened to someone else, I'd think it was impossible to love someone so fast. A girl with my upbringing who turned twenty-six a virgin, would probably never do this but this was me now, and I had no regrets.

Idem woke me up later with some food he bought at the only classy restaurant we had in town, fried yam with assorted fish and garden egg sauce. It was my best dish, and he knew. After some long kisses, we settled down to eat.

"If you didn't live with your parents, I'd ask you to move in here." He took a fleshy piece of fish and put it in my mouth then dragged it out with a kiss.

We both laughed and choked on the hot spicy sauce. Water dripped from my eyes.

"My parents will never allow you," I said.

"Not unless I marry you," he said.

"Marry! We just met...this time last week, I didn't know you existed." I gasped. "Hmm, we can't marry yet o."

"But we just made love, and I didn't use any protection," he said. "You could be about getting pregnant as we speak."

My heart dropped into my belly. He was right, and that would be so scary. I looked at his face and he had this very sweet smile that told me he really meant what he was saying in a good way. Idem wanted to marry me? Bukky and Lore had not even met him, and our families had not met. My oldest brother, Poju, in Ilorin probably had not even heard about him if Kayode or my parents didn't tell him.

Besides, *we just met.*

"I feel like I'll die if I don't wake up every morning with you," he said.

I had never been here before. I didn't even believe this kind of hot emotions existed until now, happening to me. Me wanting someone so much in my life, I ached.

I sighed. "I want to marry you too, Idem. But we need to know each other better. You have to meet my family, and I meet yours. And you have to meet my pastor."

"I totally understand that. I want to meet everyone in your life, and you meet mine too." He sighed. "It's just that I love you so much."

"Me too." I leaned over and kissed him. "I love you more."

The kiss lingered and then he said, "Is your pastor as spiritually radical as mine? Because we just committed a big sin today."

We both laughed.

"My pastor will kill you if he hears what happened today. After he suspends me."

"What unit in church are you in?" he said.

"Prayer. The over-hot one o," I said. "I used to be in praise band but my work didn't allow me attend rehearsals."

"We need to pray together for forgiveness, my love. I feel guilty but not for having you because why would something so beautiful between us be sinful? It doesn't add up, you know."

"When did you become a Christian?" I said.

"My sister, Uwana, is a firebrand. She fired me unendingly until I gave my life two years ago. I had to break up with the babe I was dating because Uwana insisted it was a sinful relationship." He chuckled. "That's why I'm so grateful to God you are born again too."

"Or you'll break up with me?"

"If you say that again, I'm going to flatten you under me until you get pregnant."

I raised my hands up in the air. "Sorry, sir."

After the sumptuous meal, we made love again, and all sore but happy, I helped Idem to unpack some of the artwork he had and hung them up in the sitting room. He had a photo frame with him, a plump, fair skinned woman and two children.

Before I could ask, Idem said, "That's Uwana shortly before I came here."

"Her kids? Or yours?"

He laughed. "Funny. Her two kids. Her husband died before the second was born so I've been there, you know, for them. She lives with our parents."

"Wow. Sorry about that."

"She's strong."

I stared at the woman. She looked happy. The picture looked like one that was taken in a light mood. The kids hugged Uwana and Idem seemed to run in just in time. The younger one looked to be three or four, while the older was about seven.

"She looks happy, despite all," I said.

"I'm trying to get her a new husband. It's been three years!"

"I don't believe it is as easy as that." I looked around. "Where do you want it?"

"Huh, anywhere. In between the artwork?"

He had small nails in the wall, so I found one and hung the frame. Inside my heart, I didn't like it. I didn't like the way Uwana looked so at peace and for me, that seemed silly.

Chapter 17

"So, you now have a boyfriend? Does Pastor know him?"

I smiled. "He met Pastor today in church, but you know how Pastor is busy on Sundays. He fixed an appointment for the week."

"Oh, my friend has found man o!" Lore clapped. "Ah, Demilade! You never cease to amaze. See you. Abeg, tell me all about him."

Since we were kids, Lore and I had been friends, all through primary and secondary schools, and university. Then she got a job and a man in Akure, and she got married two years ago, and so now every Sunday, we hung out together. I'd either make the trip to Akure, or she'd come to Owena. We had done this for four years and, I told Idem I had to go and see my friend. He offered to drop me and see some of his friends too.

Telling Lore about Idem only made my feelings more real and genuine.

"I really want to meet this guy who has swept you off your feet," Lore said. "To think it took me almost one year before I could even go on one date with Mr. Akande." She giggled.

She called her husband, Tayo, Mr. Akande when she wanted to make jokes.

"Mr. Akande sure is a strong man to get you, Lore," I said.

We made some jokes about the men who had come and gone in our lives.

"No, I think this your Idem is the strong one o, to just remove the carpet from under you like this." Lore shook her head. "I still can't believe it. This time last week, he didn't exist."

I waved my hands. "God is doing a quick work in my life. Hallelujah!"

"Idem should sha not come between us o! Demi? How many ears do you have?

I curtseyed. "Two, *Mummy*."

When Idem came to pick me, Lore walked with me to his car, and they met. My ever-cool friend had a few questions and then waved and went back inside.

"Your friend doesn't like me," Idem said, and pulled into the road.

"She's hoping you are not taking me from her," I said and laughed.

"I have already." Idem arched an eyebrow. "Me that I'm marrying you tomorrow."

"On our one-week anniversary, please, tomorrow is too soon," I said.

"Do you want exceptional suya and palmwine?"

"Huh?" I gasped. "For the wedding?"

Idem laughed so hard tears came off his eyes. "No, I mean now. There is this exceptional suya spot here in Akure, and my friend wants to meet you."

I laughed. "Oh, I was afraid that you're planning for real."

"Well, we need to get to planning, you know."

I was not too familiar with the streets in Akure and Lore had never taken me "out" in real terms. Idem manoeuvred skilfully as though he knew his way around and we continued our silly chatter until he pulled up by the road.

"If you like this suya, I will have it at our wedding reception," Idem said.

"I believe you," I said.

He came out of the car, and I followed him into a "buka" like restaurant, but with a raffia roof. Several patrons sat and watched football on a small screen while they had suya served in stainless steel plates, and palmwine in small gourds. The smell of meat roasting on a spit in the front filled the space, mixed with the heady palmwine.

I exclaimed. "I'm not drinking palmy with you, Idem!"

"You don't have to, darling." He took my hand. "Yele is already here."

A fair-skinned hunk of a man stood at a table in the middle of the buka and smiled. "Idem the great," Yele said in a heavy Yoruba accent.

"Omah-yay-lay!" Idem laughed. "I trust you to be here already. Did you order?"

"Umu Ibom." Yele laughed and they shook in a silly way. "Haba, you will not introduce me to your woman?"

"Sorry, sorry. Demi, meet my friend, Yaylay."

I smiled. "Hello, Yele." We shook hands. "Nice to meet you."

"The pleasure is mine, Demi. Idem has spoken so much about you, wow!" Yele said.

I smirked. "Thanks. Good things, I hope?"

"What else can it be?" Idem helped me sit. "I'll get our order. Yele, don't hit on my babe before I return o!"

"When I don't want to die," Yele said.

For the rest of the evening, we laughed and talked. Yele was a very jovial man who had a big laugh. At about nine in the evening, Idem and I made the half an hour journey back to his house.

"Come in for a minute, darling," he said.

"I wish. It's late and you know I have to get up early," I said.

In all sincerity, I wanted to go in, but I knew what would happen. We would make love as we did the day before. I still felt guilty about that and didn't quite know how to process it. I was happy to have given Idem my body, yet I felt ashamed and shy. It had never happened before, and I had been in more than three relationships. I couldn't even tell Lore this happened. I would in future anyway, but…

"Please, darling." Idem's voice grew husky, confirming my thoughts. "Just five minutes." He cupped my face and ran his thumb over my lower lip. "I've tried to hold myself all day."

I came out of the car and ended up in his bed.

I went in to my parents' home close to midnight, knowing the following day was going to be tough. To my surprise, I woke up on time, feeling strong and able. When I started to pray, a voice inside told me God wasn't going to hear me anyway so why bother.

Why bother?

This wasn't good for me. I didn't think it was safe to be in such a relationship just one week in and everything that mattered seemed to have been tossed to the winds. But I couldn't regret meeting Idem, or the way he made me feel, the joy that compassed me when he was with me. I had found my soulmate, and he had found me, and heaven help me if things didn't get out of my control the way they were going haywire already.

Chapter 18

"Duru! Count the bags of cement left. Be fast!"

For some strange reason, I stared at the rough-looking man Idem called to as we both sat in his site office on a Saturday morning. The man looked new on the site, but that wasn't why I noticed him. His eyes were dark and dead, like someone who could kill or do anything asked of him. He stared straight at Idem and said nothing for a second, as though he detested being shouted at, but this was the only way Idem could run a successful site. They had barely a month left before the project was commissioned and Idem wanted to present a perfect job.

The man turned and walked out of the office with a slight arrogant gait.

"I've never seen that one before," I said.

"He's a drifter. Hardworking as a horse." Idem snarled not looking up from the laptop he worked on. "Cheaper than cheap beer."

"Chai, baby, which one is cheap beer?"

"Exactly." Idem chuckled. "Yes, I'm done. I just need that moron to give me the figures and we can go to my house." He looked at me. "Or do you want to eat pounded yam? I found one Ijesa woman in you people's other Owena who is fantastic."

"Lore said she's coming today."

"Not tomorrow?"

I shrugged. "I was surprised too."

"Saturday is the only day I have you all to myself, now she's coming here."

The rugged man walked in through the open door. "36 bags," he said so low it was almost inaudible.

Idem arched an eyebrow. "Pack them on to the truck and take to the chief's compound."

The man left without a word.

"Well, when is Lore coming? And going?"

I blew Idem a kiss. "She said five. So, she can go back on time."

"And you'll still go and see her tomorrow?"

"My love, you know I belong to you alone. If she stays long, I won't go to Akure tomorrow. I'll be all yours," I said.

"After church or before." Idem stood. "If she's coming five, then I'd better drop you. It's almost four thirty. I'll just come back here and drown myself in work."

I chuckled. "Love of my life! You will be fine. Akwa Ibom, e-do okay."

Idem laughed. "You try. But it's ah-doh-kay. Like say-ing it's okay."

"Gotch ya, baby."

Outside the men loaded the cement on the truck.

"Why give it to the chief?"

Idem shrugged. "Community gift. Instead of selling it."

I smiled. "That's so kind of you."

When we got to my house, Lore was already chatting with my parents. We went into my room immediately as we normally did when we stayed indoor and didn't have somewhere to go.

"Demilade, how much about this your bobo do you know?" Lore said the minute she closed my door behind her.

My friend wasn't one who minced words, so I knew there was something.

"Why do you ask, just tell me," I said.

"Look, I'm not sure. But I made Tayo check him out after I saw him in Akure some weeks back, maybe even two months or so ago. In a hotel. With a woman."

I frowned. "In a hotel in Akure?"

"Is it impossible? He brings you every other week…"

"It's not impossible but I know every time he goes everywhere. He has friends in Akure…oh, wait." My head began to pound. "When did you see him?"

"I can't remember exactly. Seven eight weeks ago. At Sheraton," Lore said.

"Ohh!" I laughed. "It's his sister, Uwana. She wanted to visit him here, but he lodged her in Sheraton. He said our hotel here is trash." The realization was a big relief. I breathed hard. "Ah, Lore, I almost died just now."

"His sister." Lore did not smile. "Why would he take her there without you being with him?"

"I was at work."

"Did you meet this his sister during her stay?"

"She works too and had to go back..."

"Go back. Go back to where? After one day or two. To Akwa Ibom?"

"Ah, Lore, what is it now? I know you don't like Idem, but you don't have to start accusing him. Huh."

"You don't want to be reasonable about this?"

"Reasonable in what way, Lore? In what way? I have explained to you the situation. The fact that Idem gave me a detailed information is enough. Please."

"Hmm. Why are you shouting?"

"I'm not shouting." But I was. "I just don't like that you are trying to find fault with Idem. Nothing I have said about him is good enough for you."

"Huh, good enough for me, how? Am I the one marrying him? Don't I have my own husband?"

"Then mind your own business, Lore!"

"Me? Mind my own business? When I'm telling you something so important and you are just shouting at me. When you should listen. I should mind my business, Demilade."

"Yes. Lore. Mind your business."

"Well, sorry." Lore shouted. "My business is your business, and your business is mine."

"Well, no!"

"Yes!"

We stared each other down and breathed hard.

"Are you girls okay?" Mummy called out.

"We are, Mummy," we both shouted at the same time.

"What I am saying is that just as much as you think Idem is not cheating, I think he is," Lore said. "I asked Tayo to check this out, and one of his friends said this was the third time this woman was lodged in Sheraton in two years."

"And Idem has been in this area for two years. What is wrong in his sister visiting twice in three years?" I snapped.

"Two of those three times, you were already his girlfriend. And you didn't meet this woman?" Lore paced. "Huh, as in love as you two are?"

"We've been together for barely six months, and I work five sometimes six days a week. I travel, he travels, and so how much time do we really have together?"

"Every day, if you ask me."

"Look, I don't even need to explain this to you. You never liked him, but it's sad you'll try to spoil him to me," I said.

"He brought her here, Demi. To Owena. To his site. On her last trip," Lore said.

The implications hit me harder than I wanted to admit to my friend. I covered my face unsure of whether this was the time or place to come out clean with my friend.

Chapter 19

"**I**'m pregnant, Lore."

Lore remained quiet for so long I thought my confession had killed her. I had to look at her. Her mouth was open, her jaws sagging. She glared at me and then I realized it was the disappointment I saw in her eyes that really did me in. Guilt clutched on the threads of my heart and caused physical pain.

"How long?" Lore's voice finally came in a whisper.

"Three weeks." I tore my gaze from hers, unable to process the hurt in them.

"What did Idem say?"

"I haven't told him. I went to Ife yesterday during my lunch break and bought one of these pregnancy kits at the teaching hospital." I sighed. "I missed my period. Which has never happened."

"You slept with him?"

Involuntarily I laughed.

In six months, I can count on my fingers the number of times I didn't sleep with Idem. He just made it feel so right and when I agitated about getting pregnant, he took me to a private clinic in Akure and I got a thing inserted to prevent conception. Obviously, the thing had not worked this month because I was positively pregnant.

I snickered. "I think that's what makes a woman pregnant."

Tears clouded my eyes. Now Lore had a theory about Idem cheating, a new fear gripped my heart. What if he didn't want the baby? Or worse still, demand for an abortion. What was I going to do? I stretched out on my bed and closed my eyes. It was going to cause a mess in church. Sister Demilade of all people. Pregnant! It was the worst thing that could happen to me. Being caught! This was what the church cared about. The image and what would younger sisters in Christ think. But I ached. Not only for my sin but the fear of the consequences. After the first time with Idem, I had shouted down my conscience continuously until this day, when it all seemed to come down hard on me. My reality.

Lore sat beside me, but I refused to open my eyes. "See, you need to tell Idem, and for crying out loud, announce you're getting married. Can he marry you in one month?"

My eyes flew open.

"If you can marry within this next month, no one will be able to judge you," Lore said.

I gasped. "You want us to cover it up?"

"It's wrong, I know but a mistake is a mistake, and you can't just allow church to pounce on you for one mistake." She drew in a shuddering breath. "No one will hear it from me."

"Aww, Lore." I sat up and hugged her. "Thank you so much."

"What are we friends for?" She hugged me back.

I couldn't let her know it wasn't "one" mistake but a sinful lifestyle I had come to love, expect, look forward to. Shame on me, but I couldn't lie to myself about this. My conscience was seared. Dead. And to think what bothered me more wasn't sex with Idem, or what people would think about my pregnancy but the possibility that Idem would break my heart made me even more depraved. Was my faith even ever genuine? Or I just grew up following statuesque.

"Look, let's just pray about this," Lore said.

That was when I noticed she had tears in her eyes.

Oh, my darling friend. If she knew where I was, she'd be utterly heartbroken.

"Oh my God! When did you find out?"

Idem kissed my mouth again and laughed. I laughed too. His reaction was such a relief. He picked me up, kissed me and then kissed me again.

"We should celebrate this specially." He picked at the button of my blouse. "God! I'm going to be a father."

Within minutes, we were in the throes of passion, "celebrating" our continued sin. I just was so relieved, though. After what Lore told me about Uwana visiting twice in the last two months, I feared there was something Idem was not telling me. But with this reaction, and his joy at my condition, I couldn't be bothered. I loved Idem, and I believed anything he told me, and it didn't matter whatever else. Not every fact was the truth. Simple.

When we were totally spent, bathed in our sweat and leisure, Idem said, "Marry me, Demilade. It doesn't make any sense for us to be living apart anymore."

I snuggled into him. "I will, darling. I love you so much."

In that moment, as those words left my mouth, I knew I had replaced God with Idem in my heart. The realization dawned and scared me, but I quickly pushed it aside and succumbed to Idem's kisses and exciting rant.

"We can do this as soon as you want, my sweet. I know my parents will want to come but it's such a long trip and they'd rather just send a representative. Would that offend your parents? Because I know you Yoruba people like a lot of fancy and crowd. If you want, I can charter all my Ibibio people hundred-kilometre radius but oh my God! Lord, I'm going to be a father. Wait. You can't tell your pastor, our, I mean, no one in church must know. I don't want all the drama they do in that church." He cupped my face. "Let's marry in two weeks. Is that too soon for your father? I mean, we can say that we are "burning" and don't want to sin..." He punctuated his words with kisses and laughed at the last statement.

I covered his mouth with mine. When the kiss ended, he sighed noisily. "God, how I love a sexy woman in my bed."

"You are talking too much," I said. "And worrying. My parents will do anything I want. No excuses. Two weeks is fine."

"Great. Well, let's get down to it. What are your colours for the day?"

"I just want a simple wedding. People know I'm low key already. And I always told my parents, the day I decide to marry, don't let it shock you I will do it in a hurry."

Idem laughed. "You knew I will come by, right? Good. Because I've been wanting to marry you for the last six months."

When I got back to my room that night, something struck me. In all the rant and scream, and joy and love-making, and planning our wedding, Idem never once questioned the contraception, which had failed us. He was just so happy. Just too happy.

Chapter 20

"I think it is only proper for his family to visit. Even once."

I sighed. I couldn't understand why my parents were so insistent. "Daddy, it's election year. His father is running for office in the state house of reps," I said.

"But this is marriage," Daddy said. "What is the hurry? Elections is in five months. Can't you wait to marry in six- or seven-months' time?"

"I expected you to understand." I stood. "I'm just tired."

It was most unlike me and very disrespectful, but I stomped into my room and slammed the door. Five minutes later, Mummy barged in.

"What is wrong with you, Ademilade? When did you start stomping out when your father is…"

"I'm pregnant, Mummy."

Mummy's mouth dropped open, and she sagged against the wall. "Yee."

That reaction was expected. My parents were Pentecostal believers, and elders in our church. They were sterling parents who raised us right. Poju had missed a few miles along the way but after he moved to Ilorin and got a job as a graduate assistant at the university, his life started coming straight again. Kayode and I had never missed the road, and I can only imagine what this news was doing to my mother.

"We need to do a wedding before it starts to show," I said.

Mummy dragged her hands over her face. "You have killed me, Demi."

"I'm sorry. But again, I don't know. I'm sorry to be a disappointment." I shrugged. "That's why we need to marry before it comes out."

"You will fail the church pregnancy test," Mummy whispered. "Pastor will never agree to join three people."

"That's why you should give your consent quick. Talk to your husband." I sat on my bed and gave Mummy my back. "And I can do a small registry wedding."

"Ah, Ademilade. How did you allow the devil to gain control of your life?"

Maybe talk like this, which I heard consistently had hardened me. Or maybe the devil had come over me like Mummy said. Whichever it was didn't matter as long as I got my wedding day in.

"Mummy." I turned to her. "I'm sorry to come out to be what you didn't expect. But Idem and I love each other and the only reason why we want to marry quietly is to save you all the embarrassment."

"Demi!" Mummy gasped. "You're not sorry for what you did?"

"Okay, fornication. I am sorry. But Idem and I asked God for forgiveness, and we are trying to make amends by getting married right away."

"I heard everything," Daddy said from the doorway and Mummy, and I jerked towards his voice.

My father for that split moment looked ten years older and I really felt bad for him, and for Mummy, but I realized I didn't even feel bad for myself. My church, my family, the society all hammered on doing right. Yes, it was good to do right but what really was right? Each time I was with Idem, it felt right. And what society counted as wrong for us was beautiful. I really couldn't care at this point how my parents felt or how this would make them look. No one ever bothered about what I wanted or what I thought was good.

I never bothered until I met Idem, and he opened my eyes to all the good things of life.

"When do you want to do the ceremony?" Daddy said.

I looked down at my hands. Regardless, I loved and respected my parents, and I didn't want to be the source of their frustration or sadness.

"Idem is ready when you are," I said softly.

"Tell him to pick a date. I am ready too," Daddy said.

"Aha, Daddy. Ready how? She...how will...we are..."

"Mummy!" Daddy dragged the word softly. "We are ready."

"Thank you, sir," I said.

Daddy turned and walked out of my room, and Mummy followed him.

"Ready, sir!" Mummy said at the top of her voice. "Have we done the necessary investigation?"

"What nonsense necessary investigation?" Daddy shouted in response. "Does your daughter look like someone waiting to hear investigation results?"

Mummy cried. "Ah, I am finished."

The door slammed.

I felt empty, as though something major had left my life. I stared into space and in that instance, all I wished was that I was in Idem's arms.

"They will come around. If you need family, I will come."

"No, Uncle. Daddy is attending. Just that he is upset." I shrugged. "I don't know how to apologize to him."

My father's only surviving brother, Uncle Ige, shared a glance between Idem and I as we sat in his sparsely furnished sitting room in our ancestral family home in Owena Ondo. Absently, I tugged at the raffia stuffing of the leather couch where there was a little tear further causing damage.

"You don't need to apologize. Just do whatever he says from now on," Uncle Ige said.

"The only thing he has asked for is a date." I sighed. "I don't understand how he..."

"Then give him a date. Do you have one?"

"Yes, sir. We do." I nodded and looked at Idem. He nodded his consent.

"What is the date?"

"October 16, sir," Idem said.

Uncle gasped. "Next week? What is the rush?"

"It's what we want, sir." I smiled at Idem, and he smiled back.

Chapter 21

"Look, forget about fables and myths. I'm covering my veil when I walk in whether the judge likes it or yes."

"You are such a beautiful bride, Demi." Kayode smiled. "And don't worry, everything will be fine."

Tears pooled in my eyes. My big brother, so supportive and kind. I smiled. "Thank you, Bro. Kayode."

Daddy called out. "We will be late the way you people are going on!"

Despite the anger and frustration, everyone came around for me. Bro. Poju couldn't get time out of work at such short notice, according to him, though I still struggled to wrap my head around that. Idem's parents were not going to be around either but his friends in Akure were standing in for them.

Because of the way everything went, Daddy had received my dowry and gifts in a closed-door ceremony an hour before the registry wedding. Suffice to say that my pastor refused to be a part because of the pregnancy, a church I grew up in where my family did everything for. Stories for another day...

Lore covered my face with the veil. "We're ready, sir!" She called out.

She looked around my room and we hurried out.

As much as it was not meant to be a big wedding, it still was. My family and friends filled the small courthouse on this bright and beautiful Saturday morning. My groom looked dashing in a black suit and white shirt, with a blue tie, with Yele, who was his best man. I wore my beautiful white flowing gown, and Lore wore a navy-blue dress. I didn't have a train because of the way everything seemed rushed, and what was the use of a train if I wasn't having a church wedding.

After the civil marriage at the court, we had a small reception at Idem's house. My new home. My parents, Lore and her family, Bukky and a handful of my colleagues and my extended family all laughed and ate in a light celebration mood. Yele and two other guys from Akure as well as the construction site workers also came for the free food and merriment.

Finally, towards evening, people started to leave.

"No thanksgiving in church tomorrow, right?" Lore said to me as we both packed some of the food for her to take away.

I shrugged.

"That just feels wrong. I know it's wrong, what you did but…"

"It's not important, Lore. I'm married." I shrugged again. "And Idem said we could worship in the church he attended in Akure. If I really want to."

"It will be good to go."

"I don't know. If I wake up early."

Lore smiled sadly. I perfectly understood how she felt. I had been her maid of honour, and I remember how excited she was on her day. And I was too. She had been a virgin and her groom too. It was the dream we all wanted for ourselves. She had gone for honeymoon right after her wedding. Everything for her had been perfect and I had never imagined mine would be different in any way.

She hugged me tightly. "The most important thing is for you to be happy, Demi. Are you happy?"

I became emotional and sniffed. "I wanted better, but I am with the man I love so yes, I am happy."

"I am praying for you. And regardless of what Pastor or the church does, don't lose your faith. And your husband too, you have to pray for him, and both of you must forgive. Okay?"

I smiled. "Okay, ma."

We both laughed. She picked her food, and we walked out together. Idem was also seeing some other people off. I waved at Lore and her family. She shouted that we would see the following week since I'd be on honeymoon this week, and I laughed.

Idem's site was closing and there was still so much to do to ensure the project was ready for commission.

"We really should go for honeymoon," Idem held my hand as we stood and watched the cars drive away. "What do you think?"

Yele was still around with another of their friends.

"I think your baby wants to sleep. My feet are swelling, and your friends still want to gist," I said.

He placed a long kiss on my mouth. "I will let you go and rest now, so that when I come in, you will not have any excuses."

"Hmm, you wish."

We walked into the house. "What else can a brand-new groom do?"

Yele stood. "Ah, that is the cue for us to leave."

The other man stood too. I thought Idem should introduce us, but I was too lazy to point it out.

"Thanks a lot, Yele. And your friend," I said.

"Rashid."

"Oh, okay Rashid. Thanks." I yawned. "This old bride needs to sleep."

That night, I closed my eyes and refused to think about tomorrow. I don't know if Idem checked in with me as he said, but the next time I opened my eyes, it was Sunday morning. I had slept through my wedding night.

Chapter 22

“I don’t understand what the big deal is, Demi. You are just making a fuss out of nothing!”

I stared at my husband. This would be the first time he would ever raise his voice at me, and I could hear very clearly the frustrations beneath the tremor in his voice. And I wondered why. I thought it was a big deal that on our wedding day, no one from his family wanted to hear my voice, say “hi,” or welcome me into the family. The only member of my nuclear family, Poju, who couldn’t make it, called three times and spoke with Idem twice on that day.

“My family is not yours and can never be. It doesn’t make my parents less caring or concerned.” Idem paced. “I told you my father is on a campaign trail with the governor and Mummy will want him beside her when they call. Together.”

“I don’t understand that!”

“You don’t have to. Just accept it, babe. Accept it.” He stared at me, wide-eyed, as though we spoke two different languages. “Please. Just take it like that.”

I couldn't. It rankled. It was over a month already since we got married and I haven't spoken with my parents-in-law. Suffice to say, my father had relapsed to silence since our wedding day, I didn't want to ask him if Idem's parents had, in the spirit of culture and tradition, "greeted" their in-laws. Shame made me feel helpless. Was it because I was pregnant? But wasn't that even a good thing in some climes?

I swallowed. "Okay. When are we going to visit?"

"After the baby comes." Idem walked to the wardrobe and pulled out a pair of jeans.

"After the...why?"

He turned and walked over to me and kissed me on my mouth. "Because that is the earliest I plan to travel to Akwa Ibom." He kissed me again. "You don't have a clue how dangerous it gets during elections. Which is just about four months away. Things must settle down before I risk you and our baby on such a journey." He kissed me more.

I warmed into him and wrapped my arms around his waist. "I'm sorry. It's just that..."

"I know how this is. It's just a bad time but we'll be fine. I promise."

I pressed my head into his chest. "Thank you."

"I love you, Demi. Nothing else matters." He pressed a kiss on my forehead and pushed back. "The very last batch of workers are being paid off today. Then I want to dash to Akure. See Yele. Talk some business. See if I can nab a contract around there." As he talked, he got dressed.

I sat on the edge of our bed and followed him with my eyes. I loved him so much it hurt, and I didn't think he even understood the extent of my love.

"Lore coming tomorrow?"

"Yeah."

"I was thinking maybe we should go together, and I drop you at her house instead of you being alone here," he said.

So thoughtful. Always thinking about me.

"No, um, Bukky is coming later. Just to hang out with me," I said.

"Okay then love." He picked his car keys and came to cup my face. "My parents are not going anywhere. You will meet them. Soon. Sooner than you can imagine, darling."

I nodded. "Hmm."

He laughed. "I'll bring some of that crazy delicious suya for you."

I smiled just to make him feel better, but I didn't feel a lot of joy or happiness. "Thanks darling."

Shortly after he left, Bukky came to visit.

"You need to insist on this, Demi. I mean, how will you be married to a man you don't know anyone in his family." She rolled her eyes. "He's not even on social media for you to go find his people."

"Honestly Bukky, I don't know anymore."

"You have to know o. Aha, is he a spirit?" Bukky gasped. "What if he is a spirit? Yee, Demi?"

"Stop!" I laughed. "What kind yeye spirit."

"I don't know o. Why are your parents even quiet about this? They should…"

I sighed. "They are still upset with me that I got pregnant. Short of disowning me, they are leaving me to my fate."

My parents' betrayal hurt more than anything else, but I just had to live with it. My brothers kept their distance and Poju even came to town once and didn't bother to check on me. I felt so alone sometimes on this.

"That's tough," Bukky said. "But, my dear, you need to go and meet Idem's family. You need to go to Akwa Ibom. Or you will have a child and not know where your baby is from? If they eat grass, you join them and eat."

"I've brought this up with Idem and he is just as frustrated about it. This is election year, and it's not safe to be on the road. Uyo doesn't have an airport. We still have to travel from Calabar and though I understand it's not far, the road is not really good."

"I don't know what you can do. I mean, no one thinks he's a ghost or anything but…"

I burst into laughter. "He has a sister, and Lore even knew when his sister visited in Akure."

"Yeah, you said so. Anyway. Come. Wait. Is the sister on social media? What's her name?" Bukky opened her phone tentatively.

"Uwana Isong."

For a minute, Bukky searched online. "That name is very common. Like fifty of them."

"Apparently, it must be a common name." I rubbed my temple. "Thinking about it makes my head hurt."

"Well, in your condition, you should try not to think too much so you won't fall sick." Bukky frowned. "How's the morning sickness?"

My pregnancy was shy of three months and the sickness continued. I shrugged. "I hope it will get better."

Bukky wasn't married but she lived alone and with her family in Ibadan, work was her only reason for living in Owena. I and other office colleagues were her only friends.

"Stay positive. Even though I know things will get better. Worrying about it doesn't help you or the baby."

"Thanks, Bukky." I chuckled at the serious look on her face. "You look so serious. There's really no problem. Idem is not even worried at all. I'm the one making a fuss."

"And it is perfectly normal to fuss. Really." Bukky grunted. "Before my sister got married, my parents told her to go and live with the guy's family."

"Live? Huh?"

"Yes. You know he's Ibo. My mother told my sister to go and stay with her fiancé's mother during her annual leave." Bukky scoffed. "That's how she went o, and she learned so much. Hmm. You know it is a serious matter. But let me not stress you over it. As long as Idem is comfortable it's not that they don't like you." She paused. "Or they have disowned him."

I laughed. "Disown? No o."

But long after Bukky left and Idem came back. Long after fulfilling our daily lovemaking session, I remained awake and thought about Bukky's concerns. What if I was married to a ghost?

Chapter 23

"**I** have to, Demi, my father needs me."

"Then I'm coming with you," I said. "I am travelling with you."

To make my point clear, I marched into our spare room and took one of my empty suitcases. There was no way in heaven or earth my husband was travelling to Uyo and I would not follow him. We had been married for close to six months, which meant I was about six months pregnant, fit as a fox and ready to take on anything.

After he sold his sob story about being afraid for me and our baby in election period, and all, I hadn't asked about travelling again, but quietly waited for our baby to be born. I knew in my heart that the seed Bukky sowed about marrying a ghost had matured in me. I knew I was in trouble because it was definitely the most unnatural thing for a man like Idem to have no contact whatsoever with his family.

Since I never brought up the issue about his family again, he too didn't but now he wanted to go and see them? I was coming with him. I returned into our bedroom and dropped the suitcase on the floor.

Idem smiled. "Fine. We'll travel together." He pulled me into his arms and kissed me. "My beautiful, anxious wife wants to meet my family at last!"

I frowned. "Is that a lofty dream?"

He burst into laughter. "I never thought it was. I would want to meet my family." He cupped my face. "When you stomped out of the room just now, it occurred to me this must have really bothered you, and I have been insensitive. I am sorry."

I sighed. "You can't even understand. Sometimes, I wonder if you are a ghost. I... you didn't even talk about Uwana again. I just..." The thought of my fears overwhelmed me, and I crumbled. "I have been so scared."

"Oh my God, ghost? Of all things?" He chuckled, and then brought my face to his and smiled. "You are the most amazing woman on earth. I am not a ghost, heh!" He pulled me to sit on his lap on the bed and smoothed his hands over my bump. "I have a confession to make, though."

My heart thudded. Here it was! I knew there just had to be something. How was I going to handle this? Was he married to someone else? What could his confession be?

I sniffed. "You are a ghost?"

He laughed. "Of course not."

"You are married?"

"It's complicated..."

I tried to stand up from his lap, but he pulled me in. "Idem, no, I..."

"I'm not married. But my parents didn't want me to marry you, and I know I lied to you about them, I'm sorry." He turned me to look at him, into his eyes. "I love you so much, and when you told me about our baby, I called their bluff."

My teary eyes widened. "Idem?"

"Yes. My father is very powerful, and very proud, as you may imagine and now, he has won the seat in the state house, he is even more arrogant. My mum wants me to come and make up with him." He sighed. "Besides, I need another big contract. Since the last one, you see how difficult it has been to get anything sensible around here."

I felt ashamed of my doubts and fears and hugged Idem's neck. "I'm so sorry, darling. I've just been thinking of myself alone. I never knew."

"I know. And you shouldn't apologize. I was trying to protect you from the ugliness of it all. But I was wrong. You are my wife, and I should have told you." He scoffed. "Especially the way your parents treated you. I should have told you."

Tears poured down my face, and he kissed my mouth deeply.

"Stop crying," he moaned. "It kills me to see you cry."

"I'm sorry. I... you know what? You need to go on this trip alone," I said. "When baby is born, you can take me. By then, everything should have settled between..."

"No. It's not fair. You are coming with me, please. Please." He cleaned my face with his hand. "I have a flat I still maintain. We'll stay there. I can go and see my parents and then bring you later to meet them."

"Are you sure?"

"Of course, love. I am very sure."

I jumped off his laps. "This is huge. Oh, my goodness. I am so excited. Wow, Idem! I'm going to Uyo."

It was my selling point to visit my parents for the first time since I got married. Daddy was grouchy about it and thought it was high time, and Mummy was just so happy the anger between us was ending.

Lore screamed when I told her and Bukky hugged me. Suddenly, the tension around my life succumbed like ice on fire.

Idem had wanted to travel the following day but to give me some time to apply for leave, we postponed the trip by a week. I couldn't remember the last time I was so excited. And alive. What a life.

"I just feel so strongly that we should pray together."

I smiled. "Lore, the great. Why not?"

"Listen Demi, this is not even a joke anymore. You haven't been to church since you got married and I totally get that. You did not get the support you deserved. But you can't be angry forever."

"Angry? At who? For what? I'm not angry o."

"Please, spare me. Pastor and his wife, other church members. Your parents. Even God." Lore sighed. "Me, maybe?"

"Ah, why would I be angry with you?"

She shrugged. "I don't know. But it's time to let go of it all. God wants you to move on, come back to him."

"Lore, it's tough. I don't know. Sometimes, I try to pray but I can't. I end up ranting."

"That's why I want us to pray together. I know you're pregnant and can't fast, but I will fast, and we can just pray together now, before you travel tomorrow, and when you arrive. Just now and tomorrow. Okay?"

"Hmm, okay. Will I reject prayer?"

"It's not about rejecting prayer, Demi! You need to rededicate your life to Christ. You and Idem. You two need to come back to God. I mean, you were wrong to get pregnant before marriage, but you can't play victim now."

I rolled my eyes. "It is well with my soul."

Lore and I prayed. It was just the day before my trip to Uyo via a flight from Lagos to Calabar. It was big for me. I did need prayer and Lore's support was priceless. I felt something in my heart. I did feel sorry, but my anger still simmered.

"It is well with you, Demi. The Lord go with you to Uyo, and be with you and guide your every step, and lead you."

Chapter 24

"Hi! Uwana!"

"You know my name? Good."

She waltzed past me into the sitting room in Idem's flat in Uyo two days after we arrived, with two men.

"Idem talks about you every time." I ignored her coldness. "Your picture is in our parlour back home."

"Our parlour, meaning the parlour in my husband's house in Yoruba? Right?" She looked at the two men with her and they all laughed. "Can someone throw this fool out of my house before I give her miscarriage."

"Uwa..."

The two men closed up on me and took me by either arm. Before I could spell jack, they picked me up and walked out, flung me on to the concrete floor and while I struggled to my feet, slammed the door shut. The first thing I did was try to reopen the door. It was locked. I banged on it and shouted at the top of my voice.

"Idem!" I kicked the door. "Idem, open this door!"

To think we made love the night before as was our ritual and he was sleeping in late, when I stood, feeling like a good wife to prepare breakfast. After breakfast, he wanted to visit a friend but feeling lazy about it. To think while I went to check who knocked on the door, Idem was scrolling through his phone in the master bedroom of the two-bedroom apartment. There was no way he didn't hear my conversation with Uwana...*his wife*! Idem was married? How? Why would he tell such a lie to me? Live such a lie?

My head pounded as I continued to bang and kick the door. No one responded.

The flat was one of eight in a three-story building and Idem's was on the ground floor, so I could turn round to the bedroom window. I found a stone and threw it at the sliding window, but it hit the woven metal burglary proof, which sandwiched the sliding glass.

I cried. "Idem! Idem!"

This couldn't be happening. My baby started kicking hard, and I took a step back, panting. I had to think this through. Since we arrived, Idem had gone to see his parents once. He told me it was a good meeting, and I would meet them soon. It never even occurred to me to ask after Uwana. I was just way above my head with joy.

"Idem, to God who made you, open the door for me..."

"Or what?" Uwana shouted a moment before she pulled back the curtain and I could see her clearly.

Idem stood behind her.

"Idem. What is this? Are you married to Uwana?"

Uwana stepped aside so I could see the full view of my husband. The man whose gold rings sat on my finger. It was a criminal offense in Nigeria to be married to more than one woman at a time. The registrar said it at our court wedding. Did Idem understand the full import of what he was doing? I will sue him to hell and back.

"Look, Demi, I can just say now that yes, I married Uwana, but only traditionally. And..."

"Tell her how many children we have," Uwana said. "Fool."

Idem exhaled. "We have two kids. Listen..."

"You don't owe her an explanation. A woman who steals another woman's husband deserve no better," Uwana said.

"Idem, you never told me you were married." Angry tears streamed down my face.

I figured I had nothing to discuss with this woman, and my husband was the one I needed to face.

"He did not have to tell you." Uwana snapped. "Can't you find out about him? All you these desperate Yoruba girls. Ino! You have seen handsome rich guy, and you sink your teeth into him. Thief." She hissed. "A man brings you to this flat that has no furniture and you believe him. For your information, this place belongs to those two men who threw you out. They are my brothers."

I screamed. "Idem!"

"This is why I married you, Idem." Uwana snickered. "You have guts, my darling! You go Yoruba go marry! Idiot."

Idem cleared his throat. "I'm sorry, Demi, I..."

Uwana closed the curtains.

"Idem! Come and open your door now. I deserve an explanation," I said.

Instead, Uwana opened the sliding window just enough to squeeze out my purse and shoes.

"Go back to where you came from. If you try and harass us, I will have my brothers beat you to pulp and drop you by the roadside. Remember this is Uyo, not Yoruba. It is my city! And my father-in-law is a member of the state house!"

I stared at my purse and my shoes. What was this?

Lore's prayers rang in my thoughts, *it is well with you, Demi. The Lord go with you to Uyo...*

"Thank you, Lore, I don't know what we would have done without you and Tayo."

"It's the least we can do, Mummy," Lore said. "I just thank God she made it back."

"Hmm, thank God." Mummy heaved a heavy sigh. "It's now to get her to eat and stop crying."

"She'll be fine," Lore said.

I sat on my bed and starred into space as my parents stood by the entrance of my old room and Lore put the rest of my things away, after she and her husband went to my former house, break the door open and pack my things out.

"Idem is married to someone else," I said softly, and huge tears dropped on my cheeks.

TIWATOPE

Chapter 25

"When she opens her mouth, hian. You will jump and wonder where the sound is coming from." Stanley winked. "Wato is great like that."

"Stop calling her, Wato!" Mummy laughed. "You sef, you allow him to call you that!"

I shrugged. What could I do? Stan was my weakness. I was in his family house every day after school and grown so fond of him.

"What does Wato mean?" Boma looked up from reading a book on the couch.

Stanley shouted. "Her name. Ti-WATO-pe."

"Ah! Stanley!" Mummy laughed more. "The wato itself means drooling!"

"Ye!" Boma laughed. "Huh, why can't you call her Ti-watope like everyone else, Stan!"

"Is she complaining?" Stan gave me one of his winning smiles. "Huh, Wato?"

I shrugged again. "Stan can call me whatever he likes."

Boma rolled her eyes. "Abeg, not wato. No wayz!"

Boma always treated everyone as though her opinion was the best and must be taken. Stan always indulged her. I'm not sure I liked Boma so much because of just how she imposed her opinion on everyone.

For six years, since our senior secondary year, when I was on the same team with Stan for an inter-school debate, I hadn't been myself. It was strange how you went to the same primary and secondary school, and you didn't fall in love until the final year in secondary school. I worked my way around Stan. He attended a university in Lagos, and I applied to the same school and got admission and graduated. I just wanted to continue to be around him, and I was.

I am.

"Anyway," Mummy said. "Back to what I was saying about your singing. I couldn't believe it tonight. Ah, my daughter...you blessed my life."

I curtseyed. "Thank you, ma."

Boma closed the book she was reading. "How come I wasn't invited to this program?"

"It wasn't in church," Mummy said.

"It was at a studio," Stan said. "Though, my God, it was something else. The artiste was under anointing, ehn!"

Boma snickered. "Ahha, because of Wato's voice?"

"Ah, no no no, Boma, you can't call her wato!" Mummy shouted. "None of you must call her that."

"I am the only one with the right," Stan said.

I shrugged for the umpteenth time. It didn't matter to me.

"Well, if Boma is going to start calling you my special name for you, I'd better drop you off at home," Stan said.

I picked my handbag. He should have dropped me off before coming home with his mother, but she asked to come home quickly to attend to Stan's father who had a stroke. Though Boma was home, heavily pregnant, and with her husband going offshore she stayed with her parents so she would not be lonely, Mummy still preferred to take care of her husband by herself.

"Ah, Stanley, my son. This girl must not escape you o!" Mummy clapped. "She is my wife already. Any time I need comfort, she will sing for me. I see a Yoruba girl in your fate!"

"Wato, let's go, jare." Stan reached out and grabbed my elbow. "Before Mummy will start suggesting names for our unborn children." He laughed.

I smiled and curtseyed. "Bye, ma. Bye Boma."

"Bye my dear," Mummy said.

Maybe it was my mind but Boma didn't answer. Was I to call her Sister Boma? Hian!

Inside his Nissan Sunny, Stan said, "If I knew you could sing that well, I'd have invited you to my church a long time ago! Haba! Wato! And you couldn't tell me?"

"I sang, you just didn't hear it," I said.

Stan gasped. "Lailai! Wato, you never sang in my house, or in school."

"Well, maybe humming. And I came to your church a few times...more than a few," I said. "You never asked me to..."

"Because I never heard you sing!" Stan laughed. "So, now that I know, you should come for one of my special programs."

I giggled. "But I always come for your special programs."

"I mean, as a soloist," Stan said.

"Really?" My hand shot to my mouth to cover my gasp. "I don't think..."

"Come on, you like drama!" Stan said. "Even if we have enough voices, I want yours in my band."

I couldn't believe my ears. From when we were in primary school, Stan sang. Everyone liked him, including me. I believe I must have fallen in and out of love with him for as long as I could remember. Each time he showed interest in another girl, my love died and would then resuscitate again when he was over the girl.

Until six years ago.

Through university. And youth service. And now we both have jobs, him in a bank, and me in the ministry of education, as an administrative staff.

To be a part of Stan's band...

"You don't want to join us," Stan said softly.

I realized he really was expecting me to respond.

"Of course, I do!" I cried. "I just can't believe you want me."

"Like seriously, Wato!" he snickered. "You know, when that guy...what's his name?"

"Who?"

"The musician guy who we went to record for."

"Kenny?"

"Yeah, Kenny. You know when he told me he wanted to do the studio thing, and he invited you to back up, I was surprised, but I didn't say anything because I don't really know him. My pastor recommended him to..."

"We went to the same secondary school, now," I said. "He was a year our junior."

I knew Kenny well, because he wanted me to be his girl-friend and for so long, I'd been giving him a capital "no." A class year my junior but two years older in age...hmm, no.

"He said so."

My heart skipped when I saw my house ahead. I didn't want the ride to end.

"You know what, Wato. Are you going home to do any-thing in particular?"

"No. Why?"

"Let's go to church. I want to test something."

Yes! "Oh, sure." I smiled. I just wanted to be with Stan.

Chapter 26

"Sing that line again."

I did. It was unbelievable but Stan and I sang while he played different instruments. This man walked in and just sat in the pews and listened to us. It got so spiritually heavy that the man went on his knees several times and fell to his face once.

Stan.

I never imagined he was so gifted. So spiritual. So deep. He laughed around a lot. Joked. Gave everyone and everything a name. When we did a duet, I died in love with Stanley Duru. He realized how well our voices blended. My voice had never harmonized so well with anyone on earth. I squealed and jumped in excitement.

"Listen, we're going to record some of this," Stan said. "It sounds so good! And I don't really like to sing."

The man in the pews shouted. "Lucifer!"

I gasped. "Why do you say that sir?" Before I could stop myself. I looked at Stan and he laughed.

"Don't mind Austin. He thinks I am reincarnated Lucifer the archangel," Stanley put down the rhythm guitar he had been playing and smiled. "I'm famished. We should find food."

I nodded. It was very late already, and I knew my landlord would not be happy that I was getting home close to midnight, but I wanted this time to stretch.

"Where will we buy food at this time, sha?"

Stanley winked mischievously. "One iya alamala closes around three. Believe me she turns the amala while you wait."

I burst into laughter. "Amala at this time?"

"You will love it, Wato. And you can eat just one wrap."

I couldn't believe my ears. "How many wraps will you eat?"

Stanley looked up as though thinking about it. "Ah, it's late sha. Maybe three."

I laughed louder. He was tall and thin. Where will the food go? But I just shook my head and allowed him to lead me out. It was past eleven already.

Lucifer.

That was Stan's pet name in his church, and oh how so appropriate. Because he could sing so well and play all the instruments. His special programs were where artistes came to worship on Stan's band. He had a full band. And his pastor allowed him to manifest his gift. The first of the programs I attended was where I surrendered my life to Christ. Started to speak in tongues, and worshipped God non-stop for three hours for the first time in my life. The monthly program was attended by many people from other churches, and my parents never missed it, though we were members of another church.

Austin, a man I gauged to be in his thirties walked up to us, and gripped Stanley's hand with a huge smile. "You are a blessing, man of God!"

"Heh, don't call me man of God o, Austin! Then pastor is what?" He pulled the man. "Come let me drop you at your house."

I could see something strong between the two. A relationship. A deep friendship. The man couldn't be less than ten years older than Stanley.

"No, Lucifer of God. I want to do night vigil. I already told the security," Austin said.

"Pray for us o!" Stanley bowed.

We left the church. In the car, my curiosity got the best of me.

"Who is he?"

"Austin? Hmm, he came to church some time back to beg for food. Pastor gave him more. Food clothing...he was homeless, so they got him accommodation," Stanley said.

The streets were clear of traffic, and I just loved driving at this time of the day with him. He was relaxed and an aura oozed off him that drew me to him. I wanted to tell him I was in love with him. So strong was the urge.

"Wow, that's so kind of Pastor," I murmured. *Oh Stanley! I love you so much...*

"Yeah. Austin is a great guy. He just was unfortunate."

"What about his family?"

"I don't know. I guess Pastor would know though." Stanley chuckled. "We're here. Chai, parking!"

I pulled my gaze away from this guy I was dying silently over and looked at the road. We were in a small street with cars parked on both sides of the road, making it difficult for cars to pass. Still, there seemed to be traffic on this small street.

I gasped. "Are all these people here for the amala?"

He laughed. "Yes o, my dear. When you eat this amala, your life will change."

I couldn't believe my eyes.

"Lord Jesus, give me my space o," Stanley said.

As though an angel was waiting to hear the command, a man walked quickly to a car parked right in front of us with a nylon bag. He got in his car and started it. When the car in front of us moved, Stanley waited for this man to pull out and we got his parking space.

"Thank you, Jesus!" Stanley said. "You know, one day I came here and spent almost two hours waiting to park. Then I prayed and God made a way for me."

"Hallelujah!"

"Yes o, my dear Wato. I now pray for parking and God answers me every time," he said.

There you go again, Stanley called me "dear". It was music in my ears.

"Yes," I answered softly, not sure what I was responding to.

To my surprise, he took my hand, and we walked into a crowded restaurant together. The first thing that occurred to me was the amala woman must be doing some form of jazz to have so many customers at close to midnight. We found a table, and a waitress came to take our simple order – four wraps of amala and mixed meat with malt drinks. Stanley paid. He proceeded to make small talk about our music and what his band did. I was surprised to learn that he really had a full band, and they always worked with many artistes. In fact, he had a mobile band with people from all walks of life all over the country and they provided instrumental services for free. All the artistes had to do was just provide them with the logistics – transportation and accommodation when necessary. They fed themselves. Wow, I kept saying.

"We do back-ups too if they want," he said. "And you are joining us, right?"

I beamed. "Of course."

"I hope you won't want to be paid o, with a voice like yours? Na God dey pay us o," he said.

I smiled. "No, Boss. I won't need to be paid. Now or in future."

"I like the way you call me boss." Stanley winked.

For an awkward second, I just stared at him. Overwhelmed by my feelings. He glanced at me and arched an eyebrow.

"Did I say something wrong?"

"Oh, no. No." I giggled.

They brought our hot amala, and honestly, Stanley under-described this food. I ended up asking for a second wrap. It was so good. A little spicy though and perhaps, that was the caution I needed. Spicy food always made me have a running tummy.

Back on the road, Stanley asked for my thoughts.

"Please I need the address of this place," I said. "Ah, I must eat this thing tomorrow."

Stanley laughed. "Be my guest. We can come together tomorrow."

My heart sank into my stomach. He liked my company at least. That was enough.

"That will be very nice," I said.

"Let me pick you up at work, and we can do this again. Yeah?" I nodded. He smiled. "Play music and eat amala gbigbona!"

I giggled like a schoolgirl in love.

I love you, Stanley Duru, I moaned in my head.

He dropped me in front of my compound and waited for me to get inside. Then he waved and drove off.

The gateman shook his head. "Ah, o ti n gb'okunrin?"

The man never minded his own business. Already accusing me of "manizing."

"Mi o gb'okunrin o, Baba Isale!" I defended myself viciously and marched towards the house.

The house was a duplex, and my landlord, stayed in it with his family, but let out the in-law suite, which was downstairs, to me. The only way my parents agreed to have me rent close to my office, since they lived on the Island and my office was on Mainland, was if I would live with a family. They and I also, felt it would be more secure. But maybe because my parents escorted me to move in, and also met my landlord and his wife, the man had been watching over me as though I was his child. He even had rules...so annoying.

As I turned the lock on my door, which had its separate entrance from the main house, Landlord came to stand on the balcony upstairs.

"Tiwatope! Where are you just coming from? At this time!" Landlord barked.

I rolled my eyes. *What business was it of his?* Yet, my upbringing did not allow me to be rude. I curtseyed.

"Ekale sir," I greeted.

"Ale? This is not ale again o! This is oru! Almost 1 am! Haba! Don't you have work tomorrow morning? Where are you coming from?"

"I. I went to church, sir. I joined a band, so we were practicing," I half-lied.

"Band? Do your parents know about this?"

At twenty-two, almost twenty-three? What was this?

"They know, sir."

"Good. Good. Anyway, you have a visitor. She has been waiting for you since." He grunted. "I will send her to you now."

A visitor. I never had visitors, and for the person to wait in my landlord's house. I wanted to ask questions, but the man had upset me too much already. I opened my door and went inside. My room was big enough to accommodate a double couch. I wasn't much of a designer, but my colours were cool tones of purple and peach. I made my bed every morning so that when I returned home tired from work, I'd be able to sleep on a neat bed. I was a tidy person, and very clean too. Cleaning was not a difficult thing for me at all. I did my cooking myself and never ate outdoors, which changed tonight, and brought a smile to my face.

Someone knocked followed by my name. "Tiwatope?"

I couldn't recognize the voice, but this person was not from Lagos because they pronounced "p" in my name wrongly.

I jerked the door open, and gasped. "Belema! Belema Sekibbo?"

Chapter 27

"That's how I just packed my bags o, and Lagos here I come!"

I stared at my room mate in orientation camp in Delta state. I couldn't believe it. Maybe during a boring room chat, she may have gotten the gist that I was a Lagosian. Maybe not. Truth is that we never uttered more than a few sentences per time.

"How did you get my address?" My gaze flew to the huge suitcase she dragged into my room with her, and a smaller raffia bag, and a hand luggage. She had relocated!

"Guys on camp knew you." She took off her shoes by my door and yawned. "I'm so tired. Your landlord is nice o. Hmm. I ate rice and Yoruba stew. With kanda, lol." She sat on the bed and smiled at me. "It's so good to see you. I started to panic o. Did I get the wrong address? In this Lagos!"

"Wow! Well, I thank God for you for sure. But right now, I need to sleep. I have to wake up early and go to work." I sighed. "The bathroom is just right there in case you want to take a bath before you sleep. I normally can't sleep without having a bath." I hung my bag where I normally did. I wasn't a good hostess maybe because I was so shocked to see her.

I didn't know how her presence made me feel. Awkwardly, I walked to the bathroom and turned to smile at her. What guys knew me on camp? I was as quiet as they come!

"Please make yourself comfortable. When I get back from work tomorrow, we can talk," I said.

She heaved a heavy sigh, and her next words made me feel guilty. "Oh, thank you so much, Tiwa! I was so scared you will turn me away, but I really needed to move to Lagos." She ran to me and hugged my neck.

If I knew how to faint, I would have. This girl snubbed me so much on camp. And once we passed out of the orientation camp, I didn't see her again until, well, the Christian fellowship had a send forth party after the final parade...but, oh yes! She must have seen my address in the photo book the fellowship did. All in good faith, they wanted us to keep in touch and...

"Wait, how did you get my address? It's not the same one I left in the photo book," I said.

She laughed. "Photo book? Who photo book epp? I asked o. People in the fellowship who knew you," she said.

I gasped. "Nobody really knew me."

"So, you think!" She flopped on my bed, instantly rumpling the sheets. "Lagos here I am!"

My heart sank into the bottom of my stomach. I didn't want to live with this stranger and for some reason not quite clear to me, I didn't think she would be a great friend or someone I'd like to be close to. I really needed to take a bath and sleep. I walked into the bathroom and closed the door. I tried to take as much time as I could, trying to understand what to do with my guest. When I walked back out, she was fast asleep, in her travel clothes, and sprawled across the bed. Quietly, I just took a pillow and slept on my couch.

"Amala can't happen today, I'm sorry."

"Huh! Why now?"

I wanted to cry. "My friend from NYSC came in last night from home and I need to get back to her so we can discuss and plan."

"Oh well, let me know when you can go. You see, it's always better to go in the night. Late. Or should I come and pick you around ten?" Stanley chuckled. "Your friend should be asleep."

It was a great idea, but I was feeling tired already. "Maybe tomorrow or the day after."

He grunted and I knew I had given the wrong answer. For a moment, I felt my own disappointment. At the same time, Stanley's disappointment made me feel good, as though I was being chased.

"I want to eat amala with you." Stanley laughed. "Okay, we'll try again tomorrow. Take care, babe."

"Thank you."

When I hung up, a sob escaped from my lips. I wanted to eat amala with him too, but Belema would be waiting for me, and if I settled her quickly, then I could move on with my life. She had relocated to Lagos, and it was only fair to help her. If I had moved to Rivers State, I would wish to know someone who could help. I encouraged myself that amala would happen the following day. And Stanley called me "babe!" That stayed with me.

Belema had cleaned the room, and cooked jollof rice when I got home. I was the clean type, and I kept all my things neatly, but when I entered my room, I almost didn't recognize it.

"Ah ha! You've been busy," I said.

Belema was on my couch, watching my TV. She smiled. "What else can I do? Sitting alone all day. I browsed the internet for jobs until I was tired."

I dropped my bag on the bed and took my shoes off. "Wow, thank you. I thought I was neat."

"Don't mind me o, it's fake neatness. If you see my room back home." She laughed. "I wanted to impress you."

"And I am super impressed. And hungry."

I strolled into the kitchen, and it was quite clean too. It excited me. For a moment, I felt elated. Maybe I had misjudged Belema, and I felt guilty. I dished a healthy portion of jollof to my plate. The fried meat looked a little burnt but the love and thought behind it made me overlook this.

"Do you like cooking?"

Belema laughed. "Let's just say, if someone else does the cooking, I will be glad."

"I like cooking and cleaning. So, I'm happy to host you." I sat with her. "So, did you find anything interesting on the internet?"

I put a spoonful of rice in my mouth and almost spat it out. But I was good at pretending. My gaze shot to Belema, but she was scrolling through her phone, so she missed the shock on my face. The jollof was pepper and salt. I looked at the heap on my plate and knew I would not finish the food.

"Pepper, shey? Sorry!"

But she didn't look up. She pushed her phone towards me instead.

"I found this job website but I'm not sure they are real. I mean, they have so many jobs lined up. In this economy where jobs are scarce."

Thank God I brought a bottle of water with me from the kitchen. I drank for a moment and then sighed.

I groaned. "Tell me the pepper was a mistake."

Belema laughed. "It was. But you Yoruba like pepper, na!"

"Not like this o!" I sniffed.

Chapter 28

"**I** already paid for the studio."

I rolled my eyes for a third time in a row.

"Please." Kenny lowered his voice though it was soft already. "Please, dear."

"Look, I already promised Stanley something, and I disappointed yester..."

Kenny's gaze dropped to his feet. Standing in front of my desk, the posture made him look small, and I felt a tug on my heart. I wanted to shout at him and tell him once and for all it was not possible. I wanted to eat amala tonight. To think that I had put amala off for one week was insane. Belema got me so stressed taking her out every evening after work to meet different people who wanted to employ her. I could blame it on myself who was being nice and trying to get her connected. I'd told her the best way to get a job fast was through direct introduction, and in my haste to help, or not, I offered to introduce her to people I knew. The appointments were all in the evening after I closed from work, and so I jeopardized, pushed off, and apologized to Stanley to understand.

"Stanley has got nothing on you, Tiwa," Kenny said. "He's just wasting your time."

I shot to my feet. "What do you mean by that?"

Kenny's angry gaze met mine. I was surprised he looked upset. What was with the frown? I was the only one who had a right to be upset.

"What I mean is that I want you to sing for me."

"Again!"

"Yes, again!" Kenny said between clenched teeth. "It is a blessing to hear your voice. Your voice inspires my very being," he whispered harshly. "I will be...my music will be nothing without you!"

His eyes flashed with rage and mine as well, I guess. I was very angry with him to come on to me like this. And all the while asking for my help with his recording. For several seconds, we just stared each other down. Kenny gave in first.

He looked away. "I'm sorry. I get so incensed when you talk about another man." He turned his eyes back on me. "Do you forgive me? Your baby."

"Huh. You're not my baby." I sighed. *How do I get him off my case?* "I'm seriously not available."

"I paid almost five hundred thousand for four hours, please. Please, love."

There was a way he looked at me that my carnal insides liked. It infuriated me that he was looking at me like that right now.

I heaved an exaggerated heavy sigh. "Okay." Amala would just have to wait one more day.

Kenny gave a small smile, blew me a kiss, and walked out of my office. I rolled my eyes two more times and shook my head. Kenny was a great musician, and he believed so much this was his path in life. I think he could be successful. He had a great voice, and he was anointed. The music he recorded with Stanley was so soul lifting I played it every day. But that could be because Stanley was there, right?

"Ah, thank God you haven't closed."

My head shot up and I saw Belema standing in front of me. I gasped. What did she want here at my office? How did she get here? We'd talked a lot in her one week of being with me, and I had told her where I worked, of course, but how did she find me?

"Belema! How did you get here?"

"Hmm." She took the seat Kenny just vacated. "I can just say it's God o. Can you believe I got lost! I said let me come out and look for work. I have been walking around for hours trying to find you."

My eyes widened. "Trying to find me? Huh! Why?"

"So we can go home together." She lowered her voice. "My money finished." She cackled. "I left since around ten o!" She looked around. "Please do you have water?"

My mouth dropped open and only one thing came to my mind...*what kind of agbero is this girl?*

"And food." She giggled. "Huh, Belema! Your life!"

I shook my head, too dumbfounded to speak. She didn't tell me she was leaving the house. My goodness! I couldn't believe this. At least, I was grateful that tonight was not amala night or where would I have put her? Send her home? Definitely, if she would agree. She had pestered me to take her out and I told her my life was very private. Even on her first Sunday, we had not gone to church because my mother was hosting her church association, and we had gone to my family house for the weekend. She followed me around like a puppy, for the life of me! How did her mother even allow her to come to Lagos by herself?

"I don't have any food o," I said. "I can get you water sha. And I told you I was going out tonight and will return late, so why would you come here?"

"Huh! It's true o, you said you were going somewhere after office. Honestly, I'm sorry. I forgot!" She sighed. "I'm depressed and forgetting things so easily."

"You're depressed." I scoffed. I didn't believe her. How convenient. *The day I want to go out is when she is so depressed.* Chai, I wanted to beat her!

"Huh, you don't believe me? Hmm, I am o, Tiwatope. Look at you, with a federal civil service job while I'm still roaming, when we finished youth service at the same time…"

I rolled my eyes. "You can't even come with me where I'm going," I said, almost grateful to Kenny.

Dramatic Belema went on her knees. "Ah, my sister, please. Don't leave me to sit at home waiting."

Her gesture made me laugh. And she joined in too.

"Abeg, stand up jo! It's a music studio. I'm recording with my friend." I said.

She jumped up. "Ehn! Music studio. Ah, please let me come with you."

"No! Huh."

"Please now, no treat your sister like this!"

"Do you sing?"

Belema laughed. "Sing kwa."

"Exactly. It's serious. Serious work. And we will be there for four hours," I said, hoping this would discourage her.

"Still better than going to sit in that your room, listening to your landlord pound his wife," Belema said.

"Chai, Belema! He doesn't." I hated gossiping.

"So why is she always falling down the stairs or walking into the wall? Her face is always puffy or having one cut or the other."

"Is that what she told you?"

"Yes!" Belema retorted. "Plus, I hear vibrating wall every day."

"That's so sad. I never see her around."

"Because you are busy, you have a life." Belema cried. "I mope around all day!"

I sighed again. "Well, let me finish my work." I picked one of the files on my desk and opened it.

"Thanks, my darling." Belema hugged my neck. "I won't disturb you."

She took the seat opposite me and took out a novel from her bag.

Chapter 29

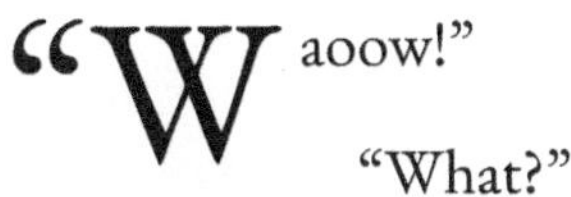

"Waoow!"

"What?"

"This bobo fine o! Chai, Tiwatope."

I looked at Belema as though she had grown horns. Which bobo? I lowered my voice. "Kenny?"

Belema nodded and breathed through her mouth.

My gaze went to Kenny who stood beside the sound engineer and stared at the settings on the mixer. He looked at us and arched an eyebrow. Belema covered her mouth over a gasp. I couldn't believe it. She blatantly gawked at him. We just walked into the small studio. We'd not even greeted the guys. The instrumentalists were ready and actually, everyone was waiting for me.

"Tell her I'm taken," Kenny said. He kept his gaze on me.

"Ewoo, sorry o," Belema said. "I'm Belema, Tiwa's friend."

Kenny snickered. "Pleased to meet you." He kept his eyes on me and added. "Can we start?"

I murmured. "Of course."

Not once did Kenny look at Belema afterwards. Recording was hard. Kenny was a gospel artiste. But the song we did that evening was more of a love song titled "After God."

After God, na you
No one can come betone (between)
After God na you
My love my life my one

The song kept ringing in me long after we got back to my house. Belema sang it over and over with her off-key voice. She kept complimenting Kenny for such a powerful song. She did not say it in any terms that she wanted to woo Kenny, but it was obvious she planned to. She told me to invite her for all other recordings.

"Are you the one he composed the song for?" Belema asked suddenly before we slept.

"No!" I gasped. "Of course not. I'm just his...a backup."

Belema laughed. "Oh, better! Kenny ooo!"

I shook my head. I didn't understand what was going on with Belema. All up to the end of the recording she had gawked and moaned. Kenny didn't even have so many lines. I did more of the singing.

After God went on to launch Kenny's career but at this time, we didn't know it would. It topped the charts all over Africa.

That night we did the recording however, Belema did not let me sleep. She went on and on and on about how handsome Kenny was. She mentioned his beautiful but gruff tenor voice, his mannerisms, his relentless hard work, his talent with music and song writing, how "sweet" the song was. Belema talked about Kenny's handsome face, and square jaws, and Adam's apple, and height and muscles, long legs, beautiful hands and nails, as he held the microphone stand and sang. His beautiful eyes. The way he arched his eyebrows. How beautiful the shaped eyebrows were.

Belema moaned. "Even the way he stared at you, Tiwa, when you were singing!"

I went to bed that night with a headache, and a tinge of jealousy. I wish I could be infatuated like that, and I also discovered something else. I hated that Belema liked Kenny.

When I got to the office the following morning, I saw a custom-made card from Kenny that read: *After God na you, Tiwa-temi.* I smiled. My colleague, Lanre, came around and saw me smiling at the card.

"Tiwa has finally been conquered o!" He shouted and two or three others came and hugged me.

I beamed. "No o, don't mind Lanre o." But it felt good.

"Put the card on your desk," Lanre said.

"No o! Please!" I laughed. It was a huge card and would crowd my desk. "I'll place it on the floor beside my seat."

All through the week, Belema sang Kenny's song – in the shower, as she cooked; around the room, outside in the compound she hummed it. I did my best to avoid discussing it. I didn't tell her about the card either.

I called Stanley about our amala, but he said he was out of town for work. He didn't return until Friday, and he didn't call about it. I decided to wait until the next day. Our amala date was growing cold so fast and that worried me.

"Can we do amala today?" I called to ask Stanley around midday.

"Hmm, I'm tired o. And I have rehearsal against tomorrow," Stanley said.

"Huh. Hmm. I didn't know about a rehearsal," I said.

"It's main church. Not the band."

My heart dropped. He sounded so flat. I'd asked Kenny why Stanley wasn't at the recording and Kenny had told me he said he was working. As true as this sounded, I found it was Stanley giving excuses and hiding.

"Huh, okay. After church?"

"We'll see."

Wow, that sounded cold and flat. He wasn't happy with me, definitely.

"Okay. See you tomorrow."

"Sure. Bye."

He hung up before I did. I could understand that he wasn't happy I had been postponing our date but for crying out loud, I was ready now. Why was he being so cold? I wanted to call back and ask but my shy self kicked in and I pushed this off. Hopefully, he would be in a better mood the following day.

The choir ministered powerfully the following day. It was Belema's first time in my church and after service, the follow-up team took her to a separate room for refreshments and I got the chance to go and talk to Stanley. He was on the drums talking with the choir master, though he'd played the rhythm guitar during service.

I cleared my throat. "Hello, Stanley."

He arched an eyebrow and smiled. "Ah, my runaway friend."

The choir master walked away as though on cue, which made me really relieved.

"I'm sorry. It's just that this girl came suddenly and..."

He chuckled. "Yeah, your imaginary friend."

Just at that moment, Belema walked up to us.

"She's not imaginary. See her." I pointed. "Belema."

In hindsight, I think time stood. But it was just a second of silence. Or maybe I imagined things, but I had played this moment over and over again in my mind and couldn't understand what happened in that lost second.

Stanley nodded. "Hello."

Belema nodded. "Hello."

"So, you're the reason Wato doesn't want to eat amala with me." He laughed. Belema laughed. I laughed.

"Amala is my worst food," Belema said.

"Typical of Ikwerre girls to spoil the things everybody liked," Stanley said.

"I'm not Ikwerre. I'm Ogoni!"

"Really? Biere? Kedu?"

"Mmuona." Belema smiled. "How did you know that?"

"I speak every language of the world." Stanley nodded. "Well, Wato and friend. I have to run. See you around."

I had never seen Stanley so detached. He stood and just walked away. It was embarrassing.

"Who is he?" Belema said.

"A friend. We went to secondary school together."

"They play well, sha. That choir piece was fantastic," Belema said.

"Yes. They call him Lucifer," I said as we left the church. I, with a hollow feeling.

"Lucifer! Na wa o." Belema shook her head. "I like your church sha. Plenty fine boys. But Kenny did not come."

I rolled my eyes. "Kenny has his own church o."

"Ah, please take me there." Belema nudged me. I slapped her hand away, and she laughed. "You don't want him, but you don't want me to have him. Na wa for you o!"

"Hey, abeg o, Belema. Please don't let someone hear you o. I don't have anybody. We're in a free world." I walked faster ahead of her.

Why would she talk like that?

Chapter 30

"Why did he call you Wato?"

I snapped. "None of your business, Belema, but please don't use that name for me."

"Huh, na wa for you this girl o! You get so touchy and angry so easily." She sighed. "Is Kenny not recording again?"

"I don't know." I shrugged. "These things take time."

Kenny did not record another song for a few weeks. Belema continued to talk about him constantly. We attended church and as the weeks went by, I rehearsed with Stanley's band, but he was so far removed from me. I didn't think it was okay to continue asking to go out and eat amala with his attitude and soon, all of that died down, and we never went to eat that amala again.

Maybe it was something I never noticed, or maybe not. Belema caught on that I had a crush on Stanley and tried to talk to me about it. I was shy but after church one Sunday, she asked directly,

"Do you like him like that?"

"Of course, I like him!"

Belema laughed. "Na wa for you o! Be liking a boy secretly. Dying secretly," she said. "If I like a boy, I tell him straight."

It got me thinking if I needed to push. Maybe take Stanley out. After the card, Kenny didn't send any other or ask me out. In fact, he was very busy for several weeks after the recording. A famous secular producer got interested in *After God*, and the story changed. In just a few weeks, Kenny was busy doing interviews and whatever. The song had not even been released.

Then Belema got a job. It was a small job as a receptionist at a local company. It was better than nothing. Better than sitting at home day in day out, roaming the street, applying. The salary was not much. It could not pay rent for Belema, so she had to continue to squat with me.

The job however, changed everything. Or maybe it wasn't the job, I'll never know.

Belema blamed everything on her job, though. She stopped helping around the house, and she started keeping late nights. At first, I was relieved to not have her in the house with me, because she wasn't great company when she was around.

Then I got an unusual visitor.

It was Ahmed, Stanley's best friend from when they were babies. He came to my house, late one evening. I had just arrived from work.

"Hi, Ahmed. Hope you haven't been here too long?" I said as I opened my door.

"Just about twenty minutes. I came straight from work," he said.

"Ah, hope everything is okay, o!"

We never talked much in the past. He attended his parents' church, which they started many years back so though the two families were close, Stanley and he never went to the same church, and by default, me neither. But the two men were always together. They worked at the same bank too. I immediately feared something had happened to Stanley, but then again, why would Ahmed be the conveyor? Why would anyone want to come to talk to me about Stanley. I was just Wato to him and his family and his friends. He treated me like a little toy he had no use of. Unfortunately.

"Everything is not okay, Tiwa," Ahmed said.

His words stopped me short, and I turned to look at him, my heart thudding. "What happened?" I swallowed. "Is Stanley okay?"

"Huh!" He dropped into my couch and covered his face. "Huh!"

My head literally exploded. "What happened to Stanley?" I screamed.

Ahmed's head shot up. "Nothing! Duru is perfectly fine..."

I shuddered and tears I didn't know had gathered, slid down my cheeks.

"No, not perfectly." He heaved. "But see how you reacted just now. See tears in your eyes just because you thought something happened to him."

"So? Why are you here?" I sounded rude but the suspense of his presence was killing me.

"Duru needs you. He's going utterly crazy! Utterly." He jumped to his feet and started to pace.

"Crazy? How?" I was so frustrated by all this strange talk...the strange visit from Ahmed.

"You don't know?" He glared at me. "What do you mean how? Is she not your friend?"

"What on earth are you talking about?"

"Your friend and flatmate. Belema. And Duru."

My head went light. "Belema?"

"Yes. And Duru. They are everywhere together." He shouted. "He eats her. Drinks her. Sleeps her. Wakes her..."

"Wait. Hold on. What do you mean Belema and Duru. Stan."

"Yes! Why do you think I'm going nuts? She's a leech!" He hurried to me and short of carrying me, stood right in front of me. "You need to save him. It's you he wants. You need to help him."

"How?" A sob escaped my lips. I covered it with my hand. "He doesn't want me."

"Wait. You see how devious Belema is? You live here together, and she didn't tell you about her and Duru?"

I was too overwhelmed to speak. I shook my head.

"You see what I'm saying?" He fell on his knees. "Tiwa, please. I'm begging you. Don't let this girl get Duru!"

I stamped my feet in anger and frustration like I had never felt and shouted at him. "What do you want me to do?"

"Love on him. Give her a fight!"

"What? Are you going crazy?" I marched to my door. "Leave my house, please."

He stood. "Wait, Tiwa. Understand. She has bewitched him. Duru is not himself..."

"There is nothing I can do about it, please go." I held my door open.

"I thought you wanted the best for Duru. I thought all that shyness around him meant you liked him," Ahmed said softly. "Don't you like Duru?"

His soft tone melted my heart and the tears I had tried to dam, burst. "I love Stanley."

"Then fight for him, Tiwa! Please." Ahmed moved closer to me. "Please."

To my surprise, he hugged me. I nodded and sniffed. When he continued to just hug me, I got uncomfortable. I stirred and he cleared his throat.

"Yes, please, Tiwa. I can't tell you how much that girl has taken from my friend." He drew in a shuddering breath that left me cold. "She's going to finish him."

"Huh, how long has this been going on?"

"Three months o!" He sighed. "It's like a vampire just sank her teeth in a man."

Chapter 31

"This one you have been waiting since, Wato, are we safe?"

"I just want to talk to Stan for a minute," I said.

We were in church, and for some reason, Stan and Belema were together as soon as church ended. If I had noticed them together pre-Ahmed's visit, I didn't pay close attention. Ahmed was right about one thing, Belema hung on Stan's sleeves. Not too obviously at first. Unless you were consistently watching and taking note, it didn't show. However, when I moved close to Stan to talk to him, Belema literally stood in front of him like a shield.

"He's going out after church, he can't talk now," Belema said.

"When did you become his PA?"

She smirked. "Hian, see question o."

I side-stepped her. "Stan, please can I see you for a minute?"

"Huh, Wato." He groaned. "Okay. One minute o." He winked at Belema, and she pouted before she walked some rows away to sit in the pews.

I didn't think she would be able to hear what Stan and I will discuss, but still, I walked a few feet farther away from where she was.

"You are dating Belema?"

Stan guffawed. "Is that what you want to talk about?"

"I'm just surprised. She didn't tell me anything and we live in the same house," I said.

"Does she owe you?"

"Stan?"

"Yes? I mean, so because she lives in your house, she must tell you what she's doing in her life?" He scoffed. "I'm just asking."

"Yes, I would expect her to tell me she's dating my friend..."

"Hold it there, Wato. I have tried to be cordial with you, but if this is about me, then stop it. Don't add my name in this equation." He paused but when I started to speak, he raised his index finger to stop me, and menacingly lowered his voice. "You don't see me as anything. You have no respect for me. So, in this case, please, stay out of my business." He then shot me his sweetest smile. "But again, maybe you are just showing concern. I appreciate. Now, don't you have other things to do? I do." He winked and raised his voice loud enough. "Belema, thanks for your patience." He started walking towards her. "Let's go, dear."

I couldn't believe what just happened. I watched them leave. Belema did not even turn to look at me for a second. I was so upset. I didn't know what to make of this.

My mum was hosting her church society again, so I had planned to go and help her after service, and I did, trying my best to push this matter behind me. When I got back to my house in the evening, all of Belema's things were gone. She didn't even leave a note to tell me "thank you."

At first, anger overcame me, and I wanted to scream. By this time, Belema had lived with me for almost a year. Not once did she pay for rent, food, or anything else. How could she? I could recount so many times that I gave her a little pocket change for clothes, and her personal needs. Sanitary towels were shared...she'd just dip her sticky fingers in my wardrobe and take what she needed. Talk of which, several times, I'd see her in church wearing my clothes or shoes or jewellery or return from work to see her in my nightie.

I had thought we could be very close friends. I had overlooked her excesses, decided to buy her a separate roll-on so she'd not use mine, pretended I didn't notice that she always used my perfume...

My phone started ringing and for a second, I thought it would be Belema, calling to apologize. I snatched my phone from my bag and answered without looking at the caller ID.

"Hello?"

"Sweetheart," Kenny said softly. "Can you step out for a second?"

"I'm sorry. Kenny?"

"Yes, love. I'm outside your house," he said.

"I'm sorry. I can't...I don't..."

"Please, honey. It won't take a minute."

"Okay, let me...I'm coming."

I looked at myself in the mirror. For some reason, I wanted to look nice. Forever, I couldn't tell myself why, but I brushed my hair, and smoothed my hand over my short dress, wore my slippers and stepped out.

A barrage of cameras flashed in my face and my hands shot up to cover my face. I stood shivering as though I had been caught stealing. I raised my face and there was Kenny, standing in front of me.

"I love you, Tiwatope. Will you marry me?"

"No! Of course not, don't be silly!"

I backed into my room, and Kenny followed me inside. I slammed the door in the face of all the photographers and cameramen and turned on him.

"Kenny, are you alright?"

"Ololufe," he said in a singing voice. "What can I do without you? I can only think about you day and night!"

"Stop it o! What is this?"

He laughed and dropped into my couch. "It's the lines of my newest song. We go to the studio next week."

I gasped. "I hope you are not planning on using that silly thing in the video?"

"If I had told you I was coming, the surprise will be fake," Kenny said.

"Not on your life." I screamed. "Kenny, stop it!"

"You looked so beautiful tonight. I could have just made it so real and..."

I burst into tears.

Kenny jumped to his feet and came to hug me. "Baby, I'm sorry! I didn't know it will upset you like this."

Uncontrollably, I sobbed in his arms, and he cooed and moaned his apology, over and over, using endearing words.

I pulled myself together. "It's not you." I sniffed.

"Huh, kilode. Who upset you, darling?"

I spat out everything that happened with Belema. How she went behind me to date Stanley. Kenny listened until I had said everything I wanted to say. He led me back to the couch and sat with me, just staring at me in that tender, special way. When I drew in a shuddering breath and kept quiet, he took my hands in his.

"Belema and I are very similar in one thing," Kenny said softly. "If we want something, we go for it without any fear or shame."

"But, I..."

"Ssh. You and Stan are not like us." He patted my hands. "You wait for what you want to come to you and life is not like that."

I gasped. "I...am I supposed to throw myself on Stanley?"

"I'm sure grateful to God you did not." He chuckled. I shrank from him, and he drew me back closer. "Tiwa-temi, what do you want me to say, I'm elated!"

I jumped to my feet. "Oya, come and go."

Kenny smiled. "I want you for myself and I'm not happy Belema treated you like this. But it's to my greatest joy. I'm glad Stanley is no longer..."

I sniffed. "No longer...?"

"No longer there." Kenny stood. "I love you, Tiwa. How does it make me feel that you are so upset about what Belema did? Unhappy. But again, I am unhappy that you are. I'm frustrated I can't come through with you. If Belema succeeds and marries Stanley, it still doesn't change my situation. I love you but you don't feel anything for me."

"You're like Belema, aren't you? You always go for what you want." I scoffed. "She wanted you first. How come she didn't get you?"

"Because again, I'm not like Stan. I know what I want, and I won't settle for less."

Kenny was giving me a headache, or maybe it was the crying I just subjected myself to.

"Okay. I hear you."

"Will you ever love me, Tiwa-temi?"

"You said I always wait for what I want to come to me, don't I? Let's see."

His gaze dropped to the floor. For a split second, I felt remorse. I wanted to tell him not to lose hope. I wanted to say I liked him at least, which should be a good starting place. But. Instead, I just gazed at him. It was a weird moment. Thinking of me telling my "huge crush" my friend just stole the one I have a crush on from me...weird in the highest manner.

Kenny looked up and nodded. "Let's see."

He didn't say a word more, and neither did I as he walked to my door and left. I felt drained. There was work the following day, but I couldn't bring myself to prepare for it or sleep. How could Belema be with Stan? They were a mismatch. She didn't even like him all that. Her eyes were on Kenny all of the time.

Chapter 32

"We're getting married."

My mouth dropped open. So soon! They were not even four months! Ahmed's eyes shot to me, and I quickly looked away from him. Belema's eyes shorn. I'd never seen anyone look so happy. In fairness to him, I think Stanley looked very happy too. He stood from where he had gone on one knee and clasped his lips on Belema's.

I couldn't look.

A loud applause went up and Belema screamed again, "I'm getting married!"

Stanley had invited his band to the restaurant. I'd thought it was just to hangout, and I'd even arrived late but not too late to miss the proposal. I wanted to die. For a strange moment, I wished Kenny was here. He would comfort me. At least, I didn't know what I thought.

A waiter passed a tray around with non-alcoholic wine, and Ahmed raised a toast. Everyone raised their glasses and after drinking to the engaged couple, everyone started to chat around.

Ahmed came to me. "I'm his best man."

Why would he say that to me? Who was contesting it?

"Congratulations," I murmured.

"I just wish..."

"Please, Ahmed. Not here." I walked away from him and went to stand with two of the female vocals, and blended in.

Stanley didn't come to speak with me, neither did Belema. After an hour or so of spitting headaches, I left the party. It was a Friday night. I didn't want to be alone and yet, I didn't have anywhere to go. My mother would know something was wrong the moment I walked into her house, and I wasn't ready to let anyone know how bitter I felt. Belema knew I had a crush on Stan, and while she ate my food, and drank my water, she schemed to take him from me.

I cuddled up on my couch and wept till I had no more tears.

Kenny heard about the engagement almost a week later and called me. By then, I was done crying but hearing him console me made me feel terrible and sort of ashamed. Meanwhile, his song was topping charts everywhere and he was becoming really popular. And I was happy for him.

"Do you want to go on a tour with me?" Kenny said out of nowhere.

"No. Tour? I mean, I have a job. I..."

"Take a leave. You've been working for more than a year and I believe there's something called annual leave in your office?"

I scoffed. "No. I don't want to take..."

"It's only twenty-one days. We go to Abuja, Kaduna, Sokoto, and then down south to Port Harcourt, Calabar, Uyo. Then come west to Akure and Ibadan. First class flight seats, five-star hotels, singing and worshipping..."

"Kenny, no."

"Please. I'm nothing without you," he said softly. "My music is nothing without you."

To date, every time Kenny said that I gave in. I think he knew too.

I heaved a heavy sigh. "No, Kenny." But I knew I would agree.

"Should I give you time to think about it?"

"When? Kenny, you know what you are doing. You are taking advantage of me. You...anyway, when?"

"It's a month away." He sighed heavily. "Thanks, my love."

I rolled my eyes. "Huh."

"It will take your mind off these people who want to get married..." he started to say.

"Abegi!"

When he hung up, I sat in the dark in my room, and really gave Kenny a thought. Why did he love me so much, and why didn't I feel the same about him. To my shame, and whatever I thought, Belema and Stanley looked good together. She hated amala, couldn't cook jack or sing a note, but she laughed a lot around him, and that I guess was enough for them. A thought in my mind showed some gratitude for Kenny. At least, I'd have a breathing space going on the tour.

A text came into my phone, and I read what Kenny sent.

I lied, love. The tour is six weeks not three. I'm sure your office can give you that much time.

For some reason, I thought first of Stanley. I had to take leave from the band too. As an entry level officer at my job, I had four weeks of leave, but I knew how to manoeuvre with my boss. Six weeks going from city to city promoting Kenny's music was exciting to me. I was happy he invited me.

I sent a text to Stanley:

Kenny invited me to tour with him. I want to take permission to be away from the band for six weeks.

Stanley responded immediately:

Take all the time you need!

Such quick discarding! I wanted to cry but, well, maybe this was better. He was getting married, and I needed to move on. There would not be a Stanley in my life. He now boasted of eating starch and gari, which were Belema's favourite swallows, no more amala! I needed to move on, and Kenny just gave me a great opportunity.

Thank you! I replied to his text.

Getting six weeks leave from work was just as easy as getting time from the band. My boss allowed me to add my casual leave and sick leave to make up the time. I told my parents about the trip, and they were more concerned about my safety, and if I would not be lonely. Mummy, especially almost offered to come with us.

The day though came, and Kenny picked me up at home to the airport. I'd never been to Abuja, and it was so exciting. We flew first class, and like Kenny had said, were lodged in a 5-star hotel. I had a beautiful room to myself, but I'd never seen any schedule so hectic. As soon as we arrived in Abuja, we went to the studio to record a new song, and then went to minister in a big church.

The following day, we were in the studio all day and then in the evening back to minister at another church. We spent four days in Abuja, and then went on a bus to Kaduna, and spent two days then went to Sokoto for three days.

On and on and on, from city to city, we held concerts, ministered in churches, recorded some music and did interviews. Kenny was something else. I had never been so close to him. He encouraged me daily and I loved the way he worked with his manager, and the crew and his instrumentalists.

I loved the way he worked with me.

I was the only vocalist who came with him. Back-up singers were organized from each city since he didn't have a band. Kenny put good thought in everything we did. He made sure I was comfortable. He checked on me each time, and the crew all showed me so much respect like I'd never thought of before. In each city, we performed *After God*, and the crowd would go wild. It was rewarding to see people scream as I sang. I never imagined there would be a thrill.

For once, as Kenny had said, I totally forgot about Stanley and Belema. Because of the tight schedules, one of the assistants kept mine and Kenny's phones and replied to only what I thought was important, which would be messages from my parents. I didn't think Stanley's band was that important or would have any news so the assistant who had our phones did not report anything to me.

When I returned from the tour, Stanley and Belema were married.

I was crushed.

Chapter 33

"We're pregnant."

What else did I expect? The mic I was holding dropped and while everyone shouted and screamed their congrats to Stanley, they also turned to check what caused the loud noise. I felt embarrassed. Stanley looked at me with that impatient look that was now the only one he ever gave me and murmured something about being careful.

His announcement as we finished rehearsals shook me more than I expected. He'd been married for a month or so and of course, this was expected. Belema never talked to me, but she glowed. She had resigned from her silly, low-paying job after the engagement and just enjoyed living her best life as Stanley's wife. Though she wasn't a member of the band, she touted herself as the manager and attended most of our rehearsals and events. I thought she just wanted to rub it in my face that she got the man I wanted. Kenny once told me to forget about her, and that she did not "steal" my man as I insinuated. That advice just annoyed me.

"We must celebrate!"

One of the men said, and within the twinkling of an eye, someone had come in with cans of malt drink. The drink was shared, and ladies hugged Belema while the men punched Stanley. I took a can and just followed through like a ghost.

On the way out, Belema caught up with me.

"Wato!"

I hated hearing that from her but despite my several protests, that was what she called me.

I turned. "Yes?"

"Won't it end?"

I frowned. "What?"

"Your jealousy! Stanley was a free man when I met him..."

I looked around and saw no one paid us any attention. Still, I whispered, "Lower your voice."

"Everyone knows. Your jealousy and bitterness are eating you alive," Belema said.

"I'm not jealous of you..."

Belema snickered. "Oh, what is this then? You cannot even congratulate us without showing how painful it is for you."

"Why are you saying all this to me?"

"Because I pity you." She shook her head. "I'm here to stay. Move on with your life. Find your own man and leave us alone!" She turned and marched away.

I couldn't leave the hall fast enough. Tears streamed down my face. I got a taxi and went home. I needed to stop, truly. My anger at Stanley made me so miserable. Belema was right. Stanley was a single man and there was no code broken by either him or Belema. He seemed genuinely happy, so why would I not move on with my life?

Kenny's tour was successful and there were now some invitations outside the country. It hit me in the face suddenly, that if Kenny started going outside the country, he would only become more popular, and he would meet many more women. Would he not decide to let me go, since I still refused to date him?

When I got to my room, I called Kenny.

"Do you like amala?"

He sounded as though he was choking. "Amala?"

"Yes. You remember that place I told you Stanley took me to eat amala?"

He grunted. "Oh yeah."

"It's always better to go late and I have been craving it for a while." It was about ten in the night.

Kenny chuckled. "I'll pick you in an hour. Be ready to stay past your bedtime."

I heaved a heavy sigh. "Thank you."

I felt silly. But it was what I needed to do.

Kenny and I got married in a big society wedding a month before Belema died.

"You should have been patient."

My mouth dropped open. "Stanley?"

"Yes. Yes. Hasn't she died now? Huh?" He shrugged. "This is all your fault, you know that?"

"Stanley!" I gasped. "Please, huh! Stop this."

"No! You stop this. You knew. You knew I liked you, but what did you do? You pushed me away." He pointed towards his front door. "For that boy! What can he sing for you that I cannot?" He panted. "Huh! He's all over singing for you. Can I not compose and sing for you?"

Tears poured from my eyes. It had taken every bit of courage within me to visit him after Belema's funeral. I'd decided not to attend, though every member of the band went. From that horrible day, when he was supposed to be carrying his baby, Stanley had not been to church or rehearsals or to work... He had not done anything with himself, from what I heard. Kenny told me I had to see him, and why not sooner than later.

Besides, we were going on a Europe tour for six months and it would be late to come afterwards. I never expected I'd find Stanley alone in his house. He looked so thin and miserable. And I never expected him to blame me for what happened.

"Kenny this, Kenny that," he continued. "Every day you're in the studio with him. Flaunting him right in front of me." Stanley raised his voice. "What did he have that I did not?"

I whispered. "Stanley."

I couldn't believe my ears. To think that I just thought I'd sit with him for a few hours just to be there for him, and he'd probably just speak about his wife, instead, this? I thought his mother, or someone would be there for him. Where was everybody? Why was he in his house alone? I wish I'd come with Kenny but we both knew Stanley may not like that.

"Don't Stanley me! Did you know she will die? Did you push a dead girl my way?"

I cried. "Of course not!"

"Then why didn't you marry me?" He started to sob. "Why? Why?"

I hurt deep into my bone. I could feel his pain and I could not help him.

"So, you are now married, and I cannot retrace my steps again to marry you..."

"Stanley, please. You shouldn't be speaking like this. You did not..."

"Get out! Leave me." He screamed. "Leave me alone, Tiwatope!"

I jumped to my feet, trembling from head to toe. "I'm sorry for your loss, Stanley."

"You're sorry for nothing. Get out!"

I walked briskly out the door with his sobs and moans following. I never saw Stanley again until that night...when his pastor blocked social media that "Lucifer" was back in concert.

CROWD

Chapter 34

"The guy is here."

Duru sat on a small stone at the back of the house and dragged deeply on his cigarette. He liked to swallow all the steam, which warmed his insides more and helped damage his lungs. He didn't care about such things. If he remembered clearly, life was fickle, and a healthy nine-month-pregnant woman today could be dead tomorrow.

He looked up at the woman he just helped to paint her kitchen. "Yes?"

"I was wondering where you went. My husband is back," she said.

Duru shrugged. "So?"

The woman chuckled. "Aren't you going to be paid?"

"Oh, sure." He stepped on the half-smoked cigarette and stood. "Thanks."

He walked around to the front of the house and waited. The man of the house came out.

"You did a good job. And your price is reasonable," the man said. "What's your number?"

"He doesn't have, interestingly," the woman said.

"How do we reach him? My boss may have a job or two. His work is really neat."

"He's usually either at the post office or the bank, especially early in the morning," she said.

"Well, since you can reach him." The man gave Duru one thousand naira. "Or can you come to my office at the new secretariat on Monday? Education unit."

"I'll be at your office on Monday. Thank you." Duru put the money in his jean pocket.

"Good."

Duru turned and walked back into the street.

"Is he a leper that he waits at a particular place every day?" the man said to his wife, but Duru had good hearing.

He blocked out the woman's response. Leper or not, he earned his own living on his own terms. Weekends were good for him because this was when the busy office workers had time to fix their stuff and over the years, he had become really good with fixing things for people.

The day was still very young. Duru had taken breakfast, but after the work in the bank-woman's kitchen, inhaling all the paint fumes, and smoking too, he felt his stomach should have some love. Besides, the whole day was lined up. Plumbing, carpentry and two car jobs. He planned to go to each job back-to-back. He also had to move into the small room he got at an old woman's house.

For the whole week he'd been back here, he had slept at the motor park while he looked for accommodation. The mere thought of it repelled him. He didn't want to settle down here, yet he couldn't help himself. The last time he came to Owena, he had worked hard, made a living while it was worth it, and moved on. Nine years ago. Nothing about the little town changed. Nothing in him, Duru, changed, yet he was here. Unsure of why. Again, he didn't care about being sure of anything.

Life is fickle.

"The toilet is outside. You share with the three other tenants."

Duru arched an eyebrow. "What if I build an extra one just for myself?"

"I won't count it as part of your rent," the woman squeezed her face. "And you can't take it with you when you're going."

"Deal."

"Aha, you have money like that?" the landlady smiled and exposed juxtaposed chipped and yellow teeth. "I have a rich tenant."

Duru pressed his lips together. He had tonight to inspect the toilets and design where his own would be. The compound was large and the part where there were four rooms must have been previously used as boys' quarters. The main house itself now had tenants living in it with the old landlady. In a small town like Owena, many families had these houses where the kids have grown up and left home. Parents who refuse to move to live with the children end up with too much space to use and acute quiet and loneliness.

This landlady had a nice yard and big rooms. Her price was reasonable too, and the house was close enough to the post office and main market. Duru collected the key to his room and entered the big space to determine what he would need, which amounted to everything. He dropped his backpack on the floor by the wall and took out his measuring tape. He knew how to work with his hands and make his own furniture.

"I kid you not, Demi, he works cars and will know a good buy."

Demi snickered. "I thought you said he painted your house. And did carpentry for your hubby's office."

"He's good," Lore said. "I mean, Tayo's engine was giving knocking sound and this guy fixed it."

Demi stared from Bukky to Lore. "He fixed Tayo's car all the way in Akure?"

"Believe me." Lore sipped her kunnu. "Hmm, this tastes so good, Bukky. Who made it for you?"

Demi rolled her eyes. "Don't tell me your mystery painter."

Bukky and Lore laughed.

"Demi, you're funny o. My mother made it, jare." Bukky sniffed. "Mystery painter. You just gave him a name now."

"Of course. Two of you are giving such glowing references." She turned to Lore. "I wonder where you even found him."

"At Daddy's old mechanic workshop. Tayo has been so worried, and his mechanic was just charging anyhow. He was there. They called him. He came to Akure. Fixed the car," Lore said. "I didn't know he does other things until I saw him at your bank the other day, and Bukky now mentioned the painting."

"He's at that bank almost every day before we resume." Demi sighed. "Looking shaggy and unkempt. Before God, I don't know how anyone can talk to him about giving him a job." She frowned at Bukky. "How did you even discover he can work?"

"Felix told me. Said he helped clear the grass in his yard and told him he can do anything," Bukky said.

Demi's eyes widened. "And you allowed him to come to your house?"

"On a Saturday when everyone was home."

"Hmm." Demi shook her head. "I need a good car. And I thought your husbands could help but I guess I'd have to go for this Duru." She scoffed. "He's scary, though."

"I think he's a drifter. You know people just come and go like that." Bukky shrugged. "I don't even think he has a house. Where..."

"The other day I saw him in Mama Oni's compound, just sitting in front of the BQ smoking." Demi gasped. "She said he was her new tenant and, in my mind, I was just wondering why she would take such a ruffian in. I mean, there's rumour her kids said they won't send money to her again because they want her to move to Lagos but then... I didn't understand it."

"Really?" Bukky's eyes widened. "I guess him and Goke don't talk much because he's still doing some carpentry work at his office."

"Well, maybe...Bukky, can you help me ask him if he comes around on Monday?" Demi pleaded with a soft voice. "The guy scares me honestly. The way he looks."

Bukky laughed. "Of course. You're funny."

Demi wondered why she was scared of the guy, as her friends chatted and laughed over other things at their regular Sunday hangout. This week was Bukky's house.

Chapter 35

"I know someone in Ilesha who gets really good cars. I can go and check him out if you want." Demi looked questioningly at Bukky.

"Can you call him first?" Bukky said. "Oh, you don't even have a phone."

"I got one but I don't have the dealer's number. But maybe I can find someone who does here. If you give me the rest of the day," Duru said.

"Thank you so much," Bukky said.

"Huh, what's your, what's your budget?" he said.

"Umm, I really don't know." Demi shrugged. "I just want a very strong, good car."

"Sure. I'll ask the Ilesha guy. I'll get back to..." he looked at Bukky. "To her."

"No problem, thanks, Duru," Bukky said.

"The pleasure is mine." Duru stepped back, then turned and walked away.

"That's the most I have ever heard him talk. Wow. He even got a phone because of you!" Bukky giggled as both entered the bank to start their workday. "His voice is sexy."

Demi gasped. "Are you normal, Bukky?"

"I tell you, Demi. He was even stammering. Heh." Bukky laughed. "He never expected such beautiful ladies will come and find him first thing on Monday morning. Nice. I have to ask all the ladies in the bank if they have anything they want to do in their lives so I can introduce them to Duru."

"You're not okay, Bukky." Demi laughed. "You silly goose."

"Thank you. As if his voice did not move you too."

Demi arched an eyebrow. "Remember me? Demi of Idem Bastard Isong?"

They both laughed and parted ways. Demi watched Bukky walk into her office, where she now worked as operations manager before she moved on to hers, where she was the relationship manager. It was another new day, a new week, but she wondered why her palms were sweaty. Bukky had been right. Demi had no clue that ragged-looking man could have such a beautiful deep voice, good diction, and decent manners.

Before the close of work, Duru returned, but Bukky was in a meeting, and Demi didn't want to talk to him alone, so she ignored him and acted as though she was very busy on her computer when she saw him enter the banking hall. He loitered for a bit and looked around but didn't talk to anyone or approach her. Then he walked out again, and she realised she had been holding her breath the whole time.

As anxious as she was to know what news he had, she waited until Bukky finished her meeting, which coincided with the closing time.

Bukky walked over to her. "Did Duru come back?"

"He did. But I formed busy." Demi laughed. "He looked around, saw you were not seated, and walked out."

Bukky laughed as well. "His sexy voice scared you, jo! I knew it. All your strong-girl façade was blown to hell by that rugged good look."

"Hmm, me I cannot shout o. If Mr. Olalekan catch you noticing sexy voice, I will say I was not there." Demi closed her door and followed Bukky out.

"Mr. Olalekan is a very happy husband. He cannot complain about what he gets here." Bukky smoothed her hands down her hips and both women laughed.

Bukky's car was just at the back of the bank where staff parked.

As they approached, Duru walked over to them. "Good evening, Ms. Olalekan."

Bukky smiled. "Oh, Duru. Good evening. Have you been waiting for long?"

"Not really." He looked at Demi. "Good evening, Ms."

"Good evening. Umm, did you get the phone number?"

"Yeah." He scoffed. "I wasn't sure what you wanted, with the price and all. But the guy was willing to allow me do a test drive."

"A test drive already." Bukky gasped. "That's nice."

"Yeah. It's a Toyota Avalon. Old but very strong. 2004 model." He half-turned. "It's over there."

Bukky and Demi exchanged wide-eyed gazes.

"Over there?" Demi burst out. "You brought it?"

"Yeah. He let me take it." Duru turned to the other side of the parking lot. "Do you want to test it?"

"Yes, thank you." Demi smiled. "Why not? Bukky?"

"I have to get home, I'm sorry," Bukky said. "We'll do our ride later."

Demi's eyes widened. "Later? If the car is still here."

"I need to go!" Bukky chuckled and got into her car.

Demi followed Duru to the Avalon. He went to the passenger's side and stretched out his hand with the key.

"I can't drive," Demi said. "I don't know how to."

He arched his eyebrows and without a word, walked to the driver's side, and took the wheel. Demi got into the passenger's seat. Her phone rang as Duru pulled out, and she picked a call from Bukky.

"Babe, are you sure you want to go on a test drive. Tonight. With him?" Bukky said.

It sounded so familiar, the risk she once took with a total stranger. A risk that left her destroyed!

"I'm in the car, and it's a smooth ride," Demi said.

She stole a glance at Duru, who concentrated on linking the main road from the bank parking lot.

"Where are you driving to?" Bukky said.

Demi shrugged. "My house."

"Let me know when you get there," Bukky said. "Take care."

"I will. Thanks, dear." Demi drew in a sharp breath and hung up. Her foolishness in the past had all the people around her so cautious, and this made her emotional.

"Where are we going?" Duru said.

"Drive towards Akure or Ilesa. I want to see how it performs on the highway," Demi said.

"Sure." Duru made the appropriate turn.

The drive was smooth. Demi enjoyed the cool breeze from the dark night when she decided to turn off the air-conditioning. It was a perfect car for her.

"Now to where?" Duru said.

"You'll drop me in my house and take it with you," Demi said.

"Okay," Duru said. "Do you like it?"

"Do you?"

Duru shrugged. "It is very smooth. A strong car too."

"Good. I'll take it." Demi sighed. "Thanks."

She described the way to her parents' home.

"I'll let the dealer know. And get his account details for you."

"Thank you."

Duru stopped outside the gate of Demi's parents' home. "Here we are. If you'd want me to teach you how to drive, I'll be happy to oblige for a small fee."

Demi turned in her seat to him. "I have only one request. I need you to drive me to Uyo."

Chapter 36

"You have a machine here, Duru! Chai."

Duru took the vehicle documents of the Avalon from Pedro, the car dealer. "Thank you."

"The woman trust you to just give you all the money like that. Two million cash," Pedro said. "Anyway sha, no be you? Duru, Duru!"

Duru got into the driver's seat. "See you later, Pedro." He tucked in the papers into the glove box.

"Wait. I suppose at least give you something for bringing me business."

Pedro took out several five naira notes and seemed to search his wallet.

Duru watched as the dealer searched his back pocket. "Don't bother. Bye."

He reversed and watched the fake surprise gesture of the businessman from his back view mirror. The Avalon was indeed a good buy. Demi would enjoy it when she started to drive, but first she had to learn. There was no way he would drive her to Uyo without her knowing how to use her car. It was his only condition to accept the offer, and though she pushed back, he had to stand his ground. As soon as she made that request, he remembered who she was.

Idem Isong's wife. Harlot, he had first called her. Idem was a bastard, and any woman with him had to be a whore. Was he surprised that nine years after he worked for Idem and met Demi, well, saw her with him, they were no longer together? For the life of him, Idem couldn't keep a decent woman. She had to be a rogue like him. Or leave, like Demi did. Duru itched to hear the break-up tale, but it was none of his business. And many years ago, when he decided to leave everything behind, he also chose to always mind his own business.

The drive back to Owena in the fully-paid-for Avalon was smooth and again enabled Duru to feel the car. He went straight to the bank, where he was sure Demi was at work. The morning was still young. He had woken early to finish up the transactions with the purchase after Demi shocked him by giving him the full amount for the vehicle in cash. She must somehow know money meant nothing to him. Or maybe she didn't care. She struck him as someone like that. She drew him to her in a way he didn't quite understand.

It wasn't noon yet and the banking hall was full. Right from the middle of the hall, Demi's small cubicle office was visible. She wasn't on her seat. Duru thought of giving her a call, or asking her friend, the outspoken Mrs. Bukky Olalekan, but thought otherwise and instead drove out with the car. He wanted his mechanic to take a look even though he had, and the car had no problems at all. He figured the beautiful woman would not relent until she got her way, and since the first time he talked to her, he had a feeling she had him in her little web. It had been a very long time since he had a desire to please a woman. He hated the feeling.

"This is a very strong engine, Duru," Olu, the mechanic said. "You just need to service it. Change oil. You need a new spare tire too."

The tall, slim mechanic closed the bonnet of the Avalon and cleaned his hands off his dirty coverall. Duru knew he was good, the best in Owena, though, why not. Olu had been a mechanic since he was born and could now be in his fifties.

"Yes, I already bought three tires. One spare and I want to move the front ones to the back, and put new ones in front," Duru said.

"You are the best mechanic I know," Olu said. "Yet, you refuse to come and work full time."

Duru smirked. "Even though I come here every day. You want me to sit down in one place."

"Sitting down in one place is not a bad idea." Olu laughed. "Can you cage an eagle?"

"Exactly." Duru shook his hand. "I will bring it for servicing tomorrow. I'll fix the tires too. And then drive to Ibadan or so just to see how it runs. Thank you."

"A a kin dupe ara eni," Olu said. "Or can I be thanking myself?"

"See you, then." Duru got into the car and drove back to the tire dealer. The man didn't have what he wanted the day before but promised he would have new consignment from Akure.

"Your tires are here, Duru." Akin said. "This your car is very fine o, Duru! Slow poison." He laughed. "Someone will see you and not know you have money for a car like this."

Duru mentally rolled his eyes. Akin was a dubious tire and spare parts dealer but he was the only one Duru could hold accountable. He could have bought the tires in Ilesha, but he wanted to be able to return them easily if they were not good enough.

"Thank you, Akin." Duru walked into his small shop, deciding not to change the man's impression the Avalon was his.

Akin, a short, fat man with yellow teeth and shrewd eyes beamed. "I knew you will come today, and I dare not disappoint. I don't want your wahala, omo Ibo."

Duru arched an eyebrow. "Call me whatever you like. Where are they?"

"Mukaila! Bring those new tires I bought from Akure this early morning." He raised his voice and spittle spattered in the air around him. Duru moved back to avoid being sprayed.

"Yes sir!" A young man shouted from afar.

Soon, Mukaila, who couldn't be more than a mid-teenager, muscled from head to toe, carried three fairly used tires into the shop.

Akin snapped. "Take them to the car. Ode! Idiot."

"No, leave them, thank you," Duru said.

Mukaila dropped the tires and hurried back to wherever he was.

Akin kissed his teeth. "The boy is too foolish. I don't understand."

Duru hit the tires one after the other and bounced them. Then he examined them to be sure they were as good as they should be.

"They are grade A. I can't cheat you, Duru," Akin said.

"The more you say that the wearier I am." Duru carried the three tires, and Akin followed behind. "If I have any problem with it, I will come and change it."

"But it is fairly used. It can't be as perfect as brand new." Akin scratched his head. "You can't return these once you take them away."

"Let's hope I don't have to." Duru got into the car.

"Na wa o. I chose the best for you," Akin said.

Duru drove off, leaving him staring after the Avalon.

Back at the bank, Demi was not on her seat. Duru decided to ask one of the security men at the door.

"She didn't come in today," the security man said.

Chapter 37

"Good evening, ma. I am asking for Mrs. Ademilade."

"Who are you?" Daddy said.

"Her mechanic, sir."

Demi stood from her bed and tiptoed to the door connecting the front door of the house to the living area. Duru's deep voice was low, but she heard him clearly.

Daddy snickered. "Ademilade doesn't have a car. How are you her mechanic?"

Demi drew in a deep breath and stepped through the door. "I forgot to tell you. I bought one yesterday." It had been two days actually, but it didn't matter.

Mummy gasped. "Aha? Forget? How does one forget to announce they bought a car?"

Demi stole a glance at Duru. His eyes were on her as she suspected. "I did." She stepped closer. "Thanks, Duru."

"I wanted to show you a few things," Duru said.

"We will wash it, dear," Daddy said.

Demi smiled and followed Duru to the car. "You could have called me," she muttered.

"I didn't think of it. Considering that you left your car in my care without thought."

She snapped. "Everything I do is with careful thought."

"I will keep that in mind going forward, Mrs. Ademilade."

"Call me Demi."

"I call you Demi in my shower."

What audacity? But that strange, mumbled statement left her almost breathless. There was chemistry here, and she couldn't believe herself already.

"I will never be in your shower."

He mumbled, "You will be."

She pretended she didn't hear him. "What do you want to show me?

"New tires. And I also got the kit for changing your tire." He walked round the car. "When do you plan to travel to Uyo?"

"Is tomorrow too soon?"

Duru arched an eyebrow. "You don't drive."

"I don't have to."

Demi looked towards the window facing the road. She could feel her parents' eyes bore through the walls of the fence. They couldn't see her or the car giving where Duru parked, but she knew.

"Let's be clear, Demi," he said. "I am not going to be held responsible for what you want to do…"

"No one knows what I plan to do," she cut in. "My parents will care for Mimi while I'm gone…"

"I am afraid, I can't be sorry for your daughter if…"

"Just shut up and listen to me. I will pay for…"

"I don't care about your money."

"I do."

He stared her down and she returned his gaze until it was ridiculous to look at each other for so long. Still, they both held on, stubbornly daringly.

"It's two whole days on the road to and fro." She looked at the new tires. "This engine looks like it can do it."

"It can," he said softly.

"I'll pay you ten thousand for every day you are not in Owena. I will pay your hotel room every night you need one." She glanced over his head. "I don't imagine we will be away for more than a week."

Duru sniffed. "Irresponsible to not let your parents know especially if they are keeping your daughter."

"Though that is none of your business, I plan to leave a letter and call them when we are on the way…"

He cut in. "Considering I have accepted your offer?"

"Considering you do not have a choice." She walked towards her gate. "Be here at 5am."

She walked through the gate and closed it behind her, her heart thudding. She let out a deep breath. She hadn't yet shared her plans with him. It was stupid and daring and she hoped she got away with it, but if she didn't, she was ready to face the consequences.

"I thought you would bring the car inside," Daddy said when she walked in.

She hated to lie to her father but under her circumstances, she needed to. "Duru needs to fix some stuff in it. He should bring it tomorrow."

"Congratulations o, though you did not tell us," Mummy said.

"Hmm," Demi grunted and returned to her room.

Her father called out with a request to pray over the car.

"When he brings it tomorrow!" She called back.

She locked the door behind her and stared at the small luggage she had open on the bed. This was a trip of her life. She needed only two T-shirts and a pair of jeans and nothing more. Everything else was intact. Nothing should go wrong.

"Demi."

Duru breathed. Her name did things to him no other woman ever had. And as he rinsed off under his shower, he dreaded what was ahead. Not for himself but for Demi. As things stood, he could kill for her, die for her. The way she affected him scared him. He ought to move away...far from Owena, but he couldn't. The minute he stepped back here, he'd felt something.

He tossed a pair of black jeans and T-shirt in a backpack, threw in his knives, extra pair of boots and a few face masks. Without looking back, he locked his door and got into Demi's car.

She stood outside the gate with her hand luggage when he pulled up fifteen minutes early.

He stepped out and opened the boot. "Good time," he said.

She grunted and put her luggage in the boot.

For the first one hour, neither said anything.

"Am I going to know what your plan is?"

Demi snickered. "On a need-to-know basis."

"So, where are we going now?"

"Uyo."

"Where in Uyo?"

She drew in a ragged breath. "When we get to Uyo, I will let you know."

"I'm not a very curious person," he said. "And I don't give a *d*mn* what you do but, in this case, I'm here, and I want to know."

She closed her eyes and a few minutes later, he heard a soft snore. If she wanted to sleep through the twelve-hour-plus-drive, then he wished her luck. Otherwise, he had to know what she was up to. That he was here alone spoke volumes about the kind of person he was. To her. Or rather, the kind of person she was, to him. He'd done many things in the last nine years, including drive through the forest in a jalopy truck with a bunch of fools engaging in illegal logging. He could have been killed many times and he didn't care. Now, though, he cared. The dying part was still not important. It was who could die with him. He wasn't ready to watch Demi die or be at risk.

Demi stayed asleep for at least two hours while he concentrated on his driving.

"Where are we?" she moaned, and he realized she had come awake.

"Somewhere in Ondo State," he murmured.

"Ondo State!" She sat up. "It's almost ten."

"We're close to Benin. The road is not fantastic. We are making good progress." He snickered. "Have you come this way before?"

"We should go through Onitsha." She snapped. "Do you know where you're going?"

Duru arched an eyebrow. "About time."

"I should have known not to sleep..."

"Onitsha roads are not good, and Aba to Ikot Ekpene is not motorable right now. We'd have to go to Umuahia first. It will be a rigmarole." He stole a glance at her.

She slouched. "Seems you know what you are doing."

"I usually do." He paused. "Do you, though?"

"I'm paying you to take me to Uyo, so I don't have to answer your questions, Stan."

His name in her voice, on her lips, sent an array of emotions down his spine to his toes. It glued his tongue to the roof of his mouth and dried his throat. Even if he had an answer for her immediately, there was no way it would come out of him.

Chapter 38

"We'll rest tonight. Tomorrow morning, we'll find the house. I have the address."

Demi stepped into her hotel room, which was two doors away from his, and closed the door. Duru stood there, just looking at the door for several seconds. He walked to the room with the key number in his hand and entered.

What was Ademilade up to?

He knew they were here to exact some revenge on Idem Isong but what? He had looked up the brute and discovered he was currently a local government chairman in Akwa Ibom State. That was no small feat. The man would have a lot of money as Duru could imagine and he didn't know what Demi could do to hurt him, at least without hurting herself.

Duru dropped his backpack on the double bed in his hotel room. It must cost Demi a lot to have such a nice luxurious hotel. It was new too. Why did she get a double room for him? He could sleep in the car, and he had told her so. He'd worked with some hunters in Kwara State for several years, sleeping in the thick forest without any ill feeling. She didn't need to spend her money like this. Yet, he couldn't get her to say a word outside of the "need-to-know" context.

He tested the bed. It was firm, well made with all-white bedding.

"Well, Miss, if you want me to enjoy tonight, I'd better, and let the morning release whatever it has for us."

He got into the shower and fantasized once more, about having her in it with him.

"I told you I'll call you."

Duru leaned against her doorway, with the rugged, clean look she liked about him, his eyes narrowed, his lips pressed together, his body-fitting black T-shirt and jeans clinging to every muscle in his body. He folded his arms across his chest. In her cliché thoughts, she wondered if he ever knew how good he looked.

"You didn't call. It's morning," he mumbled.

"Meet me at the car in ten minutes." She closed the door in his face and breathed through her mouth.

Why was he here, anyway?"

Over and over, she had hoped he would refuse to oblige her, and this would reset her brain and stop her progress on this destructive, vengeful path. Instead, his willingness fu-elled her foolishness. Did he have an idea why she was here? She hadn't told him or anyone her plan, yet he continued to assist her. She was glad he did, though. She liked being around him more than was good for her. Did she have a crazy desire for mysterious men? Or why would someone so shrouded in secrecy appeal to her for any wild reasons? After what Idem did to her! Could it be for the money? But if he was after money, he'd have cheated her on the purchase of the Avalon. No, he didn't seem like someone who cared about money.

Duru sat in the car and had the air-conditioner on when she showed up ten minutes later. She got into the car beside him.

"Here's the address." She handed him a piece of paper.

He took it and inputted it into maps. It was eighteen minutes away. He put the gear in drive and smoothly pulled out of the hotel premises.

Demi's heart thudded. Now what? When she got to Idem's house, what was she to do? Pour the acid in her bag on him, on his wife? Would they even be allowed in? She stole a glance at Duru and wondered if she should share her thoughts and fears. After all, he was here. In this, with her. But what if he disagreed and urged her to return home? She didn't want that. She had come a long way already. She had walked down the path of shame for nine years and it never got better as her parents had tried to console her it would. People still pointed at her in the market. Kids were sometimes unnecessarily mean to Mimi and teased her about her father.

Worse still, a part of Demi still wanted Idem, still prayed to wake up from the nightmare. She was that stupid. Still. Hurt. Too hurt. No, she couldn't allow Duru or anyone to turn her away from here. She had enough acid in her purse to melt Idem, and she planned to use it on him, or his wife, or his kids. She had waited long to have her revenge. She had waited this long to get someone who would bring her here to Uyo because she didn't want to come alone, knowing Uwana or Idem could harm her and no one would ever find her body...She had never met anyone able or willing to do what Duru now did for her.

"I didn't know the house would be this big."

"Or guarded," Duru said.

They parked on the other side of Idem's huge house and watched several men in regular police uniform, special mobile police uniform, and the army, lounge and parade the front of the house. The black gates were wide and high, and had spikes and electrocuting wires all around them, and the fence all the way to the end of a block.

Duru turned to her. "When are you going to tell me what we're doing here?"

"Never." Demi rolled her eyes. "Just follow my instructions."

"Yes, madam." Duru saluted but there was no humour in his voice or face.

"Think I'm crazy or not, I don't care."

Duru swallowed. "If you want to punish him, I will help you."

Demi gasped. "How? Why?"

"I'll take you back to the hotel. Leave Idem to me. If you don't like what I do with him, we'll just go back to Owena."

"And if I like it?"

Duru stared hard at her. "You'll thank me later."

Spoken in that rough hard yet soft tone, Demi's toes tingled. "What do you want to do?"

"You're not the only one who knows how to keep secrets," he said.

"How many days will it take you?"

"Only tonight," he breathed. "When you wake up in the morning, Idem will be breaking news."

She smiled spontaneously, excited by the thought that Duru actually wanted to take the burden off her. She looked away, unwilling to let him see how vulnerable she felt. This was her fight.

"No."

He arched an eyebrow. "No?"

She straightened. "This is my business, and I will handle it as I think best."

"Fine, Lady Boss." Duru shrugged. "Give me instructions."

Demi wanted to cry at the thick mockery in his tone, but this was not the time to be weak or sentimental.

She bit her lower lip. "Drop me here and drive to the end of the road. I'll call you when it's time to pick me up."

"Okay."

She came out of the car and Duru drove to the end of the road as instructed. Demi drew in a staggering breath and crossed over to the other side. To the front of the gate of Idem's house. She steeled her inner resolve. This was her moment, and she had to take it all.

Chapter 39

"Yes, thanks. Thank you."

Duru hung up on the call he made briefly as soon as he dropped Demi and stared at her walk over to the military men in front of Idem's house. There was no way she would gain entrance. He didn't think she would be convincing, but he admired her courage. Still, he didn't know how their relationship went sour, not that he couldn't have found out, but he wasn't interested if she wasn't the one telling him. He knew it had been bad from the snippets and little jeers that came in through conversations at the market, in the bank she worked, at the barber's. Even at his mechanic workshop but he refused to listen to their gossip.

Two military men spoke with Demi and soon a third and a fourth joined in the conversation. An unusual smile broke on Duru's face when one of the men opened the gate and Demi walked through.

"Wow. Lady boss!"

She would make it. Whatever she planned would be successful.

Idly, Duru sat and just stared at the gate. There were a lot of activities. Cars with tinted glasses and official plate numbers constantly went in and came out. The men jeered, stood at alert, ate, and drank. The hours went by, and Demi didn't show up or call him.

After five hours, he itched to call her, but he also knew what it was like to be at a politician's house. Idem definitely was a rich one, and the richer the busier these politicians usually were. Doling out money. Stolen money. Blood money.

"What if she was in some form of trouble?"

He couldn't afford to think like that. He came out of the car and paced, unsure of what to do. What did she go in there to do? Was she succeeding? Was Idem sorry and trying to make up? Anything could be the scenario within those walls. Or had the bastard done what Duru thought he would and arrested Demi?

As Duru toyed with his phone and the thought of calling anyway, even if she would not pick up, the small gate opened, and Demi walked out. She started to dial on her phone, and he guessed she wanted to call. He got into the car and as his phone rang, he pulled up beside her.

Demi got into the car. "We return to Owena tomorrow. 5am."

Duru nodded. "Yes, madam."

"Thank you, again."

Duru sat on the bed and tied up his boots. He tucked in his phone into his back pocket and slung his emptied backpack on his shoulder. He stepped out of his room. Since he returned to the hotel with Demi an hour earlier, he had not done anything but make several calls. He didn't think it was fair of Demi to keep him solely in the dark, but when she entered the car, he'd seen the pain and sadness in her eyes. He found himself so sensitive to her, her mood, her actions, her words. She hadn't been happy. Either her plan worked and then made her unhappy, which was quite possible. Sometimes we wanted revenge so badly but the after taste was bitter. Or her plan did not work. Either one, he wasn't going to watch Idem hurt the woman of his fantasies again. He hadn't been around when Idem did it the first time, but he would not let it pass this time. If Demi hated him for doing what he planned to do, fine. His joy would still be complete.

He walked to the road as dusk descended and took a taxi.

"Ibom hall," he murmured.

The person he'd called twice earlier in the day, Ebito, a boy who had worked on the site in Owena with Idem, came out of the hall where a ceremony was going on.

Ebito was not from Akwa Ibom state but had continued to hang around Idem for work, and somehow, Duru had just maintained contact with him. The last time Duru saw him, he was skinny and stupid.

"Wow." Duru gasped. "Ebito! You have chop up o. All the oyel money in Akwa Ibom is flowing in your veins now."

"Oh boy!" Ebito laughed. "You just dey gather muscle. E be like say you lean sef."

Duru sighed. "I told you. It's been tough. See me here na. I came all the way here. Just to see if anything will drop."

"Hmm, Oga has it o. His local government is the seat of all the oyel in this state. Dah! We see money like water." Ebito laughed. "Is funny."

"Help me, na. Mbok. I don't know what to do again."

"You're here now." Ebito slapped Duru's shoulder. "Chief fit remember you sef."

"Thank you, Ebito. I cannot thank you enough." Duru touched his finger to his tongue. "I swear, I will settle you."

Ebito laughed hard. "Leave that one. I have more than enough."

"Turn on the TV to local news."

Demi arched an eyebrow. It wasn't even four yet. What did Duru mean? Before she could snap at him for waking her up prematurely, he hung up. She had had a very bad night. After the shame of failure the day before, and uncontrollable tears alone in her hotel room, lack of appetite and stomach cramps, the last thing she needed was a call from Duru, commanding her.

She pulled herself up and turned on the TV. Truly, the local news channel had Idem in their breaking news. Demi's mouth dropped open.

Idem's child kidnapped. Ransom set at five hundred million naira.

Demi called Duru. "What did you do?"

Instead of a response, she heard the cries of a baby. Without thought, she flew off her bed and in her skimpy night gown, hurried out to Duru's room.

"Duru!" She knocked and whispered harshly so as not to raise any alarm. He opened the door to her before she finished calling him a second time and closed it.

A baby girl who couldn't be more than six months lay on the bed with a little gag in her mouth. Demi clasped a sob with her two hands.

"Duru! Oh my God. What did you do?"

"I stole their baby from their house." He stood by the door and watched her. "I told you I'll punish them for you."

Demi shuddered. "But I told you I'd handle it myself. Oh my God, Stanley Duru. Oh my God." She walked tentatively to the baby but didn't touch her.

Tears pooled in Demi's eyes. Why would he be so keen on helping her get this revenge? What did he plan to do with this baby?

A phone beside the bed started to ring and continued to for a while.

"Won't you pick your call?"

"It's them. I've told them the terms. Five hundred million in twenty-four hours or I will kill the baby and drop the body where they will find it." Duru arched an eyebrow. "They've been calling since."

Several questions ran through Demi's mind. She couldn't stop staring at Duru and the baby. She moved close to the bed but was unsure if she should carry her. The breaking news on the TV continued to show the picture of the baby and asking that anyone with information should contact the family or the police for a reward.

"You don't mean it, Duru! You can't." Demi breathed hard.

Tears stained the baby's chubby cheeks. She was such a pretty baby, so fair skinned and healthy looking.

"I do. I'll do anything you want me to do with her," he said.

"Take the gag out, please," Demi stuttered.

Duru took it out and the baby's wailing filled the room. "She cries a lot."

"She must be hungry." Demi picked the baby up. "Ssh. Don't cry, love." She cooed.

"I stole her with her bottle. She's not hungry. Just angry." There was laughter in Duru's voice. "She knows what I'm doing to her, somehow."

"It's not funny." Demi snapped. "We have to take her back. Now."

This time, Duru laughed.

Chapter 40

"**A**re you kidding me? Take her back to where?"

Duru couldn't remember the last time he laughed or felt such happiness. Demi looked petrified but he could sense her joy. The baby started to calm down and suck her hand as Demi continued to rock her.

"Her parents!"

Duru shook his head. "Idem's wife will kill you this time and nothing will happen."

"So, if this was to revenge what they did to me, how would they know it's me? This can just be random crime…"

"Watch the TV."

Demi turned to the screen, her body stiff. Duru could feel her conflict, confusion and satisfaction at the same time.

On the screen, Idem and his wife pleaded with the kidnappers to temper justice with mercy and pick up their calls to negotiate. Idem looked ten years older, and his wife looked even worse with red puffy eyes.

"Do you know they lost their son last year? What better way to hurt them?" he said.

"What happened to their son?" she whispered.

"He died in a car accident."

"How do you know?"

"I know," he mumbled.

Duru studied Demi. Her eyes remained glued to the screen. Her lips were pressed together and he only wished she could say something, tell him what she really felt, but she just continued to stare until the couple's plea was replaced by the baby's picture, and then the news anchor returned with offers for anyone who had information.

"Listen, I don't care one shred of a bit for this guy. If you want me to take the baby back, right now, I will." He paused for that to sink in. "I will take her to the motherless baby's home or a hospital or even the police station and leave her outside so they..."

"No," Demi whispered.

Duru's heart swelled. This was what he badly wanted. Her endorsement of what he did. He had been kind to the baby, fed her as soon as he entered the room, but she kept crying and the only reason why he put the small piece of handkerchief over her mouth was to reduce the noise. He followed Demi with his gaze. He would, at this point, do anything she wanted, and he had no qualms about telling her so. She continued to pace and rock the baby until she was fast asleep.

"I'm keeping her," Demi said softly.

"What?"

He expected anything but...keeping the baby?

"I'm taking her back with me. She's mine." Demi's gaze met his. "Mine."

Duru frowned. "For how long?"

Demi shrugged. "Forever."

"Stop joking. We can take Idem's money. I'm ready to double the offer, do anything but..."

Demi yelled. "I'm taking her back to Owena. She's mine now! I don't want his d*mned money!"

"We should have breakfast in Port Harcourt. I know a place."

Demi shrugged and stared at Idem's baby. She still couldn't believe herself that she decided to take her. Why would she even do this? She could never love this baby like she loved Mimi, and what would she tell people?

Duru pulled out into the early dawn of Friday morning. Within an hour, the road would start getting busy but for now, it wasn't even five o'clock yet.

"How did you steal her?" Demi said.

"This Ijaw boy, Ebito, and I worked for Idem. Ebito is still one of his thugs, following him around but I kept in touch with him." Duru sighed. "I made him believe I was desolate. Went to find him at a function in Ibom Hall where Idem was a special guest. Followed him back to Idem's house. The rest is history."

"I want to hear it. I want to know the history," she said.

Duru stole a glance at the baby. "What will you call her?"

"I don't know. I'll find a Yoruba name. Tell me how you stole her."

"I was in Idem's private parlour. Waiting for hours. I told Ebito I needed to use the toilet. He pointed one to me. But the house is so big. I knew I wanted to do something tangible like kidnap someone, the wife really, and I had a big knife to hold her hostage. So I roamed and entered the baby's room by mistake. Saw her asleep. I gagged her and put her and her bottle in my backpack."

Demi gasped. "You are callous."

"You said you wanted details."

"Go on. How did you leave?"

"I told Ebito I was pressed and having running stomach. To walk me out. He did. He didn't notice my backpack looked bigger than when I came." He chuckled. "I mean, who would? Cocky, arrogant people." He sighed. "Anyway, his car was parked outside the compound. He drove me to the motor park where I told him I was squatting with the driver who brought me to Uyo."

Demi shook her head. "That's a long tale. How would he not notice your backpack was bulkier?"

"Ebito believed. He had no reason not to believe me. Besides, who would have thought I'd steal a baby?"

"What if she had woken and cried?"

"I gagged her."

Demi couldn't wrap her head around that. "She could have died. You could have killed her!"

"I didn't. She did not die. I have carried babies bigger than her in my backpack before and I…"

"Why would you? Did you do rituals? Were you a kidnapper?"

Duru scoffed. "That's how low you think of me?"

"Who would think of stealing a baby in a backpack?"

"I worked in the forest with hunters. We carried our bounty in bags that size, and sometimes if a boy follows his father and is in danger, I put him in a sack, the size of my backpack. A ten-year-old can fit in, how much more a baby."

Despite the anger she thought he should feel, his tone was even, like a friend explaining a process.

Demi closed her eyes. "We need to buy clothes in the next town."

Duru had carried the baby with her big shawl too. That must have been warm and cosy. Still, she couldn't understand how the baby did not die of suffocation.

"The market in Eket will not be open by the time we get there, or Etinan either, and I don't think we should stop anywhere in Akwa Ibom," he said. "Port Harcourt will be okay."

"She'll be hungry when she wakes up." She worried. "I hope she is alright."

"I think she is."

Demi looked at the rosy cheeks of her new baby. The baby sucked her lips for a few seconds, which brought a half-smile to Demi's lips.

"We need to buy milk. I don't know what brand she'll like." Demi sniffed. "If we see any shops along the way and they have milk."

"So, do I get to hear what happened when you went into Idem's house. What did he say when he saw you?"

"I don't owe you an explanation."

"I have earned one," he said.

She sniffed. "You couldn't have held Idem's wife at knife point and kidnap her. His MOPOL will shoot you on your forehead and they'll dump you in the river."

"I was ready to die there."

"Oh, please. You are not telling me the truth. Your kidnap story is *sh*tty*."

Duru laughed. "I do a lot of *sh*tty* stuff. I always get away with it. I am lucky like that."

Chapter 41

"**P**lease turn away."

Duru bit the inside of his lower lip and did as he was commanded. This was incredible. His thoughts ran wild at what he found himself in right now. In the last nine years, he had seen it all but one. This. Kidnapping a baby to help a woman he lusted after get a revenge on her ex-husband for reasons he didn't know. New. Utterly. His brain must have lost many incredibly intelligent cells in the last nine years of his aimless wandering.

"Do you have milk?" he asked.

"I breastfed before." Demi snapped. "That should count."

The hungry sucking sound from the baby caught Duru's attention. He might have known what all this was about if the bastards who killed Belema had not been on duty on that awful day. His baby could have been close to twelve by now. He shook his head.

"Seems like it is working." He snickered. "The way of a babe on a nipple."

Demi didn't say anything to his silly remarks. He decided to walk to a nearby bush just to be away from the sound of the baby's suckling, which he realized was causing an unwanted stir around his loins. He wanted his lips on Demi. Crazy, this all was. He doubted if he had lusted after Belema half this much. And why was he so easily amused these days. Easily fluid with words. Now, he was even remembering his humour with scriptures. He couldn't let this happen to him. He even missed his guitar! And the object of his fascination didn't seem fazed by him in the least. He was just a handyman willing to jump at the sound of her voice.

Crazy. Extremely.

He stared at the car from a safe distance. The road was not busy, considering it was just still early in the day. They were halfway between Uyo and Port Harcourt and he hoped this baby would hold out just a little longer until they could find a baby shop to buy a few changes of clothes, diapers and milk.

Demi sat sideways with one leg on the ground and her head bent over the baby. It was a most intimate posture, and Duru hoped the baby got some milk. He really didn't know anything about this much as he itched to, and again, he smacked himself on the head for even caring a bit. Caring wasn't his thing anymore. Not about himself or any other person. Until now.

Idly, he brought out his two phones from his pocket to look through messages. There was one from Ebito.

Chai, bruh. Bad luck dey follow you o. Oga's baby was kidnapped over the night. The suspect a mopol but all of them dey deny. Mean say Oga no go fit see you today until they find the baby o. Sorry.

Duru replied.

Chai, How I go do na? The driver wey bring me from Lagos dey return this night, and I go sit attachment for free. Unless Oga settle me. How I go do na? Hep.

He smiled at the thought. Useless system. Useless people. Upon all the security and all the fanfare around Idem, his people suffered. And one could take his baby from inside his massive mansion, and they had no clue how it happened.

Duru opened the small phone with the kidnapper's number. There were sixty-three missed calls and a message. He read the message.

This number has been traced and the owner found. We will track you down shortly. Help yourself and return Chief Idem Isong's baby before noon, and we will forgive you.

Duru sent a two-word reply: *F*ck you!*

He snickered. "Hahaha. Clowns. I am afraid you will track me down shortly."

"What are you saying?"

Duru looked up and Demi stood less than a foot away, rocking the baby wrapped in her shawl. He hadn't heard her approach.

"How's she?"

Demi shrugged. "Not sure anything came out for her. But she seems comforted."

He arched an eyebrow. "How are you?"

"We should get on the road. She doesn't have anything on. If she poops..." Demi laughed.

The sound of her laughter rocked through every vein in his body, and his lips parted at the mere impact this had on him, acute pain of lust, and need.

She stopped laughing and he realized she engaged his lustful gaze with one of hers. For a split second, the urge to grab her and kiss her overwhelmed him. She turned just in time and walked back to the car. Duru drew in several calming breaths and followed her. He didn't know where this emotion was leading but he didn't feel too good about its destination. The time was not ripe. He could never love again. Least of all now.

"It must be the sour milk she sucked off your breast."

Despite herself, Demi chuckled. "You are not serious."

The baby's poop smelt so strong they had to wind down halfway for their windows and all the way down for the back windows. Soon the discomfort and extra breeze coming in made the baby start to whine, and then wail.

"Where are we? We need to badly get into a shop." Demi sighed. "Sorry, baby. Baby, sorry." She moaned.

"We're entering Ogoniland."

"Good. Please stop at any shop."

"We won't go into their towns. It's not much farther to Port."

Demi gasped. "Ah, no, please. This baby needs to clean up and her poop has soaked into my dress."

"The towns are much farther inside, and I am not very familiar with this area. We'll soon get to Port Harcourt," Duru said.

His deep, soft yet firm statement made her stomach turn. He sounded much more educated than what he did for a living. Much much more intelligent than any mechanic she knew. Who was he? She really wanted to know but it meant she'd have to talk about herself, and she wasn't ready to.

"Where are you from?"

"Rivers. My family claims Port Harcourt," he said.

She gasped. "You have family in Port Harcourt!"

"I didn't say that. I was born in Lagos. Grew up there." He stole a glance in her direction. "What about you?"

"I choose not to say," she said, despite herself.

"That's okay." He shrugged. "I don't talk a lot about myself, either."

The baby's whimpering broke an awkward silence where Demi struggled to talk about herself. She liked this cool Duru, and yet, she knew they were as far apart as the heaven was to earth. He was just a mechanic, painter, carpenter...Mr. Fixer, and she had no clue what he had done, or where he had been.

Demi scoffed. "Seems she wants to suck again."

Demi groaned at the thought of stopping, to near-undress because in her lack of thinking, she had worn a long dress on this trip.

"We can stop," Duru said, softly.

"I think I'll just change into jeans and T-shirt. Already her poop is on my dress." Demi moaned. This wasn't funny at all.

Duru pulled over by the side of the road. Demi carefully took the baby's soiled blanket to clean the soft bum, and while Duru held the naked baby, and looked away, Demi changed. She took one of her other clean dresses to wrap the baby. As soon as the clean dress touched the baby, she peed into it.

"No!" Demi screeched and laughed.

"She's punishing you." Duru laughed. "Don't worry, it's not much longer." He smoothly pulled back into the road.

Demi couldn't wait.

Chapter 42

"There, sweetheart!"

Duru half-smiled at the joy in Demi's voice after she wore the clean dress for the baby and lay her on the double bed in their hotel room in Port Harcourt.

"Never thought it will be so stressful abducting a baby," he said. "Forgive me."

Demi snickered. "Hmm, my people will say, a-seh. High-level hypocrisy."

"I happen to know what a-seh means, and yes, my request for forgiveness is very insincere." He chuckled. "My phone is swarmed with threats and pleas in equal proportion. I am actually enjoying this more than I ever thought."

Demi stared at the baby. "She is adorable, I accept."

"Have you decided on a name for her?"

"Not yet. Hopefully, I will before we arrive Owena." Demi sighed. "Right now, I am tired, and famished, and I want to see Port Harcourt. I have never been in this famous city."

Duru arched an eyebrow. "You are serious about keeping her?"

"Of course." She walked off and into the adjoining bathroom.

Duru stared thoughtfully at the baby who slept peacefully after churning down a full bottle of milk, got a warm bath and change into clean warm clothes. It was none of his business what Demi did with this child, and he didn't want to have an opinion about it, yet he felt responsible on a level he hadn't bothered to be for a very long time.

Unlike in Uyo where they had different rooms, this time, Demi paid for a suite which could afford him to sleep in a separate room, on the couch. He didn't ask why she did so, but he felt more comfortable being in the same general space with her.

His feelings for her raged, seeking expression but he could feel it would come out all wrong. There seemed to him a struggle within her. She was attracted to him, and that one time she smiled, it all became very clear she wanted him, maybe as much as he wanted her. His problem was not telling her how he felt, or what anticipated response he'd get. What about the future? He definitely wanted her in his bed and in his shower, and then what? He could not commit to a woman ever again, and Demi wasn't one he'd want to dump. Not because she'd be hurt. Because he would be scarred forever. He hadn't wanted Belema half this much if his memory served him and see how devastated her death made him.

Demi stepped out of the bathroom freshly showered and dressed in a clean dress. Her entrance squeezed out a low moan from Duru's belly.

She sighed. "Now to get food."

"I know a great restaurant in town if you are keen on local food," he said.

"Clean up first, then we'll find it."

"Sure." He walked into the bathroom she just exited and spent the first minute just soaking in her steam.

He wanted Ademilade, and no, he wasn't going to hold back on what he wanted anymore.

"I could never have imagined I will find amala this good in Port Harcourt."

"Glad it makes some sense," Duru said.

"And you said you don't know Port. Are you lying or what? There's no way you could know this joint if you never lived here." Demi licked each finger.

"I didn't say any of that. I lived here for some time. My sister lives here."

"Your sister lives here in Port? Really? Hmm."

"I haven't seen her in nine years."

Demi scoffed. "Don't tell me. I don't want to know."

Duru stared at her. "Why? It's my story. I can tell it if I want."

"Remember we are here together for a job not for reconciliation or catching up or getting to know…" She returned his gaze. "Yes?" When he said nothing, she nodded. "Yes. Now finish up and let's get back to the hotel. My baby may be awake."

She ate up as fast as she could, and he couldn't help but just stare at her. He didn't have any appetite for food. He wanted her. When she was done, she paid for the food and stood. Despite himself, Duru stood too, his food barely touched. Demi ignored the fact and hurried back to the car.

The drive back to the hotel was silent.

The baby was still fast asleep.

"I'd take a walk," Duru said.

"We leave in the morning before five," Demi said.

"Sure."

Her arrogance turned him on more than not. This wasn't the Duru he knew back in the day, soft-hearted, soft-spoken, soft in the groin mostly, Belema sometimes had to go extra to get him excited. Now, everything was opposite. What grief and anger did to people; he was a living testimony? Still, he could not be violent with a woman. He couldn't shout at her, show her how oppressed and depressed he was by her haughtiness? He wanted this woman. Simple.

The cool evening breeze refreshed him a little. He took out his pack of cigarette, which he hadn't touched in the three days of this journey and lit one. A long drag and total inhalation warmed him through. Duru closed his eyes and imagined, like he had done on many days and nights, what it would be like to have Demi in his arms, in his bed...but not in his life. That was taking it too far.

After three more sticks, Duru returned into the hotel room. He could hear the baby sucking, on her bottle, he imagined. He lay on the couch and tried to expunge the sound of the suckling from where it seemed to affect him most, in between his legs. He had to get Demi out of his head. His chest. His groin.

He knew what he had to do. Once they returned to Owena, he was leaving. He would leave that town and go far from it. To another part of Nigeria he had never lived before. Where he knew not their language or culture. As far from Demi as possible.

Sokoto. That should be far enough.

Chapter 43

"Let's go to your house, first."

"My house?" Duru arched an eyebrow. "Why?"

"I don't want my parents to see this baby tonight," Demi said.

He didn't look at her at first, now he half-turned. "Tonight. Meaning the baby will sleep in my house, tonight?"

Despite the tone he took with her, and the half-turn, he still slowed down to enter a deep porthole, and carefully turned into the road that led off the Akure-Ilesa highway to Owena.

"Yes," she said. "She will sleep in your house tonight."

"Really? Do I have a say in this?"

"You have a right to say anything you want, you know." She scoffed. "I can't stop you from saying."

Yet, he said nothing. Demi held herself together and waited.

He pulled up in front of her house and turned to face her. "I'm not sure the seatbelt will help, but we can prop her up on my backpack and I'll just have to go slow."

"I'll go with you to your house and find my way back," she said.

"I think I can manage…"

"Take me to your house, please." She snapped. "I need to know where my baby will be anyway."

He took a few seconds of tensed silence, then did as she said. Demi could feel fear creep in on her. What was she even doing? This was insane. To bring Idem's baby to Owena. The poor baby cried a lot on the trip yet, she feared to ask Duru to drive back to Uyo. It's what she should have done in Port Harcourt, but her ego and whatever else would not let her do the right thing. She did derive some pleasure from the thought that Idem and his wife were going through serious torture not having their baby.

"Did Idem try to contact you again?"

"That phone has had no peace." He chuckled. "I reply once every while with a short text."

"Short text? What do you say in it?"

"*F*ck* you, most of the time," he said.

Demi chuckled. "That should make them very happy. The *bastard* liked to *f*ck*."

The moment the words came out of her mouth, she wished she hadn't said it, and she turned to look out at the street where they turned into. Duru's neighbourhood was low-income, and what did she expect?

"I'm glad you approve," he said softly.

Shame overwhelmed Demi. She had tried her best to keep a professional profile and treat this handsome rogue like a client. She paid him in cash in full, and didn't want to make any unnecessary small talk with him or acknowledge the way his dark gazes affected her heart. Through the long tedious journey, she took care of the baby and thought of her next steps, but as soon as they got closer home, her confidence failed her. What would her parents think? She'd have to answer many questions from them, and Mimi. How would she explain a new baby sister? She couldn't even give this baby a name. She couldn't discuss her confusion with anyone. Only Duru seemed to understand, and she didn't want to get to that level of discussing her life or issues with him. She did feel shame for her actions, for telling him Idem liked sex, for being so vulnerable in that little sarcastic sentence, and knowing he understood her. She was angry he was being so understanding and conforming.

"We're here." He pulled over to the side of the road by a small dirt gutter. "My room is behind in this compound." He turned to her. "Are you sure you want your baby to spend the night in this dirty compound?"

"Let's see." She opened the door and came out. "Your house is not far from mine, that's good."

She followed him through a small, crowded compound with a big bungalow close to the gate and the fence, to a smaller one with three doors. It was late enough for everyone to be indoors. Duru unlocked the first of the three doors and turned on the light with a switch by the wall. Demi licked her lips before she entered a small room with a spring bed pushed to the wall. Such a humble abode. There was nothing else in the room except the well-made bed. Nothing. It sent a shuddering sensation through Demi's body. How could someone live like this?

Duru walked to the only wooden window and opened it. "This it."

Demi sat on the bed and rocked the baby. "Here's the truth. I can't keep this baby. I don't know why I brought her. My parents will be devastated if they know what I did. I just told them I was going away for a few days to clear my head. Mimi...I don't know how I will answer her questions about this baby."

She summoned the courage to look up at him. He just stood there by the window and stared at her. Definitely, he must think she was crazy. She thought she was.

"Do you need a few days to think this through?"

Demi laid the baby on the bed. She was still awake, but quiet. "Could you please just get her bag, and mine?"

He arched an eyebrow. "You can't stay here. The baby, yes, until you figure out what you want to..."

"I don't want to stay here. I sent Bukky a text to pick me here, and she will. So, I need to get my bag from the Avalon."

He glared at her as though she had grown horns, and then left the room. Demi covered her face and tried to breathe. This wasn't even funny. What had she done to herself?

Duru entered with her luggage, and the bag with the new things they bought for the baby.

"You can abandon this baby here. I will get rid of her for you. I will not be wicked," Duru said. "I do not have any hard feelings for her parents but trust me, she will be treated fairly, and you have nothing to worry about.

Demi stood, hesitated, and walked to Duru. She pulled down his head and took his lips with hers. He did not respond at first and didn't lift his hands to hold her. He didn't pull back or resist either.

"Hmm. Hmmm."

Demi kissed Duru until the tightness in his groin became unbearable aided by her soft moans, and then as though she knew he was at breaking point, stepped back.

"Thank you," she murmured, turned, picked her luggage, and walked out of his room.

Duru breathed hard through his mouth. He should follow her. Jack her back. Give her what she had coming.

He only breathed harder.

Chapter 44

"**W**hat on earth are you doing here, Demi?"

Bukky's question took almost a minute to sink in even as Demi got into her friend's car. She did it! She kissed Stanley Duru, and it confirmed everything she felt. She felt good. Better than Idem ever made her feel. Just that she couldn't stop her hands from trembling. Or her heart thudding. Now what? How was she going to face him tomorrow, and the day after and after then?

"Ademilade!"

"I need a house. I need accommodation." Demi drew in a shuddering breath.

"I asked what you are doing in this horrible neighbourhood, madam!" Bukky snapped. "At this time of the day."

"I just came back from my trip. That Duru guy dropped me." Demi rested her head. "He lives there."

"And why will he drop you at his house, and not yours." Bukky gasped. "Demi! When did you return and why were you there?"

Demi closed her eyes. How would she even explain? It was the stupidest thing to have followed Duru to his house. And what a house? How did a person live like that? Who was he? What did he spend his earnings on? There had to be something right there. And she had kissed him so passionately. Enjoyed it too.

"I hope you are not sleeping with that ruffian. Demi!"

"Huh?"

"You've had sex with him!" Bukky exclaimed. "Goodness gracious. Shey you see something is wrong with your head! You need deliverance. After everything that stupid Idem did to you. After dumping you like that! You know, Demi, I tried not to believe you didn't know Idem was married. I tried to think that you are smarter than that but after tonight, I think there is something very wrong with you and for crying out loud, I don't pity you again.

"Do you know this Duru from anywhere? So these past few days that you said you travelled, you were locked up in his house? Ah, aye mi! This is unbelievable. You don't even pity yourself. Where is his family? For all you know, he is married like Idem. He may even have disease. I'm going to report you to pastor..."

"I didn't sleep with him, Bukky." Demi sighed. "We just arrived this evening and I told him to drop me."

Bukky lowered her voice. "Talk to me, Demi. What's going on? Are you in some trouble?"

"Okay, look. I am really attracted to that guy, and I thought I'd spend the night, but I got sense and ran instead." Demi shrugged. "That's why I sent you a message to come."

"Huh." Bukky exhaled. "Well, thank God you left before doing something stupid."

Bukky pulled up in front of Demi's parents' home.

"I really need my own place, though," Demi said. "If you see anywhere."

"Do you think it's a good idea?" Bukky said. "With this guy around now, you know. If it was in your house, you won't be able to run."

"I know you think I'm dense, but Duru is a gentleman. He could have taken advantage of me, and he didn't," Demi said.

"Well, true. And I really think you're dense." Bukky laughed. "Though, that Duru is cute o, hmm. Huh! Yeah, hmm."

Demi laughed. "Thank you. At least my dense has a good eye."

"But do you know about him? He's not Yoruba though he speaks the language fluently. Do you know where he's from, his family?" Bukky's eyes bore deep into Demi's soul. "He looks young, but his eyes are old. I won't be surprised if he is more than forty."

"Huh! Forty?"

"Of course," Bukky said. "Look at the back of his hands. He's been around for long. I'll just advice you that before you go deeper, check him out. Meet his people. Even though again, hmm, is he even educated?" Bukky raised her hand in protest. "I know you may say that doesn't really matter but it does o. Hmm. And is he a Christian? Even if it is only going to church. That guy smokes like a chimney o."

"I made it clear to him no smoking around me," Demi said.

Bukky gasped. "So, you have really started going deeper?"

"No, I told him when I asked him to drive me. No smoking inside my car or around me. And he kept to it," Demi said.

Bukky sighed. "Hmm, just be careful. I don't trust any man again o, after what that stupid idiot did to you."

"I will be. Thanks, dear." Demi hugged Bukky.

"See you in church tomorrow," Bukky said.

Demi took out her luggage from the back seat and went into her father's compound. Bukky didn't pull away until a moment later. As expected, everyone had turned in. Demi let herself in and walked quietly to her room. Mimi was asleep on her bed. She just wanted to have a bath and weep or laugh. Maybe she should have slept in Duru's house with the baby and decide what next. Here, she felt alone, and confused, and horny. She'd thought she could never want a man again in her life.

What was Duru thinking about her? Of course, she could pick up her phone and call to find out, but she felt really embarrassed. That kiss had been good, though he didn't respond. What if he did? It would be explosive. Why didn't he respond to her kiss? Self-control? Had to be because from the first day she had a conversation with him, he had subtly flirted with her. In truth though, what could a future hold for them? She'd be the talk of the town all over again, banker marrying a mechanic. She and Duru were in two very different worlds that never mixed.

"Ah, are you back?" Mummy whispered and pushed the door open gently. "I thought I heard the door open."

Demi curtseyed. "Yes, ma. I tried to be quiet. I didn't want to disturb. Good evening."

"It's late o, you shouldn't travel so late."

"We left early. The car had problem in Ibadan," Demi said.

"Ehn, you should have just stayed with your brother and come tomorrow." Mummy moaned. "Well, thank God nothing happened. Welcome."

"Thank you, ma. Good night, ma." Demi turned even though her mother still stood at the door.

"Hmm, good night, dear."

Chapter 45

"Your baby is so beautiful."

"Thank you. Her mother travelled so I am dad and mum," Duru smiled. "Grateful she's not a fussy baby. And Mummy will be back today."

The usher lady in the church smiled. "Are you waiting for someone?"

Church had closed at least two hours earlier and Duru had patiently waited until it emptied out. He wanted badly to touch a guitar and couldn't think of anywhere else to get one. And the church was just a ten-minute walk from his house. It was a good opportunity to get out with the baby too, since Demi didn't show up in the morning and he vowed not to reach out to her. He still couldn't decipher this one.

The girl could kiss, though. He still tingled.

"I, huh, sorry. I wanted to see the guitar," Duru said.

"The guitar?" The woman frowned. "As in, guitar. Music guitar?"

"Yes, ma. I am a musician."

The woman's frown deepened. "You can come tomorrow evening. That is when the choir meets. Please, sir. I have to lock up."

Her attitude surprised Duru. People didn't generally resist musicians, but perhaps the way he looked in a black shirt and tight jeans, with a sleeping baby in his arms, and a request to "see" the guitar, made him suspicious. The town was too small for a wanderer like him. Everyone was usually wary.

"Oh, thank you, ma." Duru bowed and left the building.

He returned to his house and found Demi waiting. She wore one of those short dresses he noticed she took with her on the trip to Uyo; they made her look young, and fancy, delectable, sexy. His anatomy reacted stronger than he expected.

Demi scoffed. "Out on a stroll with baby?"

"Give her a name." He stepped by her and opened his door.

"We need to talk. Inside is not nice." She looked around. "And neither is here."

"We can go for a drive," he said.

"I can't love you."

Demi scoffed. "Thanks for telling me."

"Listen, you can't kiss me like that again and expect me to just stand there and allow you to walk away." Duru licked his lips. "Okay?"

Despite the humiliation whirling through her veins, she wanted to kiss him again. And again.

"What will you do?"

He glared at her long enough to safely keep his gaze from the road. It was a direct challenge, and she hated herself for being here, doing this, setting him up, taunting him, luring him. She wanted him. Badly. He was the last man she could have. His eyes, his words said it all. He wasn't available.

"Okay!" She drawled. "I won't kiss you again, ever. Now, let's talk about this baby. What do you want to do with her, because I don't know what to do and I am not showing her to my family."

"I'm a man." He inhaled. "And I have my limits. I know my limits."

Demi folded her arms across her chest to show false defiance. If she survived this drive, she would run as far as she could from this man. Block him totally out of her life. She couldn't afford another mistake with a man. It would kill her.

"You're pushing it, Demi. And you won't like what comes out of there, I assure you. You won't like me," he said.

She turned away and stared out. He was driving too fast. "Just tell me what you think we should do with this baby."

Duru slowed down and pulled to a stop by the shoulder. "I can't keep this baby, either. We should just take her back to where we got her from."

"To Uyo. Hell, no. Who will make that long journey for what?"

"You should have thought of that. I really thought you wanted to keep her," Duru said.

Demi heaved a sigh. "Any word from her father?"

"Just the long texts and continuous calls." He shrugged. "What else can they do?"

"I can't go all the way back to Uyo. We can take her to Akure and drop her at a motherless baby's home." Demi leaned back her head.

She couldn't stop her heart beating so hard. When did she start lusting after this guy so badly? Her palms were cold and sweaty. She didn't want to talk about this baby. She wanted to hold Stanley Duru and kiss him and make love. *Dear Lord, free me from this hungry spirit of lust.* She could feel him too. Could feel his struggle, in his tremulous voice, and the way he drove so fast. She imagined he was hard. She tried not to think or imagine anything.

"We could take her to Akwa Ibom State House in Lagos. Someone there will let her father know."

She scoffed. "How thoughtful of you."

"Do you agree?"

"Yes. I agree."

She just wanted to go under her duvet and cry and masturbate. She hated herself. She had prayed for God to take masturbation out of her life, and he had. Until now the urge was strong.

"When?"

She sighed. "I can't take another few days off so weekend."

"We leave Saturday and return Sunday," he said.

"Sounds like a plan," she muttered.

"I want you too, Demi. It's killing me. But once we return from Lagos, I'll leave town." He put the car in gear and made a U-turn to return to town.

She closed her eyes. "You can drive to your house. I'll find my way home."

"She'll be fine till Saturday? Do you think?"

Demi laid the baby on the bed. She was asleep.

Duru went to stand behind her, so close when she straightened, she fell into him. He turned her head around and fastened his lips on hers. His kiss was not wandering like hers had been. It was demanding, almost punishing. He dipped his head and deepened the kiss. Demi moaned in that same way he thought would turn him mad.

He raised his head and looked into her eyes. "You said you'll never kiss me again."

She pulled his head down. "I lied." She moaned and took his lips again.

He tore his lips from hers. "Demi! Marry me."

She staggered back. "No. Huh. Bye." She hurried out of his room.

Duru squatted and breathed hard. He couldn't do this. Couldn't stay around her for another week. He had to leave. Leave town. Go far as he decided.

Chapter 46

"Calm down, you're not making any sense."

"Look. He's here." Demi gasped. "He just walked in. I can't do this."

"I'll talk with him," Bukky said. "Pull yourself together. Don't say anything."

They stood and faced the door as Duru walked over to Demi's office. He nodded a greeting, his gaze fastened on Demi.

"I needed to see you, this afternoon," Duru said.

"She has told me everything," Bukky said. "Where's the baby?"

Duru arched an eyebrow. "With my landlady's house-girl."

"She can't talk to you. Let's go to my office," Bukky said.

Duru glared at Demi, but she looked away. She could feel her emotions creeping up on her. With Idem, things had been different. He had been in control from the start. From the first day they met, he had hit on her, made her do things she didn't know she was capable of. With Duru, it was different. Duru grew on her. He seemed unsure of her, himself and allowed her to take charge. She ordered him around, had a false sense of being in full control, but after that first kiss, it was clear Duru had her on his strings. However, Idem played the strings skilfully. Duru instead trembled with it and though he was playing it too, Demi didn't think he understood what he was doing at all.

"I didn't really come to talk," Duru said. "Just to let Demi know I'm going. Right now. I'm on my way out."

"Going to where?" Demi gasped. Her face shot to his, and their gazes locked.

For the first time since she spotted him come into the bank, she saw his face. He didn't look as though he had slept. Which made him look wild, and dangerous, and so irresistible to her.

"What will happen to the baby?" Bukky said. "You promised to take her to Lagos."

"I made arrangements with Akin. He's reliable. He's a good driver and he knows Lagos. He'll drive you on Saturday and bring you back on Sunday."

"Who on earth is Akin? You can't just dump them on a stranger!" Bukky exclaimed. "Where are you going? Look, after Sunday you can go anywhere you want for all I care..."

"Let him go," Demi said softly, though she couldn't take her eyes away from Duru's.

What had she gotten herself into? She'd die if he left but she couldn't have him around either. She wanted him yet there just couldn't be a relationship. She didn't even know anything about him and feared too much of being disappointed. If ever she got involved with anyone again, it would not be in this small town. She should have left after the Idem saga. Tucked tail and moved to Ibadan, but instead she stubbornly stayed and faced her shame. Her father told her she was brave. Her mother said she was foolish. Her mother was right.

"Thank you." He turned and left.

"What was that?" Bukky snapped. "My God! Demi! That guy did not take his eyes away from you for one second."

Demi followed his retreat until he disappeared from her view. She lowered herself into her seat.

"I told you. He was like this yesterday too." Demi moaned. "I'm so confused."

"Look, I think you are right. He should go wherever he wants. You can't do this again." Bukky sighed. "To God who made me, I have never seen a man eat up a woman with his eyes like that before. Even Mr. Olalekan in his romantic glory never looks at me like that."

"I can't laugh, Bukky. I'm finished." Demi moaned. "I'm not going to any Lagos with any Akin."

"Which rando is that abeg?" Bukky smirked. "Mehn, this Duru ooo. What kind of zekzy beast is this?"

Despite herself, the thudding in her chest, the wetness between her legs, the dryness of her throat, Demi laughed hysterically.

"He's still in his house."

Lore exchanged glances with Bukky and Demi. "He is? But he left the baby with you?"

The landlord's daughter, a skinny teenager who seemed to be only slightly bigger than the baby, nodded.

"He said I should take care of her until Mr. Akin comes on Saturday," the girl said. She seemed to enjoy this assignment too as she rocked and smiled at the baby.

"What a jerk," Lore said.

"Mr. Akin is not coming for the baby," Bukky said. "We are taking her."

If Demi expected a resistance from the landlord's daughter, she got none.

"Oga Duru said you may come too, but he wasn't sure." She looked from one woman to the other. "She's a good baby."

It was getting late before she could close from work, and Lore had insisted on driving down from Akure after Bukky called her and told her everything. The three musketeers knew everything about one another, and it was a no-brainer that as soon as Bukky knew, Lore would too. Once Duru left and Bukky could recover from the way he behaved around Demi, they had had a three-way call with Lore.

"Thank you. Where's her bag?" Demi said.

"Let me bring it."

The girl handed the baby to Lore and hurried along.

Lore hissed. "I wonder how he was able to convince these people to keep the baby."

"Hmm, he is convincing o," Bukky said. "In fact, I have never seen anyone so convincing. His eyes, ehn? Those eyes!"

"Bukky!" Demi gasped. "Chai."

"Ah, Lore, you should have been there today. It's as if a live wire was in the room. Even me I was feeling the electric."

Demi shook her head. "Let Mr. Olalekan catch you."

Bukky laughed. "Even him would have felt it. Kasa!"

Lore and Demi laughed.

The landlord's daughter came back with the travelling bag Demi bought for the baby's things.

Demi took it. "Thank you so much."

The girl curtseyed. "Yes ma."

Outside the stuffy house, the three walked to Bukky's car.

"I want to see that guy, sha," Lore said.

Bukky gasped. "Shey?"

Demi exclaimed. "For what?"

Lore snickered. "The electric, na. What else?"

"I can't believe this."

Duru sat on the bare floor of his empty room and stared at his backpack tossed against the wall. The ladies argued about whether to knock or not. Whether to see him or not. Demi sounded distressed and he clenched his fists to keep from doing anything, saying anything. He could hear Bukky's voice and from the third voice guessed it would be Lore. The three musketeers. Why would Demi involve her friends? This was between just the two of them. But again, if he had a friend he could confide in, who offered positive support, would he not jump at it? He missed Ahmed. For the first time in so long, he wished he could speak to his friend. What would Ahmed do about this Demi? About the fact Duru hated to admit to that when he thought of a woman, it wasn't Belema's face that came to him but Demi's. That he couldn't even remember Belema's face so well. She was very fair, he remembered but Demi's black beauty only appealed to him.

"I am going to knock. I want to see him."

Before Duru could get himself together, three firm knocks came through and the door opened.

"Aha, Lore. Why not wait before you open the door?" Demi cried.

Duru jumped to him feet.

Demi pushed Lore aside and walked in first. *Did she think he would be naked or what?*

"Sorry to barge in like this..." Demi stopped short and looked around the empty room. "What's going on here?"

Her two friends stepped in after her and their mouths dropped open too.

"What's going on here?" Demi took small steps into the empty space.

"I told you I'm leaving. I sold my bed," Duru said. He didn't owe her an explanation but yes, he did. He owed her. His sanity.

"No kidding." Bukky gasped. "Where are you going at this time of the night?"

It was almost nine o'clock, and Duru had been set to leave for at least five hours. But he hadn't been able to. He'd first thought of going toward Akure and then continue up north. Then he thought of going through to the east through Ore. Then he felt he didn't want to go too far, and he could go to Osogbo and onward to Ogbomosho and Ilorin. He'd just sat there on the bare floor of his room, kicked his backpack to the wall and stared into space.

For four hours.

Duru felt as though he was facing a panel. What could he tell these women that it would not seem as though he had a mental challenge, though, it seemed as if he did have? He shrugged and looked at Demi who had a frown on her face and watery eyes. The look in her eyes broke his heart. He really had to leave this environment. He had to overcome this madness. He was here nine years ago. Venting and hungry to revenge his wife's and daughter's deaths and unable to take rational decisions. Now he was back in that emotional space he vowed never to return to.

"Well, you can't go anywhere right now, and Demi needs help moving into her new house," Lore said.

By the way Demi and Bukky's eyes shot to Lore, Duru knew that offer wasn't planned.

"No, I…"

"Of course, you do." Lore rolled her eyes. "Why am I taking the baby with me until you move?"

"Lore is right," Bukky said.

Duru stared at Demi. Her mouth dropped open, and her eyes expressed some form of anger, confusion, or betrayal, Duru wasn't sure.

"What do you say, Duru? The house needs some carpentry," Lore said.

"And painting, too," Bukky said.

"Yeah, painting definitely," Lore laughed. "That's the first thing."

Chapter 47

"Honestly, this is not..."

"I will stay and help with the house," Duru said.

Demi gasped. Of course, he will stay and try to drive her to emotional shipwreck. Where did this come from? She didn't have a new house she was moving to. Why did Lore and Bukky suddenly cook up such a useless tale. Now, she had to actually look for a house but was it that easy? She wanted to tell Duru there and then that there was no house, but she'd be betraying her friends, and she couldn't do that. Yet, she had to.

"Thanks, but I don't..."

"Thanks, Duru." Lore turned to Demi. "I need to get home, and this baby is getting restless."

Duru arched an eyebrow. "Where's the house?"

"Funny, right? The place where Idem used to live." Bukky laughed. "I told Demi not to take it, but she must have a bone to pick with that house."

Demi's mouth dropped open.

"I know it. I'll check it out in the morning." Duru held Demi's gaze. "I'll let you know what needs to be done."

Demi nodded, too stunned to respond. What were her friends getting her into?

"Ah, thanks, Duru." Bukky clapped. "Oya, we need to go."

Lore checked her watch. "Yeh! Almost nine thirty."

They trooped out of Duru's room. He followed at a slower pace, but Demi could feel his gaze on the back of her neck.

As soon as Bukky pulled on to the road, Demi burst out. "What are you girls thinking?"

"The electric," Lore said. "Chai, that guy almost electrocuted me with his gaze."

Bukky laughed. "I told you."

"Listen, both of you. This is not funny." Demi snapped. "He's going to go to that Idem's house and discover people are living there."

"And then?" Bukky laughed. "I'm so excited for you."

"What are you saying? Look at the guy. He doesn't have anything. What are you two wishing for me?" Demi wanted to cry. "What kind of guy is he?"

"That is scary, though." Bukky sighed. "He doesn't have anything. He must be a drifter."

"Or running from something." Lore drew in a shuddering breath. "Chai. With that kind electric eyes."

Demi cried. "It's not funny!"

"But you too, how did you entangle yourself, now?" Bukky threw up her hands, and off the steering for a second. "He never had that look when he was working for me." She exhaled. "Hian, you just have a way of finding schmexy beasts all over the place."

Demi rolled her eyes. "Idem was not anything like Duru."

"Or maybe she brings out the schmexy in rogues," Bukky mumbled.

"Huh." Lore gasped. "You're still defending Duru."

"Look, I have to call him and tell him I'm not moving anywhere, and you ladies were just playing pranks," Demi said.

"You will do no such thing." Bukky exclaimed. "Do you want him to leave town?"

Demi shrugged. "If that is what he wants for himself." But the minute she said it, she knew she didn't want him to leave.

The baby started to fuss, and Lore patted her. "But you said he asked you to marry him."

"Oh God. How can I marry him? I don't know anything about him. I'm just tired." Demi leaned back her head and closed her eyes. "Ademilade, what's wrong with you?"

"Listen, dear," Lore said. "Just relax. Don't think. Don't do anything. Just be praying. Huh?"

"Let's see what happens when he inspects Idem's old house tomorrow," Bukky said.

▽

"The house has tenants."

Demi couldn't tear her gaze from his. "Look, I'm sorry, I..."

"But two houses from there is free. I checked around for you," Duru said. "It's a twin two-bedroom flat. Newly built. At the back of a duplex. I think there was a small BQ there, but the landlord just took it down and erected the new structure."

"Oh."

"I told the landlord I'm interested. He lives in the main house," Duru said.

Demi sighed. "That's very thoughtful of you."

"Do you want to take a look? The landlord gave me the front door key."

Demi stiffened. Bukky was in a meeting and would not be free to go with her. Did she trust herself to be with Duru alone again after Sunday? He looked stressed and his shoulder slightly sagged, and Demi could just imagine. He must have slept on the bare floor. What would he do now? Buy a new bed and mattress? She didn't understand him and wished she could. But she was too emotionally attached and didn't trust herself. It would be so easy for him to sway her and after Idem, she had to be in total control of her emotions before she could allow any man in her life and Mimi's. Already, Stanley Duru had jumped too many stages, she needed to stop him.

Demi shook her head. "This is not a good time, really."

"I can wait until you close," he said.

"I won't close until around eight..."

"I can come back then. The landlord said some other people have come to ask, but he will wait for me," Duru said. "It's a nice place."

Demi sighed. "Okay, I'll go with you after work."

In her mind, Bukky would come too, and be there. Demi wasn't ready to be alone with Duru just now. Even speaking to him like this in her office, so close, with people milling around, her heart pounded. She wanted him to hold her, kiss her, touch her...No!

"I'll see you later," he said softly and walked out of her office.

"I can't do this," Demi whispered. "He can't love me so I can't love him too."

"Bukky couldn't make it, and I have to be fast too."

Demi walked to the passenger's side of her car and got in. She could kill Bukky for running off and leaving her alone to see this fallacious accommodation alone with Duru.

"Ask him to drop you at my house..." Bukky's voice rang in her brain.

"Okay." Duru got into the driver's seat and pulled off and into the main road.

In the side mirror, Demi spied Bukky getting into her car to head home and wait for her to return with the gist.

"You aren't really looking for accommodation, are you?" Duru said. "Your friends just said so."

"Well, huh, no. I need to move out of my parents' house." Demi found herself saying. She couldn't bear the shame that Duru guessed right. "I've been wanting to move. For Mimi's sake."

"Well, I think this place I found will be good for her. There's some grassy land at the back of the new units. Where a child can play," he said.

Demi looked out of her window and tried to breathe normally. He had an aura around him that left her gasping, wanting, needy. Idem never made her feel like this. In hindsight, Idem seemed to have forced himself on her. With Duru, it was the opposite. He drew her to him like a fly to rotting fruit while resisting her. She feared the way her body reacted around him. How did she get here?

"It's not far from your office, too," he said.

Demi knew that already if it was a few houses from where she lived as Mrs. Idem Isong.

"Of course, you know that already," he added. "Demi?"

She snapped. "I hear you." She closed her eyes and breathed from her mouth.

The way he called her name made her want to hold him. This was a bad idea. She should never have agreed to come with him without Bukky. She didn't even want to live on her own. Mimi made her parents very happy. Everyone would wonder why she was moving. Besides, this Duru would feel freer to come and visit her. He obviously could see her weakness around him. Like all men, he would take advantage of her. She hated to admit it, but she had a "man" problem. She could never risk this again.

"We're here," he said.

Chapter 48

"It's really nice. But I'm not sure I want to take it. Tell the landlord to give it out."

Duru exhaled. "It comes at a great price too. Just about three thousand a month."

"Well, I don't want it. Thanks for your effort." Demi walked towards the exit.

"We've not seen the backyard. Two doors lead there. From the parlour, and the kitchen." He headed there, hoping she'd follow him. "Come."

He wanted her to have this place. For his own selfish reasons. He'd have something to do this week, and then he'd be able to take her to Lagos to return the baby. By which time he hoped he'd be able to convince her to have a relationship with him, or he'd be bold enough to walk away from her. He opened the door that led out and turned. Demi was behind him as he hoped. He'd promised himself he must not touch her while on this tour. Much as he longed to hold her, kiss her...he must not. He could feel how she reacted to him, and he wanted the same thing she wanted but after that proposal, it seemed he had put her off. Now he had to tread softly, woo her. Win her.

She gasped. "The back is big."

He chuckled. "Yes. Mimi will love it." He sighed. "And I can fix the place for you this week. Help you move in. Then take you to Lagos to return the baby."

Demi folded her arms around her waist. Duru could see her struggle. He stepped back inside with her and closed the door.

"What do you say?"

"I'll talk to my parents." She shrugged. "I'll let you know in the morning."

For a long moment he stood in front of her and stared at her. Unsure of what else he could say to convince her.

"I want you to move here," he whispered.

"Why?" She snapped. "So, you can come here and display your...your..." She swallowed. "Play your games?" She walked towards the door.

"What games? You are the one playing with me. You know that! You are teasing me..."

"Teasing you! How? What did I...?"

He stepped closer, violating her personal space. Duru thought Demi would move away but she stood her ground and glared at him, her big, beautiful eyes flashing angry daggers at him, daring him to kiss her. She licked her lips, and he swallowed hard. If he didn't move away, he would touch her and do more than he should.

Duru turned and marched to the door. "Let me know what you decide." He stepped out of the house.

Demi shouted. "What do you think you are? Who do you take me for?"

Duru could feel a rush of emotion like lightening behind his eyes. His head throbbed with need and sweat broke out on his forehead, though the evening air was cool. He clenched his fists and summoned all the energy he had to stop from responding. He really wanted to go back inside and answer her questions with explicit action. Instead, he breathed hard through his nose and mouth.

Demi marched to the car when he said nothing. He turned and noticed she left the front door open, so he went to close and lock it. Then he joined her at the car, which he opened, and they both got in to.

The ride back was in silence.

At her house, just before she opened the door, he spoke. "Demi, please."

She froze but said nothing.

"Demi, you want to know who I take you for? Huh." He exhaled. "The love of my life."

"Duru, stop."

He scoffed. "I wish I could. I sat on the floor in my room after I sold my bed. For over four hours. I couldn't leave. I want you, Ademilade."

"But you can't love me!" She turned to face him. "You said so. You only want to use me."

"Of course not!" He whispered. "I'm afraid. I fear my feelings. I know how I love and I'm afraid to go back there."

Demi closed her eyes. "Stop it! I can't love you, either. So, it's better you just leave. Go away to wherever you came from. To whoever you loved before."

"I can't. I don't want to."

"Then, leave me alone, Stanley." Her eyes flew open. "I can't be your woman."

"Why? Because I have nothing? Look, I've been thinking..."

"Don't be ridiculous. I don't need anything from you. I can take care of myself, and Mimi." She threw her hands up. "And you."

"The shame of being with a man like me, then? Your friends will not approve? Your family?"

The security light from her father's gate shone directly on her face and he could see the struggle in her eyes. He so desperately wanted to wipe this away. What could he say to convince her?

She heaved. "I am my own woman. I take my decisions."

"Then, what is it? I plan to improve myself. I've been looking into farming. I work hard, and I've spoken to some people..."

"Stanley! Stop it." Demi cried. "Just stop it."

She opened the door and stepped out.

"Demi!"

But she ran into the house.

Duru bent his head over the steering wheel. He didn't know what to do. He really was in love with her, and truly he feared for his emotions. He didn't think he would survive another heart break. He had to have her. She kissed him first, and he knew then she must have feelings for him to kiss like that. And the second time when he kissed her, he proved himself right. So, why was she fighting this?

"Are you back home?"

Goodness, she totally forgot about Bukky. Well, this was her fault. Duru would not wind her so tight if Bukky was there.

Demi rolled her eyes. "Hello, Bukky."

"You didn't call again. So, what happened? Did Duru say anything to you?"

The excitement in Bukky's voice irritated Demi. "I'm taking the house." Her eyes widened at her own words.

Where did that come from? She didn't want to take the house, of course. Or did she? She stared at Mimi, who was asleep already on the bed, and Demi felt some guilt. She was never there for her daughter, and it wasn't far from the reason why she detested her father. If Mimi did not resemble Idem so much, maybe it would have been easier. So, instead of paying attention to her child, Demi busied herself with her career and left the responsibility of raising Mimi to her parents.

Duru had noted the new place would be good for Mimi. That was so true but not for the reasons he thought. A place of her own would give Mimi her space, and her identity. And, she would be forced to take care of her daughter.

"Demi! Are you there?"

"Huh?"

Bukky snapped. "Why are you taking the house? What did Duru say?"

"This is not about Duru. I want to move out of my parents'. Mimi needs to start growing up to know me better." Demi sat on the bed and stared at the peaceful, beautiful face.

Mimi had Idem's fair complexion, thick lips and narrow eyes. Demi, at the time of her delivery, thought she was an ugly baby and up until now, still did. But thinking of the baby, who she thought was really cute, Mimi had the same features. Idem's face on a female.

"You have a point there, though. That little girl needs her mother." Bukky moaned. "So, no gist about lover boy?"

"You don't like me o, Bukky. Lover boy, sha? After what Idem did to me."

"Mimi needs a dad. And you need a man to take care of you..."

Demi moaned. "Heh, I can take care of myself, jare!"

Bukky scoffed. "Not like that, and you know what I mean. Masturbation is a sin o!"

"Hian. Let me hear word, my friend." Demi laughed. "Who masturbation epp?"

"The way that Duru is behaving around you, heaven help you if he doesn't rape you one day."

"Who, abeg? Someone who you don't know anything about his family. Another Idem loading?"

"Com'om, Demi. We will find out everything of course, before..."

"Wo, Bukky, I'm tired. We'll talk tomorrow." Demi sighed. "I have to start packing. I'll like to move before we go to Lagos on Saturday."

"Huh! Wait o! What's the rush? Is there something you're not telling me?"

"Bukky! Good night. Love you!" Demi hung up before her friend could reply.

She threw the phone on the bed and stared into space. She'd have to let her parents know about her decision in the morning. They'd be surprised, but she doubted they would discourage her. For long, her mother had wanted her to take better charge of her life.

A text entered her phone, and she checked it. From Stanley Duru. He wanted to know if she had any colour preferences for the house.

No. She texted back and threw herself on her pillow face down.

Chapter 49

"That woman really trust you, o, Duru. How you do am?"

Duru side-stepped Akin and walked out of the bedroom they just finished painting two shades of pink for Mimi.

"How I do what?"

The kitchen was last. With Demi requesting to have the house finished so she could move in on Friday, Duru had asked Akin to help with painting. He could finish it in three days alone, but the extra help gave them one more day. While the painting in the rest of the house was being done, a carpenter fixed the ready-made cabinets in the kitchen. Everything else was perfect.

Akin followed Duru into the small kitchen. "Make Madam Demilade to trust you. First to buy her car and now to do her house."

Duru snickered. "She pays for the jobs I do for her." *Add driving her to Uyo to revenge!*

"She's a tough woman o. Her father too protect her after everything she went through." Akin opened the bucket of paint for the kitchen. "You know the story?"

"No, I don't. And it's not my business." Duru opened the second bucket of paint.

He had earlier outlined the two sides and instructed Akin on what to do. In another hour, they should be done, and then he would wash the floors and by the next day, which was Thursday, Demi could inspect and make any changes she wanted. Friday looked feasible to move in.

"Hmm, when that woman dey young. Like sixteen, seventeen, chai, every young man in this town wanted her," Akin said.

Duru scoffed. "Including you."

"Ah, first, they were rich o. Her father was the strongest politician in this town." Akin laughed. "People like us no near them. Second, she and my daughter are mates. I cannot want my daughter age, God forbid."

Duru smiled. He didn't know Akin was that old. "But you saw all the people who wanted her."

"Chai. The girl fine that time o. Even though she still fine too much even now. But back then, ah, if she step out of the house like this, go to function like wedding, ah. Huh."

Duru stole a glance at Akin to be sure he was doing the right thing despite his chit-chat. He was.

"Then she go university in Ibadan. And even there, I hear all the boys wanted to go out with her."

"Akin? Were you a reporter or what?"

"Everybody talk about her, na. She was the finest girl in all of Owena. Even now, as you can see." Akin shook his head. "When she finish university, youth service, return home, this teacher in the secondary school, Mr. Alao, that time was just a young graduate, wanted to marry her."

Duru arched his eyebrow. "Mr. Alao, Geography teacher at community high school?"

Akin nodded. "The same one. The man almost die after Madam Demi."

Duru mentally rolled his eyes. "Mr. Alao is much older."

"Less than ten years o. Alao is a small boy. Not even forty yet," Akin said.

"Hmm. He looks older." Duru snickered. "Acts older too."

"He's vice principal now o. The man will go far in life." Akin stood back and looked at his work. "He love this Madam Demi ehn, even wanted to kill himself when she refused."

Duru couldn't help but laugh. "I'm sorry to laugh. Mr. Alao seems like a very cool guy. I mean, I met him when I did some carpentry jobs at the school. I didn't even know he is the vice principal."

"Yes, o. Very humble, hardworking. Even Madam Demi father and mother beg her to marry him," Akin said.

"So, what did she think was wrong with him?" Despite himself, Duru couldn't help but prod. This was about the woman he loved, and maybe this could help him in his pursuit.

"Just youthful shakara. Huh." Akin squared his shoulders. "Rich men coming from Akure, Ilesa, Ibadan, even Lagos. Na shakara all through. She was singing in church. Very beautiful, smart, working in the bank?"

"She sang in church?"

"Very well." Akin nodded. "Ah, the girl move this town."

"And Mr. Alao?"

"Then that bastard from Ibo came to do contract. Huh! E no even reach two months, he was sleeping with Madam Demi the iron lady." Akin snickered. "Before you know, she carry belle, marry the idiot."

Duru swallowed. He'd heard this tale in different ways and told himself several times it was none of his business.

"That Idem?"

"Yes."

"He's not Ibo," Duru said.

Akin grunted. "All of them are the same."

"Not at all."

"Well," Akin shrugged. "All the beauty, all the fame just die there. Alao just went to marry..."

"Just like that?"

"What can he do?" Akin sighed. "He fell sick for that girl and within seconds, she was married to someone else.

Duru focused on the edges of the wall where the newly installed cabinets were. Though he had masking tapes clearly outline where he needed to paint, what Akin was saying affected him more than he expected, and he didn't want to make a mess of the painting or the beautiful wooden cabinet.

"And you know, what, Duru. Let me ask again, are you sure that madam has not done something to you? Because that is how she start with Alao, that time."

Duru froze. "What do you mean?"

"Huh, see Alao come from a very rich and big family in Ogbomoso. He come here for Youth Service and meet Demi." Akin turned to face Duru. "He come with his own car. Every day, Demi will ask him to take her to market. Take her to Ibadan. Take her to Akure. Take her here and there."

Duru smirked. "Huh, I see what you mean. But she pays for what I do. I'm her worker not some...some..."

"Wait na. Next thing, they are appearing together everywhere. She was using Alao to chase boys away from her..."

Duru shrugged. "Okay, she's a player. How is it my business?"

"I see exactly the same thing happen to you. Shey, you say you are leaving town, why are you here, painting her house?" Akin folded his arms across his chest. "You say I am taking her to Lagos on Saturday, but I don't even know why. What is that girl doing to you, Duru?"

"Nothing!"

"Hmm, she has power o..."

"Is that why Idem came and levelled her the way he did?" Duru turned back to his work. "Please, Akin. Let's finish this painting."

"Idem levelled...hahaha." Akin laughed and then sighed. "Well, a word is enough for the wise. Just be careful."

Duru raised his voice louder than he wanted. "Well, I am not rich like Alao, and she is not interested in me even if I am."

"Ah, Duru! You have entered the fisherman net. She will use you and dump you. Since that Idem left her, it is what she now does to men. One banker boy like that, Andrew..."

"Okay, thanks for your advice, though I didn't ask for it."

Duru frowned. What was wrong with him? He knew Akin was only trying to help.

"I must advice you. I think I am the only friend you have in this town, so I must tell you the truth. Demilade is danger. Na rogue o, asewo, manizer. Leave her alone. If you want to settle down here, find another girl."

Someone knocked on the front door and Duru saw it as an excuse to escape Akin and his painful counsel. It was the landlord's daughter, Morayo, a young woman Duru had seen around in the compound several times every day. She had a food flask and wore a tight dress, garnished with a sheepish smile. Duru put her age in the mid-twenties.

"I thought you will be hungry," Morayo said. "So, I cooked rice and stew."

Duru arched an eyebrow. "Oh, thank you." He looked back. "We are still painting so I don't want you to come inside but thanks a lot." He took the flask and a spoon from her.

She batted her eyelids. "Can I come back when you have finished?"

"Huh, why?"

Morayo shrugged. "I just want to see what you people are doing?"

"Sure. I'll take you around."

Morayo licked her lips. "Aww, thanks. See you later, then."

"Okay."

Duru turned and found Akin behind him. "She brought food, funny girl."

"She's not funny. She likes you. And that is a girl you can go for. She's young, still in a polytechnic or so. She will worship you. Not that beautiful Jezebel..."

"Oh, Akin, please. Let's finish our work and leave here. You've spent almost one hour talking. You have a business to go back to."

Akin smiled. "I know how you feel. Don't worry. When she shows you her real self, you sef will run on your own."

"Thank you, Counsellor." Duru walked back into the kitchen and Akin followed. "I will remember your kind words."

Akin laughed. "Ah, Duru, but I didn't know you can be very jovial like this o. That girl has really done you something."

Duru shook his head. "You know everything about everybody."

"In this Owena? Forget. Anybody. Just give me the name I will give you low-down."

Duru flinched. It was the kind of entanglement he detested and ran from. He didn't want to know anything about anybody. But Akin was right in one thing. He was hooked. Caught in Demi's net. Could he leave and free himself now? He didn't even want to.

Chapter 50

"This guy has concept o! I'm asking him to redecorate my house."

Demi shook her head. "Why does that sound like something I've heard before?"

"Me? Ask Mr. Duru to redecorate my house?" Lore frowned. "When?"

Bukky laughed. "When did he become Mr. Duru?"

"Ah, he's an important somebori nowadays, you know." Lore winked. "Someone who kisses our friend."

Demi raised her two hands. "Ehn ehn, please don't bring me into this conversation o."

The three women walked back from the kitchen into the living room. Demi had to confess Duru did a good job with the painting. Mimi's room impressed her the most. She knew her daughter would love the colours, and the lovely posters Duru put on the wall.

"Where is he, anyway?" Bukky stretched. "Isn't he supposed to be here to receive all this our appreciation?"

"He went to service the car for me." Demi rolled her eyes. "Please, it's nothing."

They headed out of the house and Bukky unlocked her car.

"Is he going to teach you how to drive now?" Bukky said.

"No. I don't want to learn." Demi snapped. "How many times do I have to say this?"

"Huh, why are you snapping at me? Just trying to find out na." Bukky got in front and Lore sat beside her.

Demi took the back seat, and sulked.

"She just wants to use him as her errand boy, chai. Electric eyes," Lore said.

Despite herself, Demi laughed along with the other two. Bukky checked the road and would have pulled out of the compound to the main street when Morayo entered the compound through the small gate.

Lore frowned. "Who be she o, with narrow hips?" She laughed, and Bukky joined in.

Demi shook her head. "My landlord's daughter. Goodness, you two are horrible."

"We tell you the truth," Lore said.

"And truth hurts. That guy is dying to love you, and you are doing him shakara..." Bukky started. "With landlord daughter lurking..."

"I should go and fall in love with someone who has no family around here again, abi? Another south-south boy. They do me?" Demi shouted. "Thanks, but no thanks."

"South-south is in your fate," Bukky mumbled.

Lore scoffed. "So, why are you shouting. Why are you keeping him around...?"

Demi covered her ears. "I don't want to hear, jo!"

"When you guys return from Lagos, take your car back and stop using him to drop and pick you from work." Lore snapped. "If you don't want to drive your car, sell it. Stop this nonsense you are doing."

"What sort of name is Duru, sef? Ibo, shey?" Bukky glanced at Demi.

"Yes, he's Ibo," Lore said.

"Ehn, we just have to find his people na. What's social media for?"

Lore snickered. "He's not on social media. I checked."

Bukky gasped. "Hian, Demi. How do you find these species of men?"

Demi wrapped her hands around her head and closed her eyes.

"Yoruba people say that a dog that wants to go missing, will refuse to hear the owner's whistle."

"What about a dog that is already missing?" Duru glared at Akin. "How would he hear the whistle?"

"Hmm, Duru!" Akin moaned. "I should have warned you earlier."

Duru ground his teeth. "Maybe."

"You mean you helped her to capture the baby? Huh! That woman has lost you true true o." Akin arched his eyebrows. "Why did I not see it?"

"Look, Akin, can we talk about something else?" Duru breathed deeply.

He should not have told Akin about the journey to Uyo, but the man seemed to be so much more interested in him after working with him on painting Demi's new house. He offered to help move into the house, and one conversation had led to the other, and to this.

"See, when you just return her from Lagos, just leave this town. That girl will destroy you o! Do you know what Idem will do to you if he knows you are the one who stole his baby?"

"I don't care," Duru mumbled.

"Ah, you are a young man. You have to care o!"

"How young do you think I am?" Duru snapped. "I'm not a baby and I don't need your advice!"

Akin's good nature was probably the only reason Duru hung around him. Someone else would take offense by his attitude.

Instead, Akin laughed. "Omode o moogun! O n pe l'efo. Meaning, a child does not know diabolic charms, and instead calls it vegetable."

Duru shook his head. "I know what it means. And I am not a child."

Akin's eyes widened. "But you are a Ibo boy in Yorubaland."

"I am not Ibo."

Akin shrugged. "But it's all the same."

Duru mentally gave up trying to have this conversation. He had said too much already in so short a time. He missed the days when he spoke to no one, and no one bothered him. He heaved the last of Demi's boxes on to the van they hired for this event and returned into her parents' house to check if there was anything left.

From the demeanour of the parents, it seemed as though Demi had not settled the matter of leaving properly. The two old people sat in the parlour and ignored Duru and Akin as they went in and out of Demi's room to clear out her property.

"We are done, sir. Ma." Duru thought it was courteous to tell them.

Demi's father grunted and her mother nodded. When neither did more, Duru walked out.

Akin waited by the side of the van. Duru got in. He didn't want to say anything more but as soon as they got on the way to Demi's Akin resumed the conversation.

"See, it is simple. Whatever you got yourself into with this woman, stop it. Right in the middle. You can even leave now. Come back next year. Let her sort her problems."

Silence was the best answer for people like Akin, and Duru was perfected in the art of it. Akin wouldn't understand, or could he? Men like him probably didn't believe in love or why a man should fall apart if a woman broke his heart. In the case of Mr. Alao, he simply moved on. In Akin's eyes, Alao was a real man. No woman could be worth this much trouble. And Duru had enough reason to think so too. After Wato's...

A text came into Duru's phone, and he used one hand to check it.

Thanks, that will be great.

Duru inhaled softly. Akin would go crazy if he got to know the text from Demi was to accept Duru's offer to do a little shopping for her pantry pending the weekend when she could take care of that. Of course, Demi was paying for every single thing he did for her.

"At least, you were living somewhere before, go back there," Akin said. "See how you have been working for this girl since Monday. You could be making good money at the mechanic workshop."

"Demi is paying for this. Or you think the money I gave you for the painting is from my pocket?"

"Okay, okay. But even though." Akin sighed. "Huh, I like you. That is why I am telling you all this."

"Do you have land?"

Akin frowned. "Land?"

"Yes, like land that you can build a house on."

"No. Why?"

"I need land for farming," Duru said. "Preferably in the bush, you know."

Akin moaned. "You want to farm? You're not doing mechanic again?"

"I was never only a mechanic. I did other things too," Duru said defensively.

"Now farming? Because of that bank girl? You think she will ever accept a farmer, when her father is a big politician, and that her friend in the bank is married to a very rich businessman, and her other friend in Akure is married to a bank manager?"

"Yes na. If I do farming, won't that help her to push me away even more, and her spell on me will break?"

"Aha!" Akin laughed. "Omo Ibo, very smart. It's true. I have this customer who has a very big land that his father left for him. But he lives in Akure. The land is just outside Owena here."

Duru pulled into Demi's compound. "Will he want to lease it for farming?"

"He wanted to sell it, but I will talk to him. He will lease it to you if I tell him." Akin came down from the van and turned around to the back to join Duru to offload the boxes. "If only to chase that girl from your life." He hit Duru's shoulder.

"Thank you. This evening?"

"Of course, as soon as we finish here and I get back to my shop," Akin said.

Duru scoffed. "Thank you."

Morayo stepped out of her father's back door several feet away from Demi's front door. "You're here?" She called out.

No, I'm there, silly. Duru opened Demi's front door and disappeared inside as Mr. Akin politely defrayed more of Morayo's questions.

Chapter 51

"Good news. He wants to meet you. Tomorrow. Early momo."

"That's great," Duru said. "What time?"

"5am. The man wants to take you there, sef." Akin guffawed. "I told you he will accept. The way I paint you for him."

Duru mentally rolled his eyes. This sudden closeness with Akin didn't look to be going anywhere for him, but he would take it for as long as it made sense to him. Tomorrow was Lagos trip to drop off Idem's baby. The child had done so well so far, which was good, because he had made continuous contact with her parents, giving short, angry notices about their delay, though he was the one who had refused to provide a location for them to drop the money for her.

"I should be at your shop at five?"

"Ah, no o. My house. Is just on the way to Akure. We will go to the land together."

This didn't sit well with Duru. He didn't want to know Akin's house.

"Huh, okay." Duru sighed. "Text your address, please."

"Sure. Huh, come with your madam's car. My own is with mechanic."

Duru gasped. "I have handed it back to her. Are you not the one who said I should back off?"

"Ah, just this last one, please. Or how do we go the farm?"

Duru slid to his bare floor and closed his eyes. Akin was going to make him speak, request, plead with Demi again and he didn't want to go there with her. Ever again. Lagos and that would be it. But now this. His decision to cut off with Demi had nothing to do with Akin's advice but rather Demi's attitude. For all he did for her, though he got paid, she had not said a word of thanks. She also avoided his gaze all through the week, and when he told her he would drop the car, which had always been in his custody, she only told him where to leave the key for her. And what time they were leaving for Lagos the following day. He could take her teasing, her passion, her anger. Not her indifference. She was killing him.

All week, he had slept on his bare floor because he couldn't decide how to proceed with his life. Even this farm thing didn't augur well anymore. He couldn't be close to her and be ignored by her. And though it seemed like such a small thing in the whole scheme of his mad emotions, he noticed Demi skilfully prevented him from meeting Mimi.

It had been on the top of his mind to meet her, even coincidentally but Demi protected her daughter from him. The way she structured his movements around her, Mimi would never be seen where he was with her. It bothered him a great deal.

Duru groaned. "I can't go and wake her up before five."

"Go this night. It's not too late." Akin kissed his tongue. "Please, let me know if you can make it." He shouted a string of curses at someone in the background. "Call me back."

Akin hung up. Duru rolled his eyes. It was only around nine. He left Demi about two hours ago. How would she receive his request? He breathed hard. He didn't want to go but again, he did. He wanted to see her any opportunity he had.

Duru pulled himself up. He was still dressed since he returned from Demi's house. This was his life now. Sitting on the floor against the wall, or lying on his side, until sleep took him. This life had to change before he ran mad.

The small gate at Demi's compound was open and Duru wondered how safe the compound could be at night. He walked to the back and saw Bukky's car parked beside Demi's. For a moment, he thought he would not go to the front; he would not bring himself to ask to borrow her car when her friend was with her. Yet, he wanted to see the land. His years in the wild had taught him many lessons about growing food and hunting. He had an opportunity to pursue the possibility of owning a farm and building a career and a life as a farmer. The possibility of pursuing his feelings for Demi. The possibility of being a dad to Mimi. The possibility of living again.

He knocked on the door and no one answered. He turned around to where should be the window to Demi's room. As he approached, he heard her and two other voices. The one he now knew to be Bukky, screeched, and the other, Lore, laughed loud. They had loud music playing too. The curtain on the window was quite transparent, and Duru could see the room clearly. Why would she leave the window so exposed, though it was just by the fence of the compound, which only meant an intruder could jump in and her room would be the first...

Duru's eyes widened. His lips fell apart, and he breathed hard. Right before his eyes, Demi was putting up a sort of show for her friends. Mimi sat on the floor, and Duru could barely see anything but her small head. Bukky and Lore sat on the bed, laughing, screeching, and rolling intermittently. The lights were full and bright. Demi danced in front of her friends wearing a big wig and heavy make-up.

Naked.

"Olu lent me one of his cars."

"Ah, now I know your head is correct." Akin laughed. "I was waiting for you to come with the Avalon then I will know that bank girl still has a spell on you."

Duru swallowed hard. He hadn't slept much after what he saw at Demi's. For several minutes, he'd just tortured himself, staring, gasping. And then left with enough ammo for a cold shower. The girl could dance. What more, they didn't see him in the pitch blackness of the night.

"Thanks for trying to set me up," he mumbled.

Akin got into the passenger's side of the old pick-up vehicle Duru brought and they headed out.

"He wants to take hundred thousand a year, and is willing to do ten years to start," Akin said.

"Okay."

Akin gasped. "You can pay him one million?"

"No. I will speak with him. He's not a supermarket," Duru said.

"How much can you pay? I will help you talk to him."

Duru scoffed. "Thank you, but I can actually talk to him myself."

Chapter 52

"I thought we'll drop Mimi off at your parents' and then pick the baby."

Demi stepped out through the front door and handed Duru the Avalon key without looking at him. "She's with Bukky."

"You're keeping her away from me," he said.

Her first instinct was to give him a sharp answer. But instead, she scoffed. He was very right. She had promised herself never to entangle Mimi with any man if at all in her stupidest moments she fell for one. Duru would try, and now for him to make this accusation, he probably hoped to.

"We need to stop at my parents' before we pick the baby." She walked to the car. He followed her and opened the doors.

"Okay."

She really was tempted to look at him, admire him. He didn't wear anything different from what he always wore, black Tees and jeans and snickers. But he was always clean, neat, decent, handsome, and he had a nice strong smell. All the time. She just couldn't afford to fall for this beastly stranger. Not again. Once they returned from Lagos, she planned to cut him off. She had to. Bukky and Lore had helped her put perspective to it. He was dangerous to her emotions, and without any link to anyone, no social media presence at all, he could be anyone. His name may not be Duru. If she ever was going to go on with another man, he'd be someone she knew about his family to his great-great-grands. And though her friends still thought they would be great together, they were realistic about the situation.

She turned to look at the road, as he pulled out to it. Dawn had broken a couple of hours earlier and the streets were already getting busy with Saturday morning activities. Every inch of her body could feel Duru next to her. She couldn't believe how aware she always was of him. It was the only reason she had made sure she wasn't there with him when he was moving her stuff into her new house. The only time they met there, Bukky and Lore were with her, and that annoying Morayo too walked out of her father's house the moment Duru walked through the gate.

"We have to talk about us. If not now, sometime," Duru said softly. "I'm not going to go away."

Demi snickered. "Drift into thin air."

"It's not going to happen. I'm here to stay."

"Spare me."

"You'll see. I don't have to trade words with you over that," Duru said.

She continued to stare out of the window until they pulled up outside her parents' house. Demi did not invite Duru, but he came down of the car anyway and walked with her to the front of the house. She would have taken the back door but not with him there. And she sort of wanted him by her side. Her father had sent an urgent message just before Duru arrived to pick her. Her parents had been angry with her for doing several things without telling them first. Buying a car, travelling to Uyo, and then moving out. But she was old enough to make her own decisions. Demi didn't know what to expect. The message had only told her to come immediately.

Had they found out about the baby? She hated for that to happen. Whatever it was, she knocked, and within a second, as though her father had been waiting by the door, it opened.

"Ademilade. Welcome. Come in," her father said gruffly.

"Daddy." Demi knelt. "Hope nothing."

Duru prostrated and both stepped in.

Seated on the couch in her father's parlour was Idem Isong. He stood when the party walked in. Demi's mouth fell open. Her gaze shot to her mother, who sat hunched in a single chair. Demi curtseyed quickly while Duru bowed.

Demi turned to Daddy, and he shook his head.

"Hello Demi," Idem said. "I came to get my daughter."

Blood drained from all of Demi's body. How did he know? They were in trouble. Duru would definitely go to jail.

"Listen, I can explain…"

"You abandoned her for over eight years and think you can just show up?" Duru snapped. "Are you stupid?"

Idem's eyes widened. "Are you mad? My own daughter? What is this idiot doing inside here?"

"He is Demi's driver," Daddy said.

Idem pointed to the door. "Then go and wait outside!"

Idem meant Mimi not the baby. Relief washed over Demi, and she wanted to kiss Duru for real.

Demi found her voice. "He's not waiting outside!"

"Demi, where's she? Your parents said she's not here. My informant told me she lives with them, but they say she's not here!" Idem glared at Demi. "I will pay up for all you spent on her so far."

"What?" Demi gasped. "What do you take me for? Who do you think you are coming here?"

"A moment ago, you were about to explain," Idem said.

"You are not even sorry for what you did." Duru snapped. "Is it because your baby was stolen, that's why you remembered you had another daughter today?"

Idem growled. "Who told you my baby was stolen?"

"I was in your house that day, Idem. Or you forgot already? Of course, why not?" Duru snapped. "Why won't you forget anything that is important."

"This nobody...get out of here before you get into real trouble with me. What are you?" Idem turned to Demi. "Where's my daughter? I'm returning to Uyo, and she's coming with me."

Duru scoffed. "What's her name?"

Idem yelled. "Get out of here, bastard!"

"You don't know her name," Demi said.

"I will. I will also find out where you live. I will take my daughter, and there's nothing you can do about it," Idem said.

"You think this is your constituency in Akwa Ibibio, fool," Duru said.

Idem came at Duru in a flash and punched his face. Without breaking a sweat, Duru returned two harder punches in quick succession and Idem staggered back. Demi sprang in between the two as Idem recovered and lunged forward. Mummy gasped and jumped to her feet.

"Stop this!" Daddy shouted.

Idem panted. "Who is this area boy? This nobody to tell me I am a fool?"

"Let's go, Stanley." Demi walked to the door.

Duru turned and followed her out.

"Come back here!" Idem shouted. "Demi! Demi!"

"Please, Idem, you have to calm down..." Demi heard her father say. Why didn't they warn her?

She felt betrayed by her parents.

"Please, Bohda Duru. I want to follow. I will carry the baby."

Duru shook his head. "No, thank you. Aunty Demi will carry her."

"The baby is very sweet. And I never come Lagos before," the landlady's young housemaid said.

Demi smiled. "What's your name?"

The girl curtseyed. "Bola, ma."

"Okay."

"Can I carry the baby, ma?"

Duru chuckled. "I decide here, Bola. Sorry."

Demi took the baby from her arms and Duru picked the bag.

"Don't worry, Uncle Duru will take you to Lagos at another time," Demi said.

"Ehn! Thank you, ma. Thank you, sir." Bola ran back inside.

Duru and Demi walked to the car.

"She actually thought I had the power to decide if she followed us," Demi said once Duru pulled out to the road and smiled.

Duru glanced at her. "You did. You just had to command me."

"Funny." Demi idly arranged the baby's shawl. A warm feeling whorled through her body.

"I wrote a poem for you."

"Look, Stan..."

"I like the way you call my name," he said.

Demi drew in a deep breath. "Look, forget about us for a second. Shouldn't we just go and give this baby to Idem. I..."

"Is that what you want?" Duru stole a glance at her. "I can turn back right now."

Demi gasped. "You do know he will kill you for doing this. Or are you being an ignoramus."

"I don't care what he does to me, Demilade." He slowed down. "We go back?"

Demi shook her head. She cared what happened to him, but she wasn't going to tell him that. She didn't understand what was going on in his mind, but it was definitely the height of stupidity if he thought he was doing it to impress her.

"What I meant to say was that..." she drew in a deep breath. "Well, it doesn't matter."

"I want to hear it."

"Instead of driving to Lagos, we could drop this baby at the police station here and you let Idem know through the anonymous number..." she covered her face and dragged her hands down. "It will come back to us somehow. Idem is very smart."

"If that's what you want."

"No." She heaved a heavy sigh. "No. Let's go to Lagos and follow your plan."

"Okay."

They joined the Akure-Ibadan expressway, and she rocked the sleeping baby. She didn't have a clear plan even for this. Drop the baby in front of Akwa Ibom house, and sit in a car some distance away and watch what happened? It was criminal, and she feared how low she had descended, even allowing Duru to do this. She should turn back and give Idem his baby and beg him not to hurt Duru.

"Idem didn't seem to know you were in his house recently," Duru said. "You refused to tell me what happened when you went inside the compound."

Demi snapped. "Nothing happened. I sat in the gate house until I was tired." How could he sound so calm when she was dying of guilt?

"You sat in there for five or six hours, and they didn't let you see him?"

He snickered, kissed his teeth, and mumbled angry words. Demi didn't think he would gloat, and he was in more trouble with Idem if this came out, but as wrong as snatching a baby out of their home was, Idem and his wife deserved everything they got. Demi stared at the beautiful baby in her arms, peaceful, her eyes wide open, oblivious of her reality. Life was not fair, and this baby did not deserve to be kidnapped but her parents had hurt Demi while she was pregnant even, and that made Demi justified in her own sight. Hopefully, the baby would be back home soon, and no one would ever know what really happened.

Demi rolled her eyes. "What would I have done if I saw him, anyway? He was inside that mansion, with his wife, and children, and living his life to the fullest."

"What did you plan to do?"

"Tell him how badly he hurt me, and Mimi." Demi shook her head.

What was she thinking? Going to Uyo had been foolish. She just wanted closure. The baby simpered and Demi rocked her.

"You are the victim here, and believe me, I don't know what happened between you two, but no man should abandon his woman and child for any reason," Duru said.

Tears sprang to Demi's eyes. She hadn't expected him to vindicate her so. Though it did nothing to change the situation, she felt better just hearing those words.

"I didn't think I could fall for someone so hard and so fast." She scoffed, thinking about it.

She had let him have such intimacy with her on the very first night they met. How could she have? Unbelievable, but she had. Shame covered her. She couldn't tell Duru. He'd just think she was a cheap whore.

"He had the charms, and I saw him use it all the time," Duru said softly. "On you."

She turned to him. "You knew me then?"

"I saw you a few times. I worked on Idem's site as a labourer. Then I left town."

"I can't remember. But then, I wasn't around his site a lot."

"Once you drop his baby off, he'll likely not come after you or Mimi again. You know that don't you?"

"I hope so."

"You have done nothing wrong!"

Said with such force, Demi realized she indeed had done everything wrong, and Duru had encouraged her all along. She seemed to end up with the worst of men. First a married father, and now a sociopathic stranger. It must be karma...all those good men she used and turned down at the end.

Chapter 53

"I really feel like a criminal."

"That you are." Duru chuckled. "Don't worry. You just relax. The same way baby appeared in our lives in Uyo, she will disappear here in Lagos."

Demi stared at the beautiful view of the quiet Ikoyi street from her hotel room and wondered what she had gotten herself into. They had arrived Lagos late in the afternoon, and it was Duru's suggestion that she get this particular hotel, which was so hidden from everywhere. It proved just what he told her that he knew Lagos inside out. It wasn't very expensive either, and he had insisted she take only one room, for herself alone. He would stay with a friend, he'd said. They also left baby sleeping in the car...

"I'll drop baby, watch her picked up, and then be back to give you update, and probably a treat." He had smiled but she found nothing amusing. "Then tomorrow morning, I'll take you back home, and we can forget all of this episode in our lives forever."

I will forget you in my life forever, she'd thought.

She sighed. "So, what now?"

"I have to get back to baby," Duru said. "See you in a few hours. I won't leave until I see they pick her up."

"Be safe," Demi said.

She really didn't care, and the small smile that lit his eyes made her realize she shouldn't have said that.

"I will be. Thank you." He blew her a kiss and walked briskly out.

Demi lowered herself on her bed and closed her eyes. What was this? Why was she here? How could she have allowed this to happen?

"I'm coming!"

Demi hurried to the door and yanked it open. How could she have slept off under the circumstances?

"Oh, my goodness." She gasped. "Were you here for long?"

"No," Duru said. "I just knocked once, and you answered."

Demi stepped back to let him in. He had a paper bag in his hand. Duru walked in and Demi followed him. He went to the reading table in the room and placed the bag on it.

"How did it go? Did you see the person who picked baby?"

"Yea, and I even took a video." He sat down and brought out his phone.

Demi didn't want to be close to him, but he continued to hold his phone. The video of baby wrapped and placed on the front seat in a car, comes on. Duru mumbled, "Bless you, baby." He walked away and the video moved on until it showed baby through the windscreen of the car.

Demi frowned. "Was she asleep?"

"When I left her, no. But I had that dummy thing in her mouth, and she looked happy."

Demi closed her eyes for a second. Nothing happened in the video. She stared for long. "Nothing is happening."

"Yes. But just be patient," Duru said.

"How did you leave her here without anyone noticing you?"

Duru shrugged. "It's not the front of the street. And I watched for a long while before I went. Besides, I gave a wrong address to them. Thirty minutes away. When they messaged that baby wasn't there, I gave the correct address."

"Oh my goodness, Stan..."

"Look!"

Demi turned to the phone screen and her eyes widened. Two cars just pulled up in front of the building. From the first came out two military men with their guns cocked.

They looked around for a bit, and then Idem came out of the second car, dressed in black and with dark glasses that obscured his eyes, but Demi could feel his anger and apprehension even through the camera's lenses. He hurried to the baby and carried her out of the car, and up in the air. A smile broke the hardness of his lips. Demi felt a pang of guilt but also joy at the reunion. Idem hugged the baby and then took out his phone and took selfies with her. Then punched in a text or perhaps sending the picture to his wife.

Demi closed her eyes for a second. "At least, that is settled."

She returned her gaze to Duru's screen. Idem walked briskly into the car that brought him and drove away. The other car remained, along with the military men parading.

Demi frowned. "Why are they still there?"

Duru shrugged. "No idea. I left the area about two minutes after Idem. They were slashing the tires of the car when I left."

"Huh! Whose car?"

Duru shrugged. "No idea. I stole it."

"Stan," Demi whispered. *He spoke of his crimes so casually.*

She turned back to his phone with eyes wide, and her jaw sagging, and saw the video had ended. "How did Idem come himself?"

"I guessed he would prefer to, when I saw him at your parents', I sent a message to his wife's number that we were dropping baby in Lagos. I knew she'd probably compel him to go there."

"Hmm." Demi shook her head. "At least, that is settled." She walked to the bed and sat. A strange hollow feeling of despair filled her.

"I thought you'd want a treat after all this," Duru said. "I bought ewa aganyin for you. It's the best in all of Lagos."

"I can't eat anything."

"You have to try it." Duru picked the paper bag and walked over to her. "Come on." He opened the bag and brought out a food flask.

Demi shook her head and closed her eyes. Duru opened the flask, and the sweet aroma of stew and beans filled the room. Demi couldn't help herself, and her stomach grumbled.

Duru laughed. "You see?"

Demi opened her eyes. Duru had a spoon heaped with beans and fried stew right before her face.

"It's the best, trust me," he said.

He put the spoon to his mouth and took a little bite. "Hmm. Heaven."

She rolled her eyes. "I want my own spoon. And plate."

Duru threw back his head and laughed. "Of course, Madam."

He walked back to the table where a box telephone lay and called the reception. When he was done, he returned to his seat there at the table and sat down.

"They'll bring drinks too."

Demi nodded. "Thank you."

"Don't be melancholic about this. I know you may feel bad about..."

"I miss her." Demi exhaled. "I feel a funny connection to her."

"As you should like a normal person." Duru leaned forward. "She's safe with her father, and you got your revenge. Don't stress."

"Yeah, I got my revenge." Demi snickered. "As though it is that easy."

"Nothing good comes easy..."

"What good?" Demi shouted, unsure of why she was so frustrated. "How can what he did to me ever get a good revenge?"

"I believe that is a very good question," Duru said softly. "How do we measure the quality of the revenge we get? What matrix can effectively measure the weight of revenge for wrong done to us?" He scoffed. "Like now if Idem finds out I took his baby from her cot, and dropped her on the street in Lagos in a stolen car, how heavy is that crime and what will be a good revenge?"

Demi lay on her side and turned from him. She wondered what was about this guy. Who was he? He knew Port Harcourt so well, and now Lagos. He wasn't from the West but could speak Yoruba fluently, and he sounded so educated. Intelligent. Hardworker. Smooth operator. Talker. Kisser. Carpenter. Plumber. Mechanic. Mr. Fixer. Electric eyes! Demi covered her head with her hand. She didn't want to think or pay any attention to the way her anatomy responded to his sweetness. She didn't want to acknowledge the longing in her heart, and the joy at being here with him. What could possibly be in a future for them?

There was a knock on the door and Duru stood to get it. He collected a plate, a soup bowl, and a set of cutleries from a uniformed waiter, and a tray of water, and drinks.

"I got garri Ijebu for you, with ice. In case you don't want soft drink."

Demi sat up. She couldn't believe he'd do that. She loved sipping garri with water and ice cubes, and if by any chance there was roasted groundnut by the side, her day was made. Before she could stop herself, she leaped off the bed and hurried to him. He just scored the highest point with her.

"Aren't you curious about the ransom?"

"Was there?" She mumbled.

"No." He sniffed. "I mean, I told them to put it somewhere. Somewhere someone will find it and use it for greater good. I confirmed they got it before I shared the new location for the baby."

"Now you're Robin Hood," she muttered.

Duru glared at her with a half-smile as she dished the beans and prepared the garri. She pretended he wasn't too close, and she didn't feel ripples of fizziness going through her body until his hand snaked around the back of her neck and he crushed his lips to hers.

Chapter 54

"**D**um. Dum. Dum."

Duru's heart thudded as he drove into the street where his former church had held services. A force beyond his control pushed him and urged him to keep going. To the front of the church premises. He pulled to the side of the front. It was a little early for anyone to be in church yet. He just needed to be here for a second. To breathe the air in this environment.

It scared him that he wanted to be in a church again. Twelve years! The last time he entered a church was at Belema's funeral service.

He came out of the car, and walked to the side where he could peek into the church hall. It was just dawn. Contrary to what he told Demi the previous day that he'd spend the night at a friend's, he had slept in the car in the parking lot of the hotel, and through the generosity of the overnight receptionist, taken an early bath, and driven out.

Inside of the church was almost the same way he remembered it. The backdrop though now had a digital screen, and the altar seemed to have doubled in size. Three shades of deep and light blue formed the background for the altar area, just as Duru remembered. The pastor loved blue, and it was the block colour of the church logo. Two seats, for pastor and his wife, formerly to one side of the front, now had six. Whatever that meant. The whole hall was definitely bigger too, with so many more seats. There had been an expansion from what Duru could see.

"Lucifer! Ye! It's a lie. It's you?"

Duru turned sharply, and right behind him stood the man he once called Austin, who the church had taken in as a welfare case, and whom he, Duru, personally made a friend.

"Austin." Duru moaned. "What are you doing here?"

"Ah, I cannot believe it o! Lucifer..."

"Don't call me that," Duru said.

"Sorry. Sorry, sir. Ah, but you just disappeared."

Duru looked around. "Well, what are you doing here this early?"

"I work for church now. Night guard," Austin said.

Duru arched an eyebrow. He didn't expect to hear that. "Oh, that is good. Did you get to return to school. The evening school thing you started?"

"Ah ah ah, since. I did my WAEC. Passed with five credits." Austin laughed. "I am doing online university now."

Duru clapped. "Wow! That is fantastic, Austin. Good for you."

"So, come inside. People will soon start coming, and..."

"No. I was just driving past and said I should..."

"God forbid, Lucifer! I will die before I let you escape. You're playing guitar today o." Austin gripped his hand.

Duru freed himself and stepped by Austin. "Next Sunday."

"Lailai! Pastor sef will kill me if I tell him I saw..."

"Then, don't tell him." Duru walked to the road.

Austin laughed and ran after him. "Even if Pastor no vex." He gripped Duru's belt and jerked him towards the front of the church.

Austin was shorter but just as well-built as Duru, and Duru just discovered the older man was stronger too.

Duru laughed. "Austin, leave me!"

"Did you catch a thief?" Someone shouted. "You need help?"

Austin shouted back. "It's Lucifer."

A man Duru remembered as Tobi, who worked in the church cleaning team, ran to them and with Austin's help, carried Duru.

"Lucifer! In church?"

"So, when are you coming back?"

Demi breathed in deeply. "Today. He's picking me any minute from now."

"Hmm," Lore moaned over the phone. "Maybe you should come to my house before you go home. I want to see your face."

"Lore, I'm fine. Honestly." Demi sighed. "Scared of course. I have never felt like this before."

"Not even with Idem?"

"Not close." Demi laughed nervously. "He...Duru...he...we."

"What!" Lore screamed. "No. No, no, no! Demi."

"It was different. I swear. I. He." She clasped her hand over her mouth, feeling more emotional than she could remember ever. "He was...I think I'm in love with him and he knows."

"Ewoo! Demi? You can't do this again. You..."

"He said he loves me. I know he does."

"What kind of person is he? Where's he from? What do you know about him?" Lore cried. "Demi, jo, please, no."

Demi cackled. "You and Bukky started this. I was ready to let him go. You pushed me in this direction."

"Yes, I know. I never met anyone like him. Honestly, I thought he was genuine, but again, if we want to tell ourselves the truth, Demilade, this guy is too mysterious." Lore sighed. "And you said he hasn't told you a thing about himself."

Demi scoffed. "Nothing!"

"Huh, then you have to just step back from this. I'm sorry I pushed you towards this but, no."

"It's easier said than done."

Lore moaned. "I know. I know. But..."

The reception door opened, and Demi looked up to see Duru walk in with a small smile on his face.

"I have to go, Lore. He's here."

"Come to my house tonight," Lore said.

Demi hung up as Duru walked up to her. He squatted in front of her and touched her cheek.

"How's my baby?" he said softly.

Demi nodded. She was still dumbstruck by the way he looked at her the night before and told her he loved her and wanted her to be his. The vulnerability he displayed. He couldn't have been acting. She knew deep down he wasn't acting. She'd nodded then too. Overwhelmed. He'd stared hard for a long minute and told her to get a lot of rest, and he'd pick her up just before her noon checkout. Though he didn't make physical contact, Demi had never been so emotionally drawn and drained in her life. She had thought it was wiser to be ready and waiting in the lobby area when he arrived. She didn't trust herself just yet to be in the room alone with him. They'd narrowly escaped sex the night before. She didn't want to be on that battlefield again.

"I thought you'd be in the room," he said.

"I wanted to be on time," she said softly.

Their gazes locked and she could feel the same warmth all over her. He affected her in such a strange, sweet way.

"Hmm. I know you." He chuckled. "Avoiding what could be..."

A couple came to stand behind Duru. Demi looked at them for a moment but could not recognize them, yet they were close enough to be invading their privacy.

"I want to introduce someone to you." Duru straightened and held his hand to her. She put her hand in his.

Demi glanced at the couple again and stood.

"This is Ahmed. My. My best man. And his wife, Bimpe." Duru cleared his throat. "Meet Ademilade. My girlfriend."

Ahmed stuck out his hand, with a little smile, much the same way Duru smiled and shook Demi. The ladies just nodded at each other.

"You'd have to tell her, Ahmed." Duru looked down at the floor in an uncharacteristic gesture of discomfort.

"Our pastor set up a service for Duru," Ahmed said. "It starts in about an hour."

Demi turned to Duru. "A service?"

Duru stared into her eyes, into her soul, and her heart dropped into her stomach. She was about to learn something really devastating about him, and she wished she hadn't kissed him ever, or nodded when he told her he wanted her to be his.

"We called him Lucifer because he was such a minstrel." Ahmed chortled. "I'm sorry we're messing up your plans. That's why he insisted I come with him."

Demi held Duru's gaze for a little while longer and smiled. "Of course."

Duru let out a soft wheeze. "Thanks, babe."

Ahmed clapped and Bimpe laughed.

"Well," Ahmed rubbed his hands together. "This is going to be great."

Demi returned her gaze to Duru, and he blinked slowly. She knew there was going to be a conversation about this, and she couldn't wait.

"I was a worshipper. Instrumentalist," Duru said as soon as they got into the Avalon. "I just, for some reason, wanted to drive by the church, and I end up going in." Duru shook his head. "I'm so sorry. I guessed this will happen. That's why I didn't want to go into the church."

"You must be very special to them." Demi realized she wasn't even angry. "Lucifer of all names. Huh."

"It is ridiculous."

"What part do you sing?"

"All, I guess. And I play instruments too."

"Guitar?"

"Keyboard, sax, drums. I haven't tried many yet."

Demi burst into laughter. "Did you even go to church in Owena?"

Duru chuckled. "I tried once. I think the lady thought I was trying to steal when I asked to play the guitar. I went after church service."

Yet, Demi felt disgusted. But more to herself. She had gotten stuck to another stranger, whose life would in the end be her undoing. She badly wanted this guy, and yet, she knew Lore and Bukky would be totally upset with her. She was upset with herself.

Chapter 55

"I present, Duru."

The man Demi had previously been introduced to as the lead pastor, Pastor Ernest, stepped down from the altar and took the seat beside the woman earlier introduced as his wife, Pastor Mo. Demi and Duru had been led to a row of six chairs at the front side of the church and four of them, with two other pastors, had taken their seats.

Duru walked up the few steps to the altar slowly, and for a few seconds stood and stared at the array of instruments Demi was sure had been laid out just for this service, because they were lined right across the altar, and the pulpit had been moved against the wall. Right in the centre was the seven-piece drum set. Four different guitars lined up to the drumset's right side, with a trumpet and a sax at the end. On the other side was a keyboard, a local drum, a tambourine and the local sekere instrument. In front was a loan mic stand with a mic.

The whole auditorium packed full of at least five hundred people, and more walking in by the minute, waited in cold silence. Duru walked to the lead guitar and picked it. The audience erupted in an applause.

For several minutes, Duru just stood in front of the mic with the guitar slung across his shoulder, and his eyes closed, then he strung the first chord.

"Unto Jesus. I surrender. Unto him. I freely give," he sang softly. "World pleasure. I forsake now. Take me. Jesus, take me. Now."

Demi felt a lump in her throat. Who was this man? The sound of his soft, deep, sonorous voice with the deft stringing of his fingers on the guitar. She had been in many church meetings and had heard many people sing with great voices, sang herself, but the atmosphere change she experienced now was different. New. Sweet. Electric.

"I. Surrender. All." Duru sang. "My darling Jesus. I. Give up my all. All to you. All. To you. My precious. Saviour. I. Surrender. All."

With the hall so silent, a woman's sobs sounded louder than it really was. Pastor Ernest slid to his knees, and Pastor Mo fell to her face. Duru took the song two more times, by which time half of the people in the hall were either crying or moaning or singing along, while the rest sat too dumb to make a sound, probably. Demi could feel her knees buckle beneath her and she lowered herself to her seat.

"Ki le o le se. Olorun. Mi. Ki. Le o le. Se!" Duru sang at the top of his voice.

"God, please! Please. I'm sorry!" Demi wailed. "Please. Forgive me."

"Eyin. Ti. E. Da, aye at'orun! Kini. E o le. Se?"

Demi lost track of time or space. She thought she rolled on the floor. Thought she hit the wall. Thought tears flowed from her eyes. At last, it was when Duru tapped her that she came to herself.

"Let's go," he said.

Because she couldn't stand on her own, he helped her up.

Just outside, a woman came out of a car, with a man right behind her, and hurried towards them as they exited but Duru did not break his stride.

The woman shouted, "Stanley, O my God!"

They got into the Avalon and Duru sped off. Demi hadn't until then had an idea of time, but she noticed it was getting dark outside. She wished she could speak or hold a conversation, but her throat felt sour from crying all through the meeting. What manner of divine presence was that? Duru didn't seem like he wanted to talk either. Demi leaned back her head and closed her eyes.

"We're here." Duru tapped her. "Honey?"

Demi sat up. "What? We're where?"

"Yes. I brought you to your house because it's late. Bukky can bring Mimi tomorrow," Duru said.

Demi moaned. "Oh wow." She peeked out and it was all dark except for the dim security light in front of the landlord's house. "That was a lot of sleep."

Duru chuckled. "Yes. You needed it."

"What's the time?"

"Quarter to ten."

"Ten! Wow." Demi picked her bag and opened the door. "Wow."

"I wanted to tell you, you need to secure the side of the house. Where your room is at." Duru said.

"I don't understand."

"The side of the house. We need to secure it. And use thick curtains," he said.

She shrugged and stepped out of the car. Whatever he meant was unclear to her.

Duru came out of the car with her and walked to the door. But he didn't seem to want to enter the house. His face was drawn, and Demi had never seen him so quiet or melancholic.

"I'll pick you to work in the morning," he said.

She nodded. What was happening here? He seemed sad. So withdrawn. She just couldn't understand any of this, and yet all she could feel within her was affection. She wanted to cuddle him, make him know she was totally his and make him feel better.

Duru cupped her face. "I'm sorry for not telling you about my music earlier, and what happened today..."

"I'm not angry, Stan. I'm happy I was a part of it." She covered his hands with hers. "You shouldn't apologize to me." She expected a kiss, or a hug.

Instead, he stepped back. "Thank you. Goodnight."

He didn't wait for a response too. He turned and walked to the car, and without a wave, drove out. Demi heaved a heavy sigh. Her heart thudded. What was he running from? Why would he be a part of such a big congregation, yet live in a small room in Owena, working as a handy man. If Ahmed was his best man, then Stanley Duru must have been a professional of some sort. Clean. Classy. Who was Stanley Duru?

Demi trotted into her room, feeling tired in many ways. She dropped her bag on the bed, and took off her shoes, then she threw herself on the bed, and closed her eyes. A part of her didn't know what to expect from this melancholic Duru, but she feared he was on the run, and whatever he was running from caught up with him today. Was it a family? A woman? She dreaded this. Or could it be financial fraud? A real crime like murder? He was quite swift in executing that kidnap of Idem's baby. But if it was a real crime, he would not have climbed that pulpit and ministered, and in essence, exposing himself to law enforcement. Demi had to find out.

She took out her phone and saw several missed calls and texts from Lore and Bukky.

"Oh, my goodness. I forgot all about them." She sat up and placed a call.

"Oh Lord, Ademilade!" Lore screamed. "Where are you? We have called everyone. Why didn't you pick up your call now? Where are you?"

"I'm in my house. I just got here. I'm sorry."

"We're coming." She hung up.

Demi sluggishly stood and went to open the door. She should be hungry. She hadn't had anything since the morning when she ate the rest of the beans Duru bought, but she didn't want to eat anything. She wanted to talk. With Stan. Her man. She wanted to know everything about him. What did he do before? Who was the man and woman they brushed past on their way out? Why did he leave that life? How could she be the woman he wanted? She strutted back to her room and sat on her bed.

Shortly afterwards, the front door burst open. Lore and Bukky ran into her room and fell on her neck in a group hug. Demi laughed.

"Na wa for you o," Lore said. "Where did you go? What happened to you?"

"It's a long story." Demi sighed. "Stan. We went to his church."

"His church?" Bukky and Lore shouted in unison.

The ladies flanked Demi.

"Tell us everything," Bukky said.

"What are you still doing here, Lore? Isn't it too late to start..."

"Forget about me," Lore said. "Oya, what happened?"

"That's what my life is now, o."

Demi found recanting made her feel better. Her friends oohed and aahed until the very end of her tale.

"I don't even know what to say, Demi. Like, his worship, his behaviour before and after." Bukky shook her head. "What do you want to do now?"

"I'm just speechless," Lore said.

Demi sighed. "I know I'm falling in love with him, and that is not a good thing, I know."

"You deserve love, Demi." Lore rolled her eyes. "And I think this is a good bundle God gave you. You just need to unpack him. I mean, see those eyes."

The three laughed.

"Oh, Lore, stop it." Demi sniffed. "It's not funny. What have I gotten myself into?"

"It's Alao's karma," Bukky said.

The ladies laughed louder.

"Alao ko, alagbe ni," Lore said.

Demi screeched. "Leave my former bobo alone o!"

Bukky leaped to her feet and stiffened. Then feigning she had a briefcase under her armpit, she marched slowly about the room and adjusted an imaginary pair of glasses. She fell back on the bed, laughing hard.

Demi slapped Bukky on the back. "Poor boy! Leave him, jo!"

"God saved you from that joker. I see his wife in the market every day. Housewife. She does nothing but cook and clean," Bukky said.

"He didn't mind my working," Demi said. "I would not have fallen into that demon Idem's hands."

"Or this demon Duru's hand. Lucifer, shey?" Lore said. "Though, this demon is an angel o, I don't know. The guy pass me."

Demi cried. "What am I going to do?"

"First, you have to find out who this guy is. Ask him questions," Bukky said.

"No. Don't ask questions. Find out yourself." Lore took out her phone from her bag. "Do you remember the name of the church?"

"Yes, and even the pastor and his wife. And his best friend's name is Ahmed … and his wife is …"

"That's why you are my friend," Lore grinned. "Your head correct."

Chapter 56

"Come on, Iyanu, this is us now. Why are you behaving like a stranger?"

Iyanu slouched. "Bro. Ahmed. You are asking a hard thing. I can't go and start sharing a guest's information."

"Please. Please, to God who made me, I will tell no one. You are doing the work of God by giving me the address or phone number they left. Please." Ahmed lifted his hands as though in surrender. "Joo! We're talking about Duru here. Lucifer. Lost but found. I beg you! Wo, think of it like this. Why did they lodge here, at the church guest house?"

"Hmm. I didn't think of it like that o." Iyanu sighed. "I really wish I was in church yesterday."

"Ah, Iyanu, you cannot believe. It was bloody! I have never in my thirty plus years of knowing Duru seen him like that." Ahmed shook his head. "And he played a lead guitar."

"Huh!" Iyanu exclaimed. "Lead guitar? That he almost never played?" He opened the computer to the list of guests from the previous weekend.

"Believe me. When he picked that instrument, I told myself he just wanted to do 'gba je n simi' kind of worship. When he opened his mouth to sing! Oluwa o. The whole atmosphere changed!" Ahmed clapped. "Three hours! Three hours Duru was just singing and playing."

"Chai! Why this weekend that I will go and visit my mum in Ijebu!"

"But you know how that fire burns. One week it will still be there." Ahmed shrugged. "Tomorrow at Bible study, you will see."

"I know. I'm on duty tomorrow but woe betide me if I don't call off." Iyanu looked up from his computer. "Which day were they here?"

"Saturday to Sunday."

"Copy this number down." Iyanu called a cell number. "That's the only thing they left. No address."

"Ah, thank you, Iyanu. God bless you. Let me call."

"Sure. Anytime. I wish I was on duty sef."

Ahmed dialled the number. An automated response said the number did not exist.

Iyanu gasped. "Kai! He gave a fake number."

"Duru!"

Iyanu shook his head. "He still did not want to be found."

"Let me call the number from my phone. Sometimes, poor network makes the number seem as though it does not exist."

Ahmed called the number out to Bimpe, and she called. It rang. She put it on speaker.

"Yes? Who is this?" A thick male voice responded.

Bimpe shook her head. "Sorry, wrong number." She hung up.

Ahmed gasped. "Aha, honey girl! Why did you hang up?"

"That wasn't Duru," Bimpe said. "Or a female."

"Yes, but we could ask the person who…"

Bimpe's phone started to ring. "It's the number." She stiffened.

Ahmed took the phone from her. "Hello…?"

"Shut the *f*ck* up, bastard! You have the gut to call this number, right? Whoever you are, you are in deep *sh*t*!"

"Excuse me, what…?"

"I'm tracking your number right now. You think you can kidnap a baby and escape? You are a fool. You are in deep *sh*t. Bastard.* God don catch you. Idiot!"

Ahmed hung up. "My God, what number did Duru leave on that hotel registration?"

"Kidnap a baby? You know, when that guy answered, I just felt shudders go through me." Bimpe took back her phone. "I don't know what your friend is doing, honey boy, but I don't feel good about this."

"It's okay. I think we have tried and if they call back with any threats, let me know."

Bimpe smiled. "My sweet husband o, am I not the lawyer in this family? I think I can handle criminals better than you."

"Well, you're right, but I still need to know." Ahmed slouched. "And please, don't mention Duru's name. At all. You know, it may be a trap that..."

"Am I the one you are telling this?" Bimpe snickered. "I'll even send the number to one of my friends in intelligence. Let them call and find out what is going on."

"Okay, honey girl." Ahmed sighed. "God, please keep Duru."

"Amen," Bimpe murmured. "Hmm, only God knows where he has been, what he has done..."

"And where he is now." Ahmed grabbed Bimpe's hands. "Let's pray for him, joo."

The two rested back on their bed and said a short prayer for Duru and the woman they met with him.

Chapter 57

"**I** got a reply from Ahmed!"

Lore clapped. "Read it!"

"Dear Bukky, I am so blessed to hear from you. Wow, what a miracle. My wife, Bimpe and I met your friend, Demi, in Lagos with Duru. We are very happy to hang out this weekend in Ibadan as you suggested. Thank you so much, and God bless you." Bukky laughed. "He also left his number and Bimpe's."

Demi exhaled. "Dear God!"

"This is great. I'm so excited," Lore said.

"But I'm just sad, you know. Stan is..." Demi sighed. "He's been so cold. So quiet. I think he doesn't want me anymore and doesn't know how to say so."

"Hmm, I doubt that. I still see that electric look in his eyes when he is around you," Lore said.

The three ladies laughed.

"It's not funny, Lore." Demi moaned. "The zeal he had is gone. He hasn't touched me since. I mean, I don't want us to do all that physical stuff until we're married but at least, show interest." She sighed. "Not even to pat my cheek."

"Forget all that, as long as the hot gaze is still there," Lore said. "You don't want to fall into sin but you want to be tempted. Kwa! What is that?"

Bukky chuckled. "Don't mind her, jare, Demi. If he doesn't want to engage, you engage him."

"Huh," Lore exclaimed. "You're looking for trouble. Don't engage him o!"

"Then how will she get her love back?" Bukky gasped. "You have to try something."

"I'm trying. He gives me short answers, hardly smiles, and he doesn't stay a lot longer," Demi said.

"He's trying to avoid sin, don't you get it?" Lore snapped. "After what you described, definitely the guy is going through a spiritual reconnection. As you should too! Demi, didn't you say you rededicated your life?"

"I did. I'm just confused." Demi shook her head. "You can't imagine his answer when I told him everything about Idem."

Lore arched an eyebrow. "He smiled?"

Demi cried. "He shrugged and told me it was the past and not important."

Lore rolled her eyes. "And what did you tell him?"

"We got into an argument, and I asked him to leave my house."

"Ademilade!" Bukky gasped. "He left?" Demi nodded.

"Well," Lore said. "We are making progress now. It is good he has that attitude so that if after all this you need to cut him loose, it won't hurt too much."

"Lore is right," Bukky said. "Now that Ahmed has responded, let's stay focused. The meeting with Ahmed will be a deciding factor. Unless you don't want him again?"

Demi drew in a shuddering breath. "I do," she whispered. "Badly."

"The owner of this phone number is the answer to the riddle behind the baby's kidnap."

"I see," Bimpe said. "But you said the phone is registered in Uyo, to an unknown person."

She crossed and uncrossed her legs in her old friend, Detective James' office in Ikoyi.

"The address is incorrect too. You see, these registrations are not confirmed so I can buy a sim card, produce an ID, and my sim is registered," James said. "How again did you say you got the number?"

"I can't even remember where in the market. You know these people who sell kitchen slicer or something, long ago at a trade fair." Bimpe paused. "The one I had got spoiled and since they gave me the number, I thought I'd call and know where their shop is." In her heart, she whispered a prayer of forgiveness for lying.

"Oh, yes, that's what you said." James sighed. "Hmm."

"The phone number may have been stolen."

"Well, I want to keep it open especially because we may hear from the criminals again." James tapped a file on his desk. "I haven't made it official yet, but I will. It's not just a scam call as I suspected."

Bimpe leaned forward. "Please James, can you tell me exactly who that person is with the phone? They threatened me. I'm not comfortable."

James leaned back. "Apparently, about three weeks ago, a local government chairman's baby was kidnapped. The kidnapper asked for fifty million naira, and then went quiet for over a week."

"Wow."

"Then the Saturday before you got this call, the kidnapper contacted the family, said to go to a market in Ajegunle and distribute money on the streets. Same for Mushin and Oshodi," James said. "Somehow, he had them tracked to do it."

"A robin hood!"

James nodded. "Kind of. They spent fifty million naira before the kidnapper said stop."

Bimpe gasped. "For real? In this Lagos? Fifty million is a lot!" she sighed. "Hmm. But how did he know they actually gave the money?"

"He was sending them their pictures, so he was probably following them around." James shook his head. "Either that or he had people planted all over the place, which sounds huge."

Bimpe moaned. "Wow. Really well planned."

"Then he led the father of the baby on a wild chase around Lagos, and finally, they found the baby asleep in a car seat in front of the Akwa Ibom State House. She was safe. The only thing they found with her was the small phone the kidnapper had used to contact them all along. The father left two soldiers there on watch and took the phone but there was no contact with that number until you called in the following Tuesday."

"Oh, my goodness." Bimpe exclaimed. "No wonder they sounded so angry. Huh!"

James leaned forward. "I sincerely think it's an inside job by one of the politician's unhappy staff or maybe an opponent." He shrugged. "But I'll look a little more and if it's really more than a personal feud, turn it over to my office."

"Hmm, thanks so much, James. I can't even imagine what this person must have done to go to such lengths."

Bimpe pressed her lips together. "Kidnap a baby!" *Duru? Why?*

"Criminals do the least expected when they are desperate." James leaned forward. "But that's when they make the biggest mistakes."

Not if it is Duru, and he has nothing to lose. Bimpe stood. "Well, thank you so so much, James."

"Any time, Madam."

He walked her to his door.

As soon as Bimpe got inside her car, she called Ahmed. "Hmm, honey boy, you just can't imagine the *looong* story around that phone number. It's like a story from Nollywood."

She narrated the whole thing.

"Honey girl, the question is, how will Duru or that girl do anything like that?" Ahmed said. "The Duru I know is too laid back to do such criminal adventurous stuff. Robin Hood my foot."

"The Duru you know changed twelve years ago," Bimpe said. "And the Duru you know, would cry the minute the Holy Spirit starts to move during his ministration."

"Chei! You saw his face? Three hours not a teardrop! God knows what happened to him." Ahmed paused. "Everything died in him when Belema died. I think he got offended by God."

Chapter 58

"Are you not a woman? Will you let that useless asewo take a good man away?"

Morayo twisted her hands and looked down at the floor. "I have tried, sir."

"Shior. How did you try? He is a man. You are a woman." Akin snapped. "Even if you will naked yourself."

"Ha! Baba! Naked? Huh, I cannot naked myself o." Morayo stepped back as though Akin would hit her. "I cannot. The man does not even have money."

"Huh, ode. Oponu. Olosi."

"Don't call me names, sir." She took another step backwards. "I have to go now, sir. It is getting late."

"Wait! Late bawo?"

"I have things to do!"

Akin jumped to his feet. "He will soon be here. I told him I have a boy for him to help with his farm. He will soon be here. Just engage him, ha. Morayo, don't you like him?" Akin turned around his small work desk and moved closer to her. "And you say he doesn't have money?" He snickered.

"Is it because he is living in the ghetto? You don't even know anything. He has a very big farm now. Hmm, Morayo! Are you stupid? Can't you see that he is very hardworking? With a man like that, you will just be sleeping and enjoying. He will be worshipping you and your children."

Morayo breathed hard. "He doesn't like me. He is always in the house with Aunty Demi. What am I supposed to do?"

"Behave like a woman. When he comes now, I will use style and say I am going to get that boy, Umoru. Tell him you like him if you don't know what to say." He brushed past her to the door, just as Duru walked in.

"Good morning," Duru said. He shared a glance between Morayo and Akin. "Sorry, I stayed a little later than I thought."

"Good morning," Morayo said.

"Good morning, not a problem." Akin waved. "Let me get Umoru for you." Akin walked out of his office quickly.

Duru arched an eyebrow. "How old are you, Morayo?"

Morayo frowned, then smiled. "Twenty-four. How about you?"

"You are a very beautiful girl, and Akin is too old for you. Why are you here?"

Morayo gasped, and then laughed. "I am here...huh, Baba Akin? God forbid."

"I'm too old for you too. Go back to school, I heard you didn't finish," Duru said.

Morayo looked away.

"Exactly, you're not this type of girl. Hmm, Morayo. Go on. Be on your way back home now. Get a career. Akin said you were doing some sewing lessons with…"

"Agbaya ni Baba Akin!" Morayo burst into tears. "Goodbye." She ran out of the office.

Duru shook his head and leaned against the wall to wait for Akin. Silly, shameless, old man. He knew Akin was up to some mischief with the girl and he had refused to care to know more. He had more than enough to cope with the farm and his relationship with Demi. Akin's wiles were the least of his problems.

Akin walked in. "Where's iyawo kekere?"

"Listen, Akin." Duru snapped. "Morayo is too young for me, so stop pushing her around. I don't even know how she lets you do that. At her age, I was already working."

"Haba, are we fighting? You need a young woman to…"

Duru knew it. Akin leave his small dirty office to go and call a subordinate? How?

"I don't! I know what I need, and I know how to get it." Duru looked around. "Where's the boy? Or that was just a fluke?"

Akin shrugged. "He's in your truck with the others."
He walked to his desk. "Am I not trying to help you to
better your...?"

"Thank you. Bye."

Duru stepped out.

Akin stood with arms akimbo and stared at the door
long after he was gone. "Ode. You think that bank girl will
marry a poor farmer like you. Shior. We are trying to help
you, you are doing like arindin. Oponu!" He sat at his desk
for a second, then jumped up. "Alabi! Where is this fool
with the new invoice?" He stomped out of his office.

"I don't know the full details of how he returned the baby.
But I don't want him to be in any trouble, please."

Demi looked at everyone in Kayode's sitting room with
the hope that they would believe her. She had nothing to
hide at this point. She just wanted to be with Stan. She
didn't think she had ever wanted anything this badly.

"It's a criminal offence but no one is prosecuting," Kayode said.

His wife had strategically taken their kids to her parents' for the "weekend." Demi knew she just didn't want
to be in the meeting or be involved with their family issues.

Lore took her hand and squeezed it for reassurance. Tears came to Demi's eyes, and she sniffed. She didn't know what she could do without her best friend. On a day like this, she needed all the support she could get. Bukky had not been able to make the trip because there was an occasion in her husband's family, she couldn't take an excuse from. Ironically, the only other person Demi trusted more had not been invited here. Duru, the reason for all this, had been mandated to babysit Mimi while Demi came to Ibadan to visit Kayode. Another reason was to take Nini, Mimi's twin home, but this was not a reason she declared to Duru. He had no idea a Nini existed anywhere.

"And no one will," Bimpe said.

"We love Duru so much, and you don't know how glad we are to be here, meeting you," Ahmed looked at Demi, and then at Lore and Kayode. "Duru is an amazing person, and I still don't know how people deal with grief, but Duru took it so hard."

Lore sighed. "Thank you for this. For keeping this, this date, I mean."

"Can you tell me what happened?" Demi said. "He has refused to say, and I don't know how to get him. To get to him...has been." Demi blinked several times to fight tears. "I love him so much. And he just makes himself distant. I don't know what to do."

Ahmed shook his head. "Duru. Duru is not distant. He is your go-to guy. He tells everything about himself to everyone. An open life, if I may say."

Bimpe nodded. "I saw a little of that too."

"Wow. He's the opposite now," Lore said. "Never smiles, doesn't talk too much. He smoked a lot before Demi asked him to stop it."

Ahmed shouted. "Smoke? Never!"

"Igbo sef!" Lore said.

Bimpe gasped. "Weed! My God!"

"He was a chain-smoker when I first met him," Demi said. "But he stopped when I told him I didn't like it."

"What is the guarantee he won't go back to it after he gets what he wants. Marries you," Kayode growled.

"I don't think he wants to marry me. I'm the one keeping this relationship going as it is," Demi said softly. "After Lagos...he's changed a lot."

"This is not like Duru at all." Ahmed shook his head. "You see, Duru. Duru is a greater lover, and he's not shy about it. When he's with a woman, he's faithful, strong by her. Bold. I saw that when I met you in Lagos. I saw the way he looked at you."

Lore grunted. "That's what I've been telling her. But something is wrong definitely. Since that Lagos trip, he hasn't been the same."

"Duru is the fun guy in the building. He looks out for everyone. He ensures there's a smile on every face. He has one on his face too. If you're crying Duru cries with you. We used to call him cry-baby in university," Ahmed said. "But there was something so endearing, so personal about it that you just love him for it."

"I didn't meet Duru until after Belema, but from what I found out, he loved his late wife very much, and she took every advantage of him..." Bimpe said.

Ahmed raised his hand. "Honey girl..."

"No, Honey boy." Bimpe cut in. "Let me just talk so that Demi understands who this guy is, and why I will advise her today to hold on to him."

Demi and Lore exchanged glares.

"Duru must have loved Belema a lot," Bimpe said. "And after she died, he was devastated. He wanted justice at all cost for her, and their unborn baby. He fought hard. He sold everything. Borrowed. He stole from his bank where he had just recently been named best banking staff."

Kayode's mouth fell open. "He was a banker?"

"The best," Ahmed said. "In 2013, he won banker of the year."

"You don't recall the name? As a banker too..." Lore shook her head. "Of course, you wouldn't."

Demi scoffed. "I don't even follow that news. Unless I was the awardee..."

Lore chuckled. "Right."

"He hired me at the time to prosecute her killers, but I failed. They were too powerful," Bimpe said.

"Who killed her?" Demi whispered.

Bimpe sighed. "A nurse. Professional negligence. Hospital owned by a rich doctor who also has political might."

Lore moaned. "Eeyah. No wonder Duru hated Idem like that."

"When Duru could not get the law, he went after them himself, almost got locked up. The first opportunity he had, he left. He just walked out of the house, and no one ever saw him again until that day in Lagos he came to the church." Bimpe clasped her hands. "Now, we found out that Belema left a will. Named her daughter, whoever she will be, as the sole beneficiary. Duru knew nothing about that."

Lore gasped. "Really?"

"That's not the worst part. Belema while alive, had been acquiring some property in Rivers State. And here in Lagos." Bimpe snickered. "Her lawyer was an acquaintance. And that's how I got to know."

"My guy did everything for that woman. He bent over backwards. Did over time, worked the jobs nobody wanted just to make more money to satisfy her." Ahmed sighed. "She always wanted more. Money for this or that. She started different businesses, and they all failed. But you dare not criticize her to Duru."

"So, how do we get back this amazing person? Because it's just what my friend, Demi, deserves. I see the way he serves her. He's at her beck and call, but he is emotionless. Demi needs the emotions too," Lore said.

Kayode leaned forward. "I guess that is why we are all here."

Demi covered her head with her arms and wept.

Chapter 59

"**I** can start immediately."

Akin shrugged. "I told you he will work hard."

The landowner, a man in his thirties Duru got to know as Charlie, nodded. "I was just hoping he can pay for all the ten years at once."

"Bros, he will pay by end of next year," Akin said.

"Before then," Duru said. "I just need to put in money to clear and do all the preparations. The land has been abandoned and not tillable as it is."

Charlie shrugged. "Anyway, Mr. Akin. You're the referee o. If he doesn't pay up, I will hold you."

Akin laughed. "I trust Duru with my life."

"Thank you, Akin." Duru arched an eyebrow. "Hmm, I'll like to take my leave now." He stood and Akin, too.

Charlie remained seated. "No problem."

Duru clutched the sighed documents of the contract to lease Charlie's land for the next ten years, which he had paid a mere fifteen thousand per year for. Akin had thought it was the most incredulous bargain. A hundred plots of land for just fifteen thousand a year? And Charlie also let Duru pay for the first five years, the rest to be paid before the first-year cycle. It was really a miracle.

"That's like one-fifty naira per plot per year," Akin had said. "He may have just dashed you the land ke."

They walked out of Charlie's law office in Akure and headed back to Owena in the truck Duru borrowed from Olu's workshop.

"You are the luckiest man on earth, Duru," Akin said. "I have never seen anyone like you o."

Duru smirked. "Why do you say so?"

"Haba, see how Charlie just give you this land for kobo kobo, and that Madam Demi is now your woman. Everything is just going well for you."

Duru shook his head. He didn't want to say too much. Akin had been very helpful but he still didn't want to get too close to anyone. Not after what his life had been like, full of people. His solo existence was fading out again and the slower it did, the better for him. Two weeks now since Lagos and he just wanted to take things one day and one step at a time.

Holy Spirit is back full force, waking him to pray in the morning and chatting him up before he slept at night. Like before. Before Belema. It scared and excited him. God didn't do threesomes. That was what it felt like the minute he started dating Belema. She literally pushed his comforter aside. Like a tug of war. Midnight worship was replaced with sex. Morning quiet time with sleep. Belema did what she called "round-up" prayer, which lasted five minutes. Five minutes round-up replaced five hours of personal fellowship...

He loved Demi now more than ever or anyone he could ever imagine but he hadn't been able to tell her since that event. He needed to make sure this would not be another threesome! She was keeping things low too. Maybe she had regrets about him already. Or maybe she was respecting God's place in his life. God didn't hate marriage...he instituted it. But marriage should not replace God.

No one and nothing should replace God.

Duru didn't want to think of anything more than the moment. He feared to. If Demi broke up with him now, he'd leave. He'd go far for good. It would be the end of him, he knew. Yet, she was treading on eggshells around him, around the Lagos trip...she probably expected him to come up with the issues, at least explain. But he couldn't. The wound opening would kill him.

"Duru! What are you thinking?"

"Olu said he will talk to some labourers. See if they can start tomorrow." Duru sighed. "Do you mind if I just drive through the farm again?"

Akin shrugged. "It's on the way, why not?"

"Okay."

"I can arrange labour for you too. And you need a good truck," Akin said.

"Olu is talking to the owner of this one." Duru chuckled. "He told the man only a mechanic can manage this truck. It is always in and out of the workshop. But the man is asking for two hundred."

Akin exclaimed. "Two hundred what? For this scrap? I will get you a fine truck for hundred."

"It's not even in my budget now. I will just have to borrow this or take transport until I can buy."

Duru didn't want to tell Akin he had offered the owner fifty thousand payable whenable. The man had not yet agreed but Duru had a feeling he would. Holy Spirit told him he would.

Duru took the turning off the highway and soon drove into the land that would be his farm, right on the outskirts of Owena. He'd been here every day for almost two weeks, doing a little clearing here and there, mentally mapping out the place and feeling out the whole process. He parked the truck along the road, carried the big cutlass he recently bought, and walked in with Akin.

"There are some plantain trees with mature plantain," Duru said. "At least I have a gift for you today for all your trouble."

Akin clapped. "Ewoo! And you never told me."

"But I am telling you now."

Duru knew where those trees were. Four of them in total. He cut down the harvest of thick, mature plantain, and they returned to the truck. He planned to give two to Demi to share with her parents and friends, one to Akin, and one to his landlady.

Once in town, Duru dropped Akin off and returned to the mechanic workshop. He'd work a little with Olu, and then go off to pick Demi. Olu walked out into the open as Duru parked the Avalon.

"Ah, you're back. Congratulations. The truck is yours," Olu said. "The owner said you can have it. Pay when you wish."

"Huh, thank you." Duru stared at Olu unable to quantify his joy. "I owe you." He hurried to the truck and brought out a bunch of plantain. His landlady would have to wait until next time.

Olu gasped. "Aha, when I was about to discourage you from farming. This is big!"

Duru smiled. "It's too late. To discourage me."

He moved the two remaining bunches into Demi's car and spent the rest of the time working for Olu. He had several hours left of the day and with this, he earned a little income.

When he got to Demi's bank, he was told she had left with Bukky. He wondered why she didn't wait for him or tell him of her plans. He worried about her because she was quite predictable. He hoped nothing was wrong.

At Demi's house, he parked at the back and walked in through the back door with the plantains. Demi was in the kitchen, cooking.

"Baby."

"Welcome! Plantains! Wow! So big. Thanks."

"You're welcome." He dropped the bunches and gave her a peck. "I went to pick you up."

Demi smiled. Her eyes lit up with some excitement Duru hadn't ever seen before. His heart leaped with anticipation, but he cautioned himself. He still wasn't sure where the relationship would go to.

"Come," Demi said. She took his hand and walked him into the sitting room.

Chapter 60

"Are you my daddy?"

"Huh. Well, yes, I hope to be."

"Good. Because all the boys and girls in my class have daddies and mummies, and I only have my grandpa and my grandma, and my mummy."

"I will definitely love to be your daddy."

"Good. So. Come, let me show you around our house. Because a daddy should know everywhere in the house."

"Oh, yes, thank you so much, Mimi."

Duru threw an emotion-laden glance at Demi before he followed Mimi. They entered the room he had painted and arranged for her.

"Your room is very pretty," Duru said.

"Yes, I like it very much. In my old house," Mimi said, "my mummy and I slept in the same room because she was afraid of boogieman at night and did not want to sleep alone." She smiled at him. "Now, I can sleep in my room alone. Because you are here now. You can sleep with my mummy, and she won't be afraid of boogieman."

Duru nodded, unable to believe how overwhelmed he was being with Mimi.

"Are you afraid of boogieman too?"

"Me? No. Daddies are not afraid of anything."

"I think so too. Olamide said his daddy used to kill boogieman every time he comes to their house," Mimi said. "Olamide's daddy must be very strong."

"Who is Olamide?"

Mimi giggled. "He is my boyfriend. His mummy is my mummy's friend. And we go to their house every day."

"Oh okay. But aren't you too young to have a boyfriend?"

"I'm eight!" Mimi threw her head back and laughed. "Oh no. It is okay for me to have a friend who is a boy. Olamide said his daddy told him so."

Duru nodded. "Oh, really. Okay, I get you now. Is Olamide eight too?"

"He's seven! Do you have any children? Because my mummy said that if a man is old like you, they should have children because they are very old..."

"Mimi, that's enough." Demi called out from the corridor. "Come and finish your homework and Daddy wants to eat."

Mimi rolled her eyes and Duru almost burst into laughter. "Okay. Mummy." She trudged out of her room and Duru followed her.

Mimi returned to her small desk and resumed her work, the same way before Duru came in. His legs feeling like jelly, he walked into the kitchen.

"She told me Olamide is her boyfriend," Duru whispered and smiled. "Who is Olamide?"

"Bukky's son." Demi chuckled. "This plantain is really nice. I'll give one to Mummy and some to Bukky too," Demi said. "Thank you."

"You're welcome." Duru sat at the small kitchen island where Demi had two chairs tucked in. His heart thudded at what he had to say. "Mimi is such a wonderful girl. Thanks for introducing us."

"It is something I've wanted to do in a while." Demi placed a plate of hot rice and stew in front of him. "I'm so happy I could finally do it."

"Thank you," he said. "Means a lot to me."

"You're welcome, love." She sat beside him with a plate of food.

"You called me Daddy to her..."

"I know. I just don't want to confuse her by saying uncle or something," Demi said. "Don't be scared. It doesn't mean you have to marry me tomorrow."

"I'm not under any pressure." Duru stared at his plate. "You have questions about Lagos, and you have not asked them."

"I thought you'd tell me when you're ready." She dug into her food. "Eat, love."

"I don't plan to tell you anything, Demilade." He scoffed. "In fact, I..."

"Eat, please. On the other hand, I have stuff to tell you, and I want to discuss them, more important things about me. My past, and...and Idem."

Duru shrugged. "I don't want to know about you and Idem."

"But I want to tell. I made wrong choices, and I want us to talk about them."

Duru ate for a few seconds and moaned. "Tastes so good. You're a great cook."

"Thank you." Demi sighed. "So, I want you to know Idem was my first..."

Duru pushed the plate aside. "I said I don't want to hear it. If my memory serves me, you told me about this before and I told you I didn't care about your past." He meant it. He didn't want to know her past. He refused to care.

"But you have to. And you have to tell me about your past too."

He flew to his feet. "That is the reason, right? You tell me, I tell you."

"Yes! That is the reason, and it is a good reason…"

"It is not, Demi! What are you trying to do with me? Did you make me meet Mimi today so you can manipulate me?" He whispered.

"What are you talking about?" Demi heaved. "Why would you even…?"

"I'm not going to let you choose how this relationship…"

Demi cried. "Let me make my own choices, for heaven's sake, Stan!"

"You make *sh*tty* choices! You fell for that *bastard* Idem. *D*mn*. You fell for me!"

"What?" Demi gasped. "Get out! Get out of my house."

Duru didn't want to say more. This was the second time she was asking him to leave, and he didn't like it. He strode out and gritted his teeth when he caught sight of Mimi studying at her little desk. He would make it up to her, but not today.

Chapter 61

"**D**o you know you are wanted?"

Duru looked up and for a second, his eyes widened. He straightened from the bed of vegetables he was tending. "Hello, Lore."

Lore looked at the shed behind the vegetable garden and sighed. "Duru, why? Why are you doing this to yourself? Your landlady told me you haven't been around for weeks."

Duru dusted his hands on his dirty baggy jeans. "I moved here to pay more attention to the farm."

Lore took in the environment more closely. A white jalopy truck was parked beside the shed. In the shed itself, was just a long bench made from tree barks and branches. A mat was rolled up at one side, with Duru's backpack beside it. She had not believed it when she went to look for him at home and was told he didn't stay there anymore. Thankfully, he had at least shown Demi the farm previously and Lore knew where to look.

"It took me almost thirty minutes driving around here before I saw the shed and decided to check it out," Lore said.

He arched an eyebrow. "I'm sorry about that."

Lore caught his gaze. "Who knows you are here?"

Duru shrugged. "My boys, I guess. They come here every day. Why? Who wants me?"

Lore wanted to scream, Demi! But she swallowed instead. "Idem. Idem Isong."

That seemed to surprise Duru. He smirked. "For what?"

"He wants to arrest you for kidnapping his baby," Demi said.

For a moment she thought he smiled but then he turned his back on her. "Then why is he not here to do it?"

"Duru! It's none of my business but you are hurting Demi very much and..."

"If it's none of your business, then don't talk about it." He heaved a sigh. "Let Idem know where I am." He started to walk to the shed.

Lore shouted. "It's rude of you to walk away while I'm still talking to you."

Duru turned to face her. "I am sorry, Lore."

Lore breathed hard. "Akin told Idem what you did. Don't ask me how he found Idem. I guess you must have told him because Demi didn't."

"You came to warn me?"

"Demi is sick with worry. Idem wants to kill you. He thinks you are hiding…"

"Akin knows I'm here. Tell him to bring Idem to face me."

Lore gasped. "Please, Duru. If you don't care about your life, other people do."

Duru bit his lower lip. "Demi told me to go away. I'm just fulfilling her wishes."

The clouds gathered and a thunder struck. Lore looked up at the sky for a moment then looked at Duru.

"Demi sent me here."

Duru scoffed. "Thanks for coming."

"Do you know Mr. Alao? Vice principal of the community school?"

"I do. Why?"

"He always wanted to marry Demi. She didn't like him. She tried to, but it just didn't work. Since she married Idem, he'd tried to get a sort of revenge on her. Sabotage her." Lore shook her head. "Tried to get her to lose her job."

"Love is not by force."

"Well, Alao makes everyone think Demi led him on but it's not true," Lore said.

"Why are you telling me? I don't care about Alao or what he thinks of Demi."

"Akin is related to Alao's wife. The VP is abusive and Akin thinks it's because he didn't get over Demi."

Duru narrowed his eyes. "And I made friends with the snake."

"Akin is not a good person, and when Idem left, he was the go-to person for all the gossip. He made sure Demi didn't walk the streets in peace."

Duru clenched his fists. "And now he has our secret."

"Idem warned Demi to produce you, or he will take her," Lore said. "But he can't do anything to Demi. Her father will..."

"I'm sorry but I'm not going to sit here and let that mad man hurt my woman," he marched into the shed.

"Duru!" Lore followed him. "Maybe you should see Demi first."

"No, I'll go to Akin." Duru picked his backpack and pulled out a clean pair of jeans and T-shirt from it.

"I think, please, you should see Demi first, please."

Duru frowned. "Okay. I'll go to her house before I go and see Akin."

The thunder struck again, and this time, louder.

"Thank you. I have to go."

"Lore." Duru closed his eyes for a second. "Thank you," he swallowed. "For being such a great friend to Demi. Thank you."

"She makes being her friend easy." Lore turned and ran to the car she parked a few metres away from the shed.

As soon as she entered her car, she called Demi.

"He's coming to you."

"He's here!"

Demi licked her lips and wiped her sweaty hands off her simple red dress. She drew in a ragged deep breath and stood facing the door. Duru must have left almost as soon as Lore did because Lore hadn't been back for fifteen minutes before she spotted Duru's truck drive into the compound.

She heard his quick footsteps and then a sharp knock. Demi pulled the door open and stood in the middle of her sitting room. She hadn't seen him for three weeks and she didn't believe how much she missed him until he stepped through her door.

"Ademilade," Duru breathed. "Are you alright, love?"

Demi rushed into his arms, and he kissed the top of her head.

"My love," he moaned. "Did he do anything to you?"

"No. We made sure he didn't." Bimpe walked into the sitting room from the kitchen with a smile on her face. "I must confess, Duru, you should join the CID. You know how a criminal's mind works."

Duru gasped and frowned.

Demi looked up at his face with tears on hers.

"What's going on?" Duru said.

Ahmed followed his wife in. "We found you. We were not going to lose you, Duru."

Lore and Bukky followed the couple. Boma, Tonye, John, and Duru's mother, who pushed his father on a wheelchair proceeded after them.

Duru let out a cry when his parents walked in. Demi cupped his face and tried to catch his gaze.

"My sweetheart, look at me. Look at me," Demi said.

Everyone found a place to sit, and with the small available space, Ahmed ended up leaning against the wall. Lore and Bukky sat on stools.

Duru glared at Lore. "You lied to me."

"I was telling tales." Lore shrugged. "I didn't know what else to tell you. How else to get you here."

Duru heaved. "How could you?"

"Akin did rat you out, but we stopped Idem before he could get here," Lore said. "Bimpe's friends in law enforcement has the case wrapped up with no physical evidence against you two."

Duru shook his head. "I can't be here. I'm sorry."

"You have to be," Demi said. "Sweetie, you have to be. I'm not going to lose you, and you have been running too long. Please, darling."

Duru buried his head in the crook of her neck, and tears slid from her eyes when she heard his deep sobs.

ROGUE

Chapter 62

"**T**wo road! Ife!"

I got into the half-filled rickety bus, in between the conductor and another traveller, and pushed my rucksack between my legs. I leaned my head forward over my chest and closed my eyes.

"One chance!" The conductor shouted and half-ran as the bus continued to move. "Park! O l'eru."

The driver pulled over roughly and someone entered to sit beside me. I instantly could smell the strong body odour before the person half-sat on me. Without giving it a second thought, I snatched up my bundle and jumped off the bus as it pulled away.

The conductor yelled. "Were! Olosi!"

Abusive terms I realized meant nothing to me. With the program starting the following morning, many commercial vehicles were pulling up and away at the camp. I could still hear Ahmed asking about me, with Boma and Mummy. I couldn't believe they came for me after I told Ahmed I was going back home. If they already thought so little of me, then there was no use going back there. I wanted to be on my own for a while and started to walk down the busy road, until I left the traffic behind. With the lights from the camp and the vehicles behind, it was risky to continue walking in the dark. Though I couldn't care less as it were.

I stopped walking and stood at the edge of the road.

A 14-seater bus slowed down close to me. "Ibadan, 'badan, 'badan!" A thick voice yelled. I waved it down.

The bus was not full, and it served my purpose. I closed my eyes and didn't open them until the bus stopped at its final destination. I didn't have any contact in Ibadan. Where would I go? I checked my phone, and the time was close to midnight. I found a shed, which I believed was probably used to peddle wares during the day and sat on the lone bench there. With my chin lowered on to my chest, I slept off and only came awake to shouts of transporters calling the town they planned to travel to. The junction got busy in a moment with different conductors yelling different town names.

"Akure! 'Kure..'kure...kure."

"O-sha, sha, sha."

"Ikire-Ife-Ilesha."

There was nothing for me in Ibadan.

"Come down. E bo'le!!!"

I actually slept off. That sounded like a dream come true. I hadn't slept a good night in three years, save last night and now. With people around me, strangers, I slept. Maybe my new life suited me well, then. I looked around. I had never been in this part of the country before, at least, not to visit. The houses by the road were mostly old, but we were in a town. This couldn't be Akure for sure. Or could it be?

The driver got busy with the conductor, and they started to change a back tire. Passengers stretched. A couple men walked to the hedge and opened their pants to pee. Belema hated that male habit with her whole heart. Poor Belema. What would she even think of me now? My wife would throw a tantrum and denounce me in a minute!

This thought had my heart beating fast. What did it mean? Could I now freely think about the woman I married? It scared hell out of me. Since I set my eyes on Belema for the first time in church, I didn't think I'd dared think contrary about her. She was perfect in all her imperfections.

I stared at the road. It was narrow but seemed a bit busy. A buka several feet down the road filled up with the passengers from the bus. The sun was just rising on this beautiful October day and it seemed it would be a very hot day. I took out my phone to check the time, and the battery was dead. What did I need a phone for anyway?

I could sell it. I took out the sim card and threw it aside.

"So childish, Duru. I don't even know how I married a baby like you…"

I shook Belema's voice out of my head. How many times had I heard that? The sweet voice had me drooling every time I heard it. Now she was gone, maybe I could judge her words. Childish. Baby. Though I was two years older than her, had a university degree while she couldn't decide yet if she wanted to proceed after her HND or not, and I had a job that served her every whim.

"Ki lo de ke?" An angry voice snapped. "Are we going to sleep here?"

"Ah, calm down, jo. Are we not trying our best?" the tough-looking bus conductor said. He couldn't be much older than me.

The driver dusted his hands. "Don't be angry. We have finished." He turned to the conductor. "Call everybody."

Due to the seat I had in the middle of the bus, people in the back had to go in first. I watched the first and second of four people go in, and just walked away.

No one called on me. Maybe they didn't notice. Or maybe they didn't care. I crossed the road to the other side and watched the bus pull away. I had no clue what the name of this town was, or what time of the day it was. But I could see a construction site just off the road. It was an old government building and a truck with men in it pulled in.

I walked briskly to them. I did need a job anyway. And money.

"Asewo!"

The useless contractor slapped the heavy backside of the girl as she walked out of the office. It reminded me I needed one of those badly. What were a man's basal needs? A widower, at that? Ahmed had teased about sleeping with Udari, knowing we didn't believe in sex outside of marriage. But who gave an eff about all that now?

"Oga Idem! Leave me o!" The girl derogatorily called a whore responded with a laugh.

"Come and take fifty naira," the contractor, Idem said.

I hated his guts. He was rude, flirtatious, and annoying, arrogant. I didn't have enough words for him. But for at least one week since I walked away from the Akure-bound bus at this little town called Owena, he paid and fed me. And he allowed me to sleep in the site shed, indirectly using me as a night watch without pay.

The girl stopped in her tracks. "Pere!"

"Okay, hundred."

"You're too stingy," she said.

She returned to him where he sat on his wooden boss-seat. He pointed to his lap. From where I took stock of site materials, I couldn't see what he was pointing at until she snatched up the hundred naira note. He caught her hand before she escaped as his phone started to ring.

"God help you today. My woman is calling." He slapped her backside again, as she walked away, and he picked his call.

"My love." He chuckled. "Are you serious? Of course. When? Now? Of course, darling. Ask one of the men to bring you in…"

I walked out, disgusted at anyone who would bear the title of Idem's woman. She must be as desperate as the harlots he picked and dropped every day.

Despite his reckless lifestyle, Idem did the work, unlike many Nigerian contractors and I had to give it to him, he kept good records and paid on time. As soon as he employed me, I had thrown myself into the job and within a week, he did recognize I was strong, focused and good with numbers. I didn't feel cheated by him since I agreed to my wages. It wasn't a lot, but in essence, I didn't think I needed much besides food and an extra pair of clothes.

Dusk fast approached and I returned to the shed to put my daily account together. Idem had me do this every single day. It was work discipline like I'd never seen.

Done, I trudged back to Idem's office with my report, and there she was. Idem's woman whom he had been speaking to on the phone. The first thing that struck me was how beautiful she was, nothing like the girl he gave a hundred bucks after disrespecting her anyhow.

This woman looked clean, polished, educated even. She wore a butter-colour silk shirt that was teasingly unbuttoned one button too low, but still decent enough, over a grey straight skirt and her figure had me throbbing. She was dark-skinned and so smooth with light make-up. A small smile teased her lips, and her gaze was on Idem. Stupid guy. How did he get this girl...woman...lady.

"Drop it," Idem said without looking at me.

His gaze was all on this woman. The snake.

I couldn't wait. I could not watch. Idem didn't deserve such a woman unless she wasn't what she seemed.

Chapter 63

"Hey. How much?"

The prostitute looked at me. She chewed noisily on mint gum, which helped to tone down the smell of her cheap perfume, but mint just didn't do enough justice to it. She however reminded me of the other woman. The one who seemed to be in my head every day since I saw her standing beside Idem's table, talking with him. Three full months, three towns, daily cold showers. Who cared what I did with my body. I was a nobody. No one in this town called Iseyin knew me. I knew no one too.

"Ole. Apayan. Ika."

"Pardon me?"

She turned to her fellow prostitute who stood a few feet away in the red zone.

"Come and see this *bastard* o! Who do you think I am?" The girl chewed noisily and stomped off. "A kill joy?"

I frowned. What did I say wrong? It was my first time of walking up to a prostitute. It took some courage to do it.

It wasn't like asking a girl out to dinner. Was I rude? Why call me a killer? Wicked. Thief. Just because I asked how much? Was there something else I should have asked? Was there a way to ask prostitutes their wage. A code for talking to whores in the red zone? I didn't know!

Like I did back in Owena, I worked on a construction site. It wasn't a lot of money, but it was more than enough. I didn't have a phone, or a bank account, or a house, and I didn't want any. I had my backpack and my life. That was more than enough. This town was not difficult to live in either. I understood Yoruba fluently but hardly spoke it. I hardly spoke.

The day before, I had roamed town and found this red zone just because I made up my mind, I wasn't committing any sin by getting a woman for myself. I didn't care if I committed sin, though. Still, that little voice would just not go away much as I tried to send it off. On second thoughts, maybe fornicating would finally grieve him, the Holy Spirit, and he would leave me alone.

Besides, Idem's woman was in my daily sleeping and waking. I should have left town that first day I saw her, but I wanted to see her again. And I did. Every working day, after I found out she worked in the only bank, I went there just to see her arrive before I went back to the site. It was an obsession, and it was very stupid.

The other prostitutes moved further down the road. I swallowed my pride. I really needed a woman tonight. I couldn't masturbate one more day. I hated porn with my whole heart, and it was now more torturous to read the porn magazines I had than not to. I walked up to another woman.

"Good evening. I need a woman."

She wasn't half as good looking as the first but what did I care? She would serve the purpose.

She looked me over twice. "Five thousand."

That took me aback. For what? "Huh, just an hour."

"Ehen, five thousand."

"I don't have that much." I sighed. Really? "How much last?"

"Ah, olosi!" She clapped. "You are pricing. Pricing what?"

I snickered. "I'm not paying you five thousand for one hour."

"Even one minute! One second sef."

This was ridiculous. I took a step back. Cold shower it would be for the night then. What if I could pay? I ground my teeth. Of course, I had more than five thousand for one hour. I didn't spend my income on anything except food, and I ate little.

"Okay," I said. "I'll pay."

She screeched. "Ewoo! Aye mi o. Oya, it's cash and carry."

Two other prostitutes came closer. One of them was my first choice and for a moment I wanted to revert to her but that would be stupid. I took out five thousand naira from my back pocket and gave her. She counted the amount and tucked it in her purse.

"I dey collect full money o." She turned away.

"That's five."

My first choice shook her head. "You this thief. You want to sleep with an oracle." She turned and walked off.

The girl I was negotiating with shouted. "Ashawo!"

"I paid you five thousand," my patience fast running out, I snapped.

"Ehn, take your money."

She threw the money at me and walked off. A car pulled over by the road, she got in and the car sped off.

I stood shivering to my toes. My five thousand was on the dirt ground, and I feared to touch it. Everything around me faded. The prostitutes moved further away, and I was alone by myself, and in myself. What did the other one mean by "sleep with an oracle?"

The small voice within me seemed to snicker. I stepped back and turned and walked away from the red zone. I could take a bus or a motorcycle back to the site I worked at where I also served as the night watch. And forget all of this ever happened. Have my usual cold shower. Instead, I decided to walk. It was a long walk.

An angry long walk and over an hour later, I lay on the mat in the site shed and stared into the darkness. Pretty much the same way I had done too many nights to count.

"They told me you are needing a woman."

A young woman stood in front of the room I recently rented from an Alhaji whose compound had a big bungalow where his three wives and eight children lived, and another big bungalow with fifteen rooms, which he rented out. All tenants shared two bathrooms, and two pit latrines built at the back of the two bungalows. It was early evening, and I just returned from work. I liked to sit outside and get some air before turning in for the night.

She looked like a teenager; too young was my first thought but who cared? I guessed she lived in the main bungalow with the family, but I never bothered to know who she was. I bothered no one. I didn't even know any of the other tenants so maybe she was a co-tenant. Since I decided to try and live in Iseyin, I thought it was good to have a room of my own, especially after the site I worked at closed. I had another site job, but it was much smaller, and the pay was less, so I did other things, odd things. Carpentry, plumbing, electricals, much of what I picked up at the sites I worked at.

I arched an eyebrow. "Who told you?"

Maybe she was a prostitute and didn't live in Alhaji's house. She smiled and exposed a big front gap tooth. She was pretty in a local, dense, organic way. Many of the Iseyin girls sort of had this look. Maybe because I was a Lagos boy, it wasn't my type. Creamy chocolate complexion bordering fair, thick lips, small boobs, big hips, and they all seemed to have no cheekbones, and lots of hair, bushy eyebrows, long lashes and thick dark tresses, which this one had neatly plaited in rows.

"Word gets around." She pouted. "I can help you this evening." She shrugged. "You can give me anything you like."

As though the still small voice in my life was finally dead and everything carnal alive. Like the way you switch on the light in a dark room. I really looked at her face for the first time and she winked. This was Friday evening, like any other evening for me. Nothing. It had been many months since the prostitute saga. I had not gone to ask any woman for anything again, watching porn on my new phone, and making do.

"Why?" I sat there and questioned myself more than I questioned her.

She slid her hands over her round hips. "You're a fine boy." She snickered. "I like you."

I clenched my teeth. My body was responding to her flirting, and I had no reason to resist. Who was she anyway? Alhaji's daughter? Who cared? I didn't.

I stood. "Okay."

I opened the door, and she walked in. My room was sparse. Just my neatly made single bed, a table and a chair, and my backpack.

She gasped. "Haba, nothing in here. No radio or TV."

She wore a dress with a zip at the back, and I went for the zip.

"Your body don full, abi?" She laughed. "Don't tear me o."

Only one thing was on my mind.

"Biliki!" A loud knocking followed by a young breathless voice shouted from outside my room. "Alhaji ti de o!" I heard footsteps hurry away.

The young woman swung away from me and zipped up her dress. She dashed for the door while I tried to understand what was going on.

"What?"

"Sorry. I'm going." She opened the door and stepped out.

I could die! As triggered and engorged as I was? No way.

"Hey, wait."

I followed her out and right there in front of my door stood a young man, about my age. I was taller though but the angry frown on his face meant he would be motivated to harm me more than I was to protect myself.

"Leave Alhaji's wife alone," he snarled.

"She came to me," I said.

His eyes bulged. "Well, leave Bilikisu alone. She's eleha. Do you know what that means, Ibo?"

"No." Truly.

"She's a kept woman. She is supposed to be covered all the time, and she belongs to my father." He breathed hard. "If you ever let her into your room again, you'll be dead before you see me coming." He stomped away.

The man next door to my room, who I had never bothered to find out his name, came over to me.

"Just leave. Go. Now!"

I looked at his face. Middle age, if I could judge. "Go where?"

"Anywhere. You see that boy leaving like that? He's coming back with four more of his brothers, and they are going to each hold a sharpened machete." He turned round. "Even me, I'm going out to visit friends. I don't want to see them cut off your head."

I didn't think. I got back into my room. Picked everything I thought I could need and walked out of the compound. Eleha, what? Bilikisu truly may be in a lot of trouble and woe-betide-me the infidel who dared allow an eleha into his room. *Eleha!* Wow! Wasn't this a female Muslim who wore a special cloth that covered her entire body, including her face? My goodness! I thought I didn't know what it meant but I did! No wonder I didn't recognise her. She had always been covered. What a mischievous woman! Girl, actually. What horrible society permitted such a child to be wife to an old man like Alhaji who could not be younger than sixty! I'd heard that if you spoke to or touched an eleha, you would be lynched. Whether it was true or not, I wasn't about to find out. This one actually entered my room? My neighbour was right. Even I didn't want to see my head cut off.

It was getting dark, and it didn't make sense to choose to leave town at this time. All the same, I went to the motor park, got into a bus headed somewhere. Anywhere. I didn't care. My time in Iseyin was done. I'd had it with the town, anyway!

Chapter 64

"**I** didn't deserve that! I didn't!"

First, I kicked a broken bucket at the deserted market. Then I kicked a stick. The village market didn't have a lot, so it was difficult to express more of my frustrations. And despite my anger, I wasn't blinded to the fact that this could be the only livelihood of the owners of the stalls. So, besides kicking dust and stones, my anger just came off of my throat.

"Why did you do it? Why did you kill Belema? Did I not serve you enough?" I wailed. "The only thing. The only thing I had all to myself. You took her, you wicked God! I hate you! I hate you! Kill me. Kill me now if you are God. Kill me!!!"

A dog barked in a near distance, and I turned to the sound. There sat a man in a nearby stall, his chin balanced on his knuckles. He stared at me. He couldn't be real. It was the middle of the night in the small market of a small village.

It was dark, but his eyes shone with a fiery anger that caught my spirit and made me lurch backwards.

"Who are you?" He growled. "Because of woman, you are cursing God. Are you mad?"

"He killed my wife." I sobbed.

"Your wife? Which one?"

"The one."

I startled awake and gazed at my surroundings. I was in the same market, and it was still deserted. Was that a dream or a vision? I hadn't cried in almost a year since I left Lagos. I didn't care anymore, or did I? I sniffed from a blocked nose, and yet, my t-shirt was soaked in sweat and tears. This was a bad sign. It couldn't be the place for me. I didn't need ugly, confusing visions upon my dilemma. I'd never had any since Belema died. Morning was breaking and I saw a taxi drive to the side of the market by the village road. As I contemplated leaving, a bus drove to the other side of the road opposite the taxi. This was the exact place the taxi from Iseyin dropped me last night. I needed to move on.

I walked over to the driver and spoke Yoruba. "Where is this taxi going?"

The driver looked me up and down, as he chewed on a stick. "Ilorin, Offa."

"How much?" I didn't even know how far but I was ready for the next stop.

"Mi o se mo, oluku!"

That word, oluku! I had never heard it before. The dusty ruffian who said it threw a dustier head gear to the ground and stomped off. Oluku, or the supervisor standing by a cement truck yelled something at the departing figure, but the labourer did not acknowledge or stop.

I hurried over to Oluku. I didn't think it was a name. I must have heard it used in Lagos in a derogatory way, but I couldn't be sure.

"Eskis sir, I can work. I need work."

Oluku gazed at me from head to toe and back up. "What can you do?"

"Everything." I lowered my backpack. "But for now, I can offload cement for you until the other guy returns."

"I'll pay fifteen per bag."

I pulled off my shirt. "Yes sir."

He pointed at the open warehouse by the truck. "You take it there."

I walked the few feet to the entrance and found a corner by the wall to drop my backpack and shirt, rolled up my trousers and returned to the truck.

Oluku handed me the gear the other guy used. "You will need this."

"I use my shoulder," I said and turned to the truck to join two other men to offload cement.

By the end of my first workday in Ilorin, I had three thousand naira, and I thought my lungs would burst. I picked my backpack and put on my shirt.

"You are very hardworking," Oluku, who I got to know was named Lawal, said behind me. "I have a job for you tomorrow."

I turned to face him. "Okay."

"Come here, before 7am and we will go to the site."

I nodded and watched him walk to a Toyota jeep parked beside the empty trailer. He got in, spoke to some other people who came by, and then drove off. One of the men locked up the warehouse, and one by one, the arena became deserted.

Dusk descended, and the kiosk where we bought food emptied. The warehouse was not far from the park where I arrived at much earlier in the day, but the bed of the trailer seemed more appealing. I looked up in the sky and it was cloudy. No, I wasn't going to sleep under the heavens and risk a wrath of God through a downpour.

A halogen lamp lit up the place momentarily, and I walked to the road. In my sojourn, people always slept in the markets and parks. I was familiar with the way that worked.

I walked about ten minutes back to the motor park, and found the gate locked. It wasn't so late. And where on earth did they lock up such a public place? I banged the gate, and within a second, the small gate opened.

"No moto again for today o," a gruffy voice said.

"I dey find shelter. I just arrive town today," I said.

"You from where?"

"Iseyin."

"So?"

I shrugged. "I need a place. Just a shed."

"No shed here o. Na moto park. No be hotel."

It dawned on me I had some money. I could afford a hotel. A cheap one. "Abeg where I fit get cheap hotel. Like five hundred, one thousand."

Gruffy voice cackled. "Five hundred? Where you wan find five hundred hotel. Unless you carry ashawo go her room."

Great idea! "Ashawo, huh?"

"Walk down to you get to traffic light. Turn left, then left, then left. They go rush you sef." He laughed and closed the small gate.

It had been five years since I slept with a woman. My late wife. Ilorin surprised me. It was a large city, and beautiful, clean unlike many towns I'd been to. A brothel here was the last thing I hoped for, but it definitely was a welcome option. To say I needed a woman was now a ridiculous understatement.

"Thank you," I murmured and went my way to find a bed for the night. And a woman.

Chapter 65

"Thank you."

The prostitute girl who accepted five hundred naira for the whole night, took the money from me, and laid it down on a dressing table with several cosmetics. I did not want to look at her face, know her, assess her body. My spirit grieved. A spirit I had tried to quench long ago with my misbehaviour. Where was all this guilt coming from? I no longer belonged to God. My body was wholly mine. I could do what I liked with it. Yet.

"Get me a cup of water. Please," I said.

"Of course." She opened a small fridge beside the dressing table and brought out a sachet of cold pure water. "Do you want to bath?"

"Yes." I took the water and drank up.

She pointed at a door I had not noticed earlier. "Water runs from the tap. Hot and cold."

"Oh."

Interesting. Like a hotel. The bed was small and only a standing fan cooled the room, but hot and cold water running? Great!

I walked into the bathroom with my backpack. It had a small shower cubicle, and a sink. A big towel hung off a hook behind the door. I replaced it with my rucksack and hung the towel on the doorknob. Then peeled off my clothes and for almost ten minutes indulged under the cold shower. It was a most relaxing bath after such a long day.

When I stepped back into the room, my hostess had a wrapper tied around her body.

"I will take a bath too," she said.

Her soft-spoken way confused me. She treated me like a guest. My eyes shot to the money I gave her, which was still on her dresser, and back to her.

"Of course."

It felt awkward to lay in a stranger's room naked, but it was what I did. I had to get service for my money, yes? The bed was firm under me, and the sheets smelt fresh, but my head sank into the soft pillow. I heard the shower and for a moment thought of joining her. But she wasn't my lover. She was a total stranger I had a contract with. I had fulfilled my part, and she had to fulfil hers.

I closed my eyes to shut out the waging war in my head and heart. When I opened them, it was 5 a.m. and my hostess was nowhere in sight.

▽

"I didn't know we would be able to build this shed so fast." Lawal told the site foreman, a burly of a man called Afonja. "I can bring the cement here straight instead of paying for storage."

"Then you pay for security. Oga, either way, you pay," Afonja said in a soft voice that did not match his tough physical profile.

Lawal coasted the area with shrewd eyes. "Unless I get the labourers to spend the night. This area already has vigilantes."

Afonja started shaking his head. "Oga, see it is better to…"

Lawal stepped out of the long shed to the side where we washed our faces and prepared to hop on the site truck Afonja drove to return us to the warehouse, which was the meeting point in the morning.

"Who can sleep here tonight? I will pay you two hundred this first night."

I stepped forward. "Me."

"I need one more person," Lawal said.

Yahaya, a young man of about twenty years old, raised his hand.

Lawal glanced past him, just as he'd done for me. "Someone else."

"I can stay, Oga Lawal. I will not sleep. Please, the extra money will…"

Afonja, who had come to stand at the window, cut in from inside. "Engineer, this place will…"

"Okay. Duru and Yahaya will stay tonight. Let's see how it goes." Lawal walked towards his jeep and the others went to the truck.

Afonja came out of the shed and shaking his head, went to the truck he would drive. With no instructions about anything, within minutes, only Yahaya and I were left.

I somewhat wished I had gone back to the brothel. The prostitute had not showed up until I left her room. Why didn't she wake me up? Or did she? There was no way I would not know. I wasn't all that a deep sleeper although I had slept too deeply the night before. She must have come out of the bathroom and seen how tired I was. Still, I felt I owed her. Or was she the one who owed? If so, then I could go back and demand for what I paid for. But didn't I pay for a room, and got a room?

Yahaya walked into the empty shed without a word to me, which suited me perfectly. I carried my backpack and followed him shortly. The neighbourhood was developing but several new houses already had occupants. The site we were on looked like a building project for a huge house. The foundation was already started and at least I knew I'd have a job for a few more weeks. By which time I knew I'd have enough money to rent a room and know if this was a place I wanted to live in, or it was time to move on.

Yahaya groaned. "My wife get belle. No f*cking for two months now."

He looked too young to have a wife, but wasn't I like this just a few years ago. A young man, with a wife. His rant was none of my business. I dropped my backpack against the side of the shed closest to the road, and at least several feet from where Yahaya stood. I reckoned if we were guarding, then, we should at least stay on different sides. Also, we should stay awake and have a plan.

"If you're feeling sleepy now, you can sleep. I'll walk around and keep watch for a few hours. Then you can take over," I said.

"Walk?" Yahaya snickered. "You no dey hear me? I dey go find ashawo for town."

I arched an eyebrow and wanted to charge at him. No wonder Engineer Lawal wanted someone else. Irresponsible. Young. Married. Those didn't go well at all. But I wasn't his father or mother, and I didn't care what he did. The Lawal himself couldn't care less. Leaving two labourers on his site without any form of security gadget or even flashlight. We could use our phone for illumination but what kind of engineer did that? Probably because the land was basically still empty, as well as the shed.

Yahaya stretched. "The ones behind the market." He chuckled. "I hear say na dem get action pass. But I never go before. You wan make we try dere?"

My first instinct was to call him off. "I'll pass."

"You get wife for house?"

"I'll pass. Go."

I didn't mean to let off so much steam, but regardless of what I was or did, I wasn't irresponsible.

"You go soon tire." Yahaya stepped out of the shed.

I waited a little bit until I was sure he was gone, then I picked my two knives and my phone, and proceeded to walk around the site.

Yahaya did not return until the early hours of the following morning when dawn started to break. The night had gone on well without any event, and because I had a day job, I lay on the bare wooden floor and caught a two-hour sleep. My co-guard never said anything to me about the night.

Engineer Lawal thought it was a successful trial and kept Yahaya and I as guards for another six months while the house project continued and reached a successful completion. He eventually got machetes, and flashlights to aid us, but the neighbourhood was safe, and we never had an incident.

Several times, Yahaya took off at night, and my mind always went back to the prostitute I paid five hundred on my first night in Ilorin. She was different, I knew, which was all the more reason to go after her.

On the final day of work, with a beautiful twin triplex completed; I felt so proud to be a part of it, and my money paid in full, I got on a public motorcycle and despite myself, followed Yahaya to his house, where he promised his landlord could give me a room to rent.

True to the promise, I got a small, empty room in a low-income part of town for four thousand naira a month. I was responsible for my own electricity and water. The one-story building had eight rooms, and we all shared one toilet and one bathroom. Yahaya asked a man in the neighbourhood to connect me to a metre so I could have power. Afterward, I went to the market and got some plastic furniture, a table, and a chair, and a single mattress.

For the first time in six months, I had my own space again. The night felt humid and lonely, and my thought went back to the prostitute. I knew that if I didn't go back to her, I'd not have any peace.

Chapter 66

"No room with that number here."

"But I was here six months ago. I am very sure." I glared at the young man at the bar in the brothel, who I had met the last time. "You were here. This girl took me to her room. She greeted you as we passed, you answered."

"In this place, we have five rooms. Since five years I have worked in this bar. Five. Room one, two, three, four, five. No room 7." He sighed. "Wetin be her name?"

I never asked! "I. I can't remember. She's slim. Tall small, not too tall. Fair." I could still see her face. A gentle face, not hardened like those of the other girls around.

"No be here. We get Flora, Princess, Destiny, Precious and Beauty. All of them get fat yansh. Not slim. Unless you want to say..." He pointed at the entrance. "Flora. See her. Abi na dat one. Na only she slim."

I turned, knowing it wasn't my girl. No room seven. I remembered so well. This was the house. Everything was the same. No room seven. Was she an angel? But we entered a room. In this bungalow. No one could convince me otherwise.

"No be she." I shook my head. "Is there another...another place like this around here?"

"Only the hotel down the street. And you no fit pay for the girls there. No insult."

"None taken." I sighed. Wow. She didn't exist. I should have known. "How much does ...do they charge. Like that Flora."

"For one night or just per hour?"

"The night."

"Two five."

I gasped. "Two thousand, five hundred?"

"Hmm, for whole night, or how much you wan pay?" The barman laughed. "Five hundred?"

It was as though I got doused in petrol. She must have been an angel, I shuddered. Despite my insistence on offending God, he still sent me an angel. An angel who created a room for me in a brothel. She left my five hundred on the dresser and allowed me to sleep. I ran out of the brothel, not caring about the barman.

My heart thudded as I returned to my house. I couldn't stay here. I couldn't. I wasn't running anymore because of my anger. I was now running from my shadow. It was my first night at my new accommodation, and I knew I couldn't stay.

I picked my backpack, which contained all of my life's possessions. To think I thought Ilorin was my place. I had the mind to be with that prostitute tonight, and tomorrow night and the following night, and the night after. It was only a dream. Going to six years without even a kiss. I was burned over. I was tired of living. When I had desires, there was no woman. And when there was a woman...something always messed me up. I was done.

I stepped out of the room I just set up and walked into the night. The landlord just got free money off me, but he wouldn't know that yet. I didn't know where to go. Where could I run to? The newest trending song by some group called Housefires "*Where can I run from your presence...*" began to ring in my head. This was insane. I hadn't listened to Gospel music in five years. Not prayed or thought about God...well, He had been thinking about me and seeping into my memory. He sent an angel. I've not been able to commit fornication! That almost drove me crazy. And now a song I'd heard in passing once or so was running through my mind like I had scored it.

Where can I run from Your presence
Where can I flee from You
Even if I hide on the highest mountain
You are there

Where can I run from Your presence
Where can I flee from You
Even if I lie on the lowest valley
You will find me there
Deeper than any ocean
Your love goes on and on
And on and on
Higher than any mountains
Your love goes on and on
And on and on
Your love goes on and on
And on and on and on

Definitely, I was going crazy now! This was insane. I had heard that song only once or so when one of the workers on my site played it. Once or so!

For several hours I was just walking, with the song ringing in my head. I didn't know what direction I was going or where I was headed. Darkness descended and I started to shout into the night like a mad man.

"Leave me alone, Jesus! I don't know you anymore. We broke up, remember? You gave my Wato to someone else and stuck me with a dead woman! She didn't even like me! You remembered to take my baby too, right? So, we're done. Leave me! I don't know you. Let go. Move on without me! I've moved on without you. Kill me! Kill me then.

Hopefully, that will make you happy. Kill me!" I yelled into the night. "Kill me!"

I didn't hear any sound but a strong burning sensation and unbearable pain. Before the scream left my lungs, I passed out.

"He's awake."

The first thing was the burning again. And pain so strong like I had never felt in my life. I opened my eyes and tried to figure out where I was and who spoke. I couldn't recognize either. But the pain...

"Ahh, pain!" I groaned and squeezed my eyes shut. "Pain!"

"Give him the ogogoro," the voice said.

Someone put a bottle to my mouth and poured some awful and bitter liquid down my throat. I gagged but he kept pouring it. The liquid ran through my throat to my stomach, burning everything it touched including the pain.

The first man shouted. "O ti to! O fe pa ni?"

The man pouring the hot liquor down my throat stopped. My throat, nose and eyes burned, and tears slid out of my eyes, but I couldn't feel the pain anymore.

"So le s'oro?" The first man said, asking if I could speak.

I nodded. I could speak but with the burning, it may be difficult.

I stuttered. "Where...where am I?"

"So, here's the story," First man said. "We are hunters. We thought you were game, and we shot you. You're lucky you did not die, only flesh wound, and we are treating it already. The question is, what are you doing in this thick bush in the night?"

Another gruffy and muffled voice said, "Ah, why are you interrogating him? Shebi you thought he was an oracle."

Several men laughed. It was impossible to know their number. Hunters. Thick bush. Only one thought crossed my mind.

I'm home!

THE DURUS

Chapter 67

"**I**'m sorry. I'm so sorry."

Demi rocked Duru like a baby and murmured soft words of love to him as he cried in her arms. It was true what Ahmed said about Duru's emotions. He had kept it under control and now the dam broke.

He stepped out of her embrace and went to kneel in front of his father. "I messed up, Daddy. Please forgive me."

The old man was so frail, Demi marvelled at what it must have taken to bring him all the way from Lagos. Ahmed had thought the road trip would be too much and instead flown Duru's parents to Akure. Lore had picked them up at the airport and driven them down.

Duru's father could not speak well or lift his arms high but the small smile on his face made this grand scheme worth all the while. Duru hugged his neck, and wept until his mother gently untangled him. Then he clung to her neck.

Boma, the woman Demi remembered had called Duru as they left the church over a month earlier, stood and hugged them, and cried along.

Then Duru went to his brother John, and hugged him, and Boma's husband.

Demi walked over to Lore and Bukky and sat with them. She oddly felt lonely. Was she going to like this "soft, weepy" Duru as against the "hard" one she fell for? She didn't know. Maybe she didn't care. He still had that "electric" look in his eyes when he stared at her, and that was all that mattered.

"I lived in that forest for six years!"

Boma exclaimed. "Wow! All through COVID?"

"Yep." Duru sighed. "We had no clue what was happening in the world. Tofeek, the one who poured the ogogoro down my throat was our PRO, along with one other Adekunle. They constantly went to town to negotiate with buyers. They told us about COVID. We were a band of fifteen men. We lived in the villages on the edge of the forest." Duru arched an eyebrow. "I just remained inside the forest. Others who had families would return home for a day or two."

Everyone sat comfortably after the emotional reunion. Bukky had arranged for a caterer to bring food and drinks, and it was served by two waiters. Demi and Duru sat on the floor by the wall, and Duru told the story from the night he walked off from the camp and got into a bus going to Ibadan.

"What took you out of there?" Bimpe asked. "The forest, I mean?"

"I don't know." Duru looked at Demi fondly. "Maybe it was just time. I'd not had a phone for six years. I wanted to see other people. It was such a strong yearning. I told Tofeek I wanted to go with him to sell our hunt. He agreed. We were close to a town called Saki in Oyo state. When we got there, I told Tofeek it was time for me to go home. I went to Osogbo. But didn't feel like leaving the park, so I got into a vehicle going to Akure." He scoffed. "The vehicle stopped at Owena for people to eat, and I came down." He placed a peck on Demi's forehead. "When I saw you again, I knew I'd never leave."

"God ordered every step you took from the day you left," Boma said. "He made sure your love for Belema didn't go to waste."

"It may sound weird," Ahmed said. "But I think all that reaction was for Tiwatope. Yes, Duru really loved Belema, but his lost love was Tiwa."

"Tiwa is someone's wife now, and I guess she's doing well?" Duru looked at Ahmed.

Ahmed nodded. "She's doing very well. Two kids. Travels the world with her husband, making gospel music and lots of money and getting awards."

"Do we know this person?" Bukky said. "Sounds like a famous star."

Bimpe shrugged. "Possibly. The Kenny is his stage name. Tiwa, his wife, sings with him."

"What? The Kenny?" Bukky screeched. "I have all his albums. I'm a huge fan. Wow! Demi too!"

"Wow, Demi! We were dancing the other day in..." Lore gasped. "You're kidding right?"

Demi moaned. "Wow! What a life."

"I thought I loved her. Then I thought I loved Belema." Duru gripped Demi's hands. "But what I have felt for you is so different and so pure. I love you, Ademilade. So much."

"I love you more," Demi whispered.

"I'll say, though, Belema did not love you," Bimpe said. "She just used you. God bless the soul of the dead." She did a quick sign of the cross.

"According to her brother, they didn't touch her things for three years. Then on her third anniversary, they opened her suitcases. I had packed them but not looked at her files or documents. I just assumed they were her certificates," Duru said. "Alas, the papers for her properties were in there.

Just before I left home, her brother called me. He wanted me to take him to see the land. Three plots in Aja area. Five plots on the outskirts of PH, which they already saw."

Bimpe gasped. "You didn't know about any of this?"

"Not a clue. She never showed interest in anything except her self-image." Duru chuckled. "She'd ask for money for her mother, her father, her parents' church back in Port. She'd ask for money for dues for her primary school association, secondary school reunion. Anything and everything. I just sign cheques, do transfers, swipe cards without thinking."

"What did you do when you got to know?" Lore said.

Duru scoffed. "Nothing. She used me. And then died on me. I feel cheated."

Bimpe sighed. "I got all the property back and in your name."

Duru nodded. "And why would you do that?"

"Because it's yours..." Ahmed clapped.

"No, Ahmed! It's not and you don't..."

"I owe you, Duru." Bimpe grimaced. "I didn't fight hard enough for you. I..."

"You did your best, Bimpe." Duru chuckled. "I didn't tell you Ahmed tried to make me date you. To forget about Belema."

Demi clasped her hand over her mouth.

Bimpe gasped, and punched Ahmed. "Did you?"

Ahmed threw his hands up in the air. "Well, I was just trying to get my friend out of the blue funk!"

Demi winked. "You got yourself out, instead." She turned to Duru with tearful eyes. "You still love her don't you? Tiwa. Belema. You still love them."

"I never loved Belema. She lured me, and I obliged her. She was tone-deaf. How could Lucifer love a tone-deaf woman?" He scoffed. "And Wato. It took me a minute but the moment I proposed to Belema, the love I had for her died a natural death. I love one woman. Her name is Ademilade. I love you so much, babe."

Duru slid to one knee in front of Demi. "I don't have a ring, but this is something I've wanted to do from the get-go." He took both of her hands and pressed a kiss into them. "I love you so much, Ademilade. I can't say it enough. And I am sorry for being a mess these past few weeks."

Tears dropped from Demi's eyes unbidden. Bimpe and Ahmed held each other and stared into each other's eyes.

"Will you marry me?"

Demi nodded. Duru always managed to make her speechless when she needed to speak most.

"Yes." Demi's voice cracked. "Yes!"

The room erupted in cheers and claps, and laughter.

"We wanted you to meet someone," Bukky said.

Duru glared at her. "There's so much my heart can take in one day."

Lore laughed. "Don't worry. Your heart will take this." She looked at her phone. "They'd been here. I just told them to wait in the car."

Bukky walked over to open the front door for Kayode, and Demi's parents. Behind them, Mimi followed holding hands with her identical twin sister, Nini.

"Good afternoon, family," Demi's family greeted, and got a chorus of responses.

Duru's eyes shot to Demi, who nodded. It was rude not to greet Demi's brother and parents, but Duru seemed overwhelmed by the new arrivals.

"Mimi has a twin, Nini," Demi said. "My parents thought it was better to have Bro. Kayode keep her until I found my feet. I took Mimi to spend weekends in Ibadan."

Duru walked quickly to the twins and crouched in front of them. "Mimi. Nini." He crushed both in a bear hug, and they returned his hug.

"I wanted to tell you, Daddy, but Mummy said to surprise you," Mimi said, eliciting a laugh-sob from Duru.

"Hello, Daddy," Nini said with a big smile.

Demi proceeded to do introductions around the room, stealing glances as her fiancé acquainted himself with their twin girls.

Chapter 68

"**G**o back to sleep, it's midnight."

"But we want to worship with you," Nini said.

Demi shook her head. She knew her second twin was forward, to put it nicely. But coming into their bedroom to join her and Stan for their midnight worship, was too much.

"Let them join us," Duru murmured.

"They have school in the morning. They will be sleeping in class," Demi said.

Duru smiled. "I know how that works, darling. The Holy Spirit always replenishes."

The girls didn't wait to get permission. Nini started swinging her tambourine. Mimi added hers. Demi opened her mouth to complain about noise but Duru shook his head. For thirty minutes, the family worshipped. Demi thought the girls would be tired, but they stayed alert.

It was the start of a frenzy family culture. The midnight worship of the Durus.

Since the quiet wedding in her pastor's office, which had only close family and friends in attendance, and a private celebration lunch thirty kilometres away at the Ikogosi Warm Spring Resort, where the new couple spent another week alone, life had been different. Demi was happy. Not just happy but she had a joy in her spirit like she had never imagined possible.

On their wedding night, seated in bed, Duru had had a quiet conversation with her. On hindsight, she knew it was a conversation that should have been had before marriage, but she didn't mind. His ground rules were exactly what she wanted for herself and her family.

"I have some power habits I had," he'd said softly. "Power habits I threw away, but I have resumed."

"Okay." She nodded. When he didn't say more, she added. "Do you want to share them with me?"

"Hmm." He grunted. "I worship every night for about an hour, could be more or less, usually less," he'd said. "You don't have to join me, but you can't stop me from having it. I'll go outside so I won't disturb your sleep."

"I want to join you," she'd said.

He scoffed. "Well, thank you, my love. But I do it at midnight, and you'd have work in the morning and..."

She'd cut in. "I'll join you for our midnight worship. Every day. Starting tonight."

Duru swallowed. "The first night of my first wedding," he whispered. "Belema told me we couldn't worship at night. She said the night was for sex."

"We'll worship at night and have sex any other time," Demi said and laughed.

Duru closed his eyes for a moment. "One by one, I dropped my power habits. There was always something more important to do."

She clasped her hand over his chin and turned his face towards her. "You won't drop any…I won't let you drop any of your power habits."

"I appreciate that," Duru groaned. "But there's more. In the morning, I pray. I can leave for my farm to do that, but we must have a daily devotion. If it's too much for you in the morning, we can do it before bedtime. With the girls, please."

"Bedtime with the girls, please."

"Thank you," he said.

"Thank you," she said.

He laughed. "Stop teasing me."

She dropped her hand to her laps. "On the first night of my first wedding, I slept all through the night. The man I married had no spiritual goals for our family. I sacrificed my faith for him and suffered greatly," she said. "No, I am not teasing. I am sincerely grateful to God for you. For this second chance."

"And I you. I thank God daily for this second chance," Duru said. "But there's more."

"Okay, I'm all ears sweetheart."

"I don't want to preach at you..."

"Preach, husband!"

Duru laughed. "Okay. Well." He drew in a shuddering breath. "I feel like Job. I lost a Belema and Agbani but God replaced them with Ademilade, Emioluwa and Inioluwa. I worked for banks before but now I have a huge farm of my own, which though renting now, Charles has agreed to new terms for me to rent-to-own."

Demi screeched. "What? You didn't tell me."

"I just got the message this morning. Right before we took our vows," Duru said.

"Congratulations to us, baby!" She hugged his neck. "We're buying it out in no time! That farm is a big deal."

"It is. It is." He sniffed. Tears gathered in his eyes. "It is. You see, God does not do threesomes. When you are with him, he wants all your attention to be on him. I learned that the hard way." Demi wiped the tears off his eyes, and he pressed a kiss to her hand. "But look at my life. There is nothing I did that I did not succeed. Even running away from God!"

"You didn't succeed in running," she chuckled. "He put me along your path, and you fell flat on your face!"

He laughed and then heaved a heavy sigh. "We will not be a threesome with God. He is the head of our home. I will not compete with him for you, and you will not compete with God, for me."

"Yes sir!!!"

"I love you so much, Ademilade." He pulled her to him. "And unlike your first husband, I'm not letting you sleep through our wedding night."

The End.

Acknowledgements

I am eternally grateful to God for the completion of this novel, which took me over three years to write.

I want to also thank my beta readers, Ekama, Confidence, Treasure, Auntie Elsie, Auntie Shunt, Busi, Fidel D'Machine, my editor, Abimbola, my models Chux and Michael (yes, the animeified guys are real models), and Auntie Elsie again, for being there for me.

Also, I wish to thank my husband, Fola, and my adult kids for their support of my person, and for helping me choose the cover (Actually, this cover is one of about 10 that I'd struggled with.)

Thank you, my reader, who inspires me always to keep writing.

NOVELS BY THE AUTHOR

SCENT OF WATER

PEPPER

FRAIL FLESH

THE DAYS AFTER THAT NIGHT

THE TRUTH, THE LIE, AND THE DARE

UNDER A RED DELTA SUN

FOREVERLAND

TISHA

WAY OF THE UNFAITHFUL

HER LOVER

I LOVED A SLAVE

BLUE DAWN

ROUTING FOR GRACE

I'LL TELL MY STORY

TRUE DREAM SERIES:

DUMPED

YOUR WISH IS MINE

EVEN THE LAWFUL CAPTIVE

HE TAKETH THE FIRST

THE OTHER SISTER

WHAT'S GOOD FOR THE GOOSE

SHATTERED

SCATTERED

BATTERED

IYKE'S REVENGE

ÌKA

SUCH A PROPOSAL

LOVE COME BY

JUST LIKE PLAY

SERVE A KOBO

BOSS LADY

A BOTCHED VALENTINE

EIBA FAMILY SAGA:

TO WHERE THE WIND BLEW

PROMISE TOMORROW

TILL DAY BREAKS